A BODY ON THE DOORSTEP

BOOKS BY MARTY WINGATE

LONDON LADIES' MURDER CLUB SERIES

A Body at the Séance

A BODY ON THE DOORSTEP

MARTY WINGATE

bookouture

Published by Bookouture in 2024

An imprint of Storyfire Ltd.
Carmelite House
50 Victoria Embankment
London EC4Y 0DZ

www.bookouture.com

ISBN: 978-1-80314-966-0
eBook ISBN: 978-1-80314-965-3

To Leighton

ONE

LONDON

September 1921

Mabel made her way down Piccadilly, around the Wellington
Arch and into Belgravia. She turned a corner to find another
leafy square where residents were taking advantage of a
Saturday morning with a piercing blue sky after a showery
night. With only a glance, she saw a man in a homburg lingering
by the gate, an older woman holding tight to the lead of a Scottie
that barked at a squirrel, and a nanny pushing a pram, her
charge sitting up and tossing a small soft toy overboard. Mabel
turned back to business, to the white stucco terrace. She found
the right house number and took one step up to the door,
pausing to brush off her skirt and adjust her hat. She then
arranged an expression suitable for a house in mourning and
pulled the bell.

While she waited, she turned to look at the square again.
The man in the homburg had gone, the nanny riffled in the
shrubbery, and the woman with the Scottie gave Mabel a nod of
good morning. She smiled and nodded back.

The door behind her flew open, and Mabel whirled round.

A maid filled the doorway. Mabel was not a short person, but she had to look up to this woman, whose faded red hair seemed to explode out the top of her starched frilled cap like a volcano erupting. She had red-rimmed, watery blue eyes, and a firm mouth that flattened into a thin line as she looked down at Mabel.

'What d'ya want?' she demanded.

Momentarily taken aback, Mabel recovered quickly. 'Hello, I'm Mabel Canning.'

'You are, are you?' was the maid's response.

'I'm from the Useful Women agency. Mrs Despard rang to ask for assistance at the wake today, and... here I am.'

The maid stepped out – causing Mabel to move aside – and looked up and down the empty pavement. 'All right then,' she said, 'come in.'

The maid led and Mabel followed her in just far enough for the woman to close the door.

'Herself isn't down yet,' the maid said. 'What is it you're to do?'

Mabel felt quite sure that the first thing to do was to get on this woman's good side.

'What do you need me to do?' she asked.

The maid cocked her head and narrowed her eyes. 'There's a load of fiddly tea sandwiches to be made, and my arm is that tired from slicing the bread,' she said, as if throwing out a challenge.

'Right,' Mabel replied. 'Show me to the bread and butter.'

Mabel followed the maid – she'd missed the chance to ask the woman's name – to the back of the house, down the servants' stairs and along a corridor well lit by electric sconces instead of gas. Mabel appreciated the modernity of London. She'd moved from a village in Sussex where her papa had been one of the first to switch on an electric light in their cottage and a good few residents still regarded electricity with a cautious eye.

The kitchen lay to the right, across from a door that had been pulled just to but not closed. As they passed, Mabel heard a whine and saw a dog's nose appear in the gap.

'Hello there,' she said, leaning over the wriggling dog that had followed its nose out. She gave it a good scratch behind its ears. 'Who are you?'

'That's Gladys,' the maid said.

'Ah, Gladys – you're lovely.' Gladys responded to Mabel's compliment by covering her hand in kisses. The dog had a rough coat and a dark saddle marking on her back. 'She's a terrier?'

'Of sorts.'

'How lovely for you to have a dog,' Mabel said.

'She isn't mine,' the maid replied, and shooed Gladys back into the room whence she had emerged – the maid's living quarters, Mabel thought, as she caught a glimpse of a fireplace and chairs before the door closed. 'Now, about those sandwiches.'

The large kitchen table was stacked with platters and already sliced loaves of bread, bowls of chopped egg, a mountain of cress, a tray of salmon and what looked like two pounds of butter. They set to work.

Mabel hadn't anticipated making up platters of sandwiches, but the Useful Women agency provided such a breadth of services that she wasn't surprised. Also, she lacked details of any sort about this assignment. The day before, in the office, proprietress Miss Lillian Kerr had spoken in hushed tones – even though Mabel was the only other person in the room – getting as far as saying that the event was the wake for Mr Guy Despard and Mabel was needed to 'help.' Then the telephone had jangled, and Miss Kerr had nodded her dismissal, leaving Mabel with only the address in hand.

Now, as she buttered the bread and reached for a slice of salmon, she ventured to learn more.

'I'm very sorry about Mr Despard,' she said to the maid. 'Was it sudden?'

The maid returned a look as if Mabel had two heads.

'How should I know?' she asked. 'How should anyone know?'

Mabel opened her mouth but couldn't work out how to reply. Before anything came to her, a woman walked into the kitchen.

She was about Mabel's age and wore a long silk dressing gown in a Chinese print with a kingfisher-blue background. Her dark hair was cut in the latest stylish bob, causing Mabel to give a thought to her own golden-brown hair, still quite long and pinned up in a bun with only the curls round her face short. Although the dressing gown was quite striking, the dark circles under the woman's eyes were her most prominent feature, standing out against her pale skin.

Mabel stood and said, 'Hello, I'm Mabel Canning from the Useful Women agency.'

The woman flashed a brilliant smile that transformed her countenance. She reached out and took both Mabel's hands in hers. 'You're very welcome, Mabel. I'm Rosalind Despard – Rosalind, please.' She took in the scene at the kitchen table, dropped Mabel's hands and put one of her own on her hip. 'Oh, Bridget, I didn't mean for Mabel to work in the kitchen. She's hired to keep me company today.'

'Well then,' Bridget said, 'sit down at the table and lend a hand, and she can do just that.'

'Oh, all right,' Rosalind said without rancour. She sat at the table, took up a knife and started in.

Mabel marvelled at Mrs Despard's – Rosalind's – acquiescence to her maid's command. Perhaps she'd begun as Rosalind's nanny. Nannies retained that sense of discipline no matter how grown their charges were. Mabel's ayah – her nanny from India – had remained with them as a housekeeper as Mabel grew, and even now when Mrs Chandekar told Mabel to do something, Mabel, thirty-two years old, did so without question.

'You'll have to excuse Bridget's ways,' Rosalind said. 'She hasn't always been a maid – she took care of the young girls backstage when I started in the music hall. We were a handful, I might add.'

'You needed watching out for then,' Bridget remarked. 'Just a slip of a thing.'

'I was fifteen when I started,' Rosalind said to Mabel. 'And on the stage until I was twenty-two. I left the stage for good when Guy and I married, and he asked Bridget if she wouldn't mind coming along and doing a bit for us at home.'

'And I said I wouldn't mind at all,' Bridget added.

'Guy and I didn't grow up with personal servants,' Rosalind explained, in a chatty manner as she ate one of the sandwiches she'd just made. 'He refused to have a valet because he said he'd learnt to dress himself at an early age and his father had taught him to shave and he could do so for himself. So it's been only Bridget taking care of us... and now me.' Rosalind toyed with the butter knife and grew solemn.

Here was Mabel's chance. 'I'm very sorry for your loss.'

Rosalind looked at her without speaking, her gaze vacant. The distant sound of a clock striking the quarter hour drifted down from somewhere upstairs, and her face drained of colour. 'Oh dear, is it time already?'

'Near enough,' Bridget said, standing. 'You go on and I'll be up to help you dress. Why don't you show Miss Canning around on your way?'

. . .

Rosalind took Mabel up to the ground floor and paused. 'There won't be enough room in the study or the dining room, so we'll have everyone in the drawing room,' she said, and continued up the next set of stairs and into a large, elegant room. 'Plenty of space here.'

Mabel could only murmur an agreement because her gaze had fallen on a grand piano on the far side of the room set in the front of the oriel windows.

'You've a piano,' she said.

'Yes,' Rosalind replied. 'Do you play?'

'I did,' Mabel said. She'd been gone from her village for only a week, but her fingers itched at their lack of use. 'I've no room for a piano. I've just moved up to London, you see.'

'From where?' Rosalind asked.

'From Peasmarsh in Sussex. Now I live at New River House in Islington. I've a lovely small flat of my own.' Mabel caught herself – this day was not about her. She nodded to a large, framed photograph. 'Is that your husband?'

'Yes,' Rosalind said, and smiled. 'That's Guy.' She led Mabel over to the fireplace and took the photo down.

He had been a dapper fellow with his high collar and swept-back dark hair that had a great deal of silver in it. He smiled at the camera – a half-smile, as if they shared a secret.

Rosalind ran a finger down the edge of the frame. 'He's been gone seven years.'

'Oh, I didn't realise,' Mabel said, wishing she'd stayed in the office until Miss Kerr had given her these details. 'Do you have a remembrance every year?'

'What? No. I'm sorry – I should've explained. It's just that it feels as if the entire world must know, must be watching my every move.' Rosalind swayed slightly and put one hand on the mantel. 'Guy disappeared seven years ago. Vanished without a word – not to me or anyone.' She searched Mabel's face and whispered, 'Where did he go?'

Mabel had no answer, but none was expected.

Rosalind continued. 'There was an enquiry, but as far as the police were concerned, I was the only suspect, and so, for months, they wouldn't leave me alone. They believed I'd killed him for his money. Park – my brother, Park Winstone. I'm sure he'll be along later. At least I hope he will. Park didn't believe I'd killed Guy, of course, but the rest of them did. They did their best to try to prove it until I swear I almost confessed just to make them leave me alone. After that, I... It's only now, you see, seven years on, that Guy can be declared legally dead.'

Seven years not knowing, not being able to live your life. It was as if Mabel felt the heaviness in Rosalind's heart.

'Here's our wedding,' Rosalind said, brightening as she reached for another photo.

Mabel looked at it and smiled. It was not the usual wedding image where the couple stared at the photographer, staid and serious. Here, the happy couple truly looked happy as they gazed into each other's eyes.

Mabel glanced round and spotted a small photo on a table near the piano. 'Is that you?'

'I'm afraid so,' Rosalind said, and laughed. 'From when I was on stage.'

She looked barely more than a girl, and wore an old-fashioned dress, replete with a bustle. Even in the photograph, the dress appeared to shimmer, giving the impression of being almost see-through. Rosalind posed with her hands atop a closed parasol with its tip on the floor, her head cocked and a perky smile.

'I was younger then – I wouldn't wear that today,' Rosalind remarked.

'Do you still sing?' asked Mabel.

'No, but I owe the music hall a great deal because that's how we met – Guy saw me on stage. He said I didn't even need a spotlight because I was bright enough all on my own.' She exhaled a small laugh. 'He exaggerated, of course. I was never that good. Not like Cyril.'

Bridget popped her head in the door. 'What are you doing in here? You need to dress.'

Rosalind seemed to lose what energy she'd found. 'I won't wear widow's weeds,' she said – a declaration, but in a weak voice.

'No one's saying you have to,' the maid replied softly. 'Now, come along.'

Without further instructions, Mabel remained in the drawing room studying the photographs and furniture and paintings on the wall. She made her way to the piano, lifted the fallboard and ran a finger over the keys lightly. It wasn't polite to play some-one's piano without being invited, however much she would like to. Mabel sighed and kept her hands to herself.

The longcase clock in the corner sounded three-quarters of an hour. *When were people expected?* As if in answer to her question, she heard the doorbell pulled. She listened, but there were no hurrying footsteps down the stairs, and so when the bell was pulled again, Mabel went down to answer.

The man on the doorstep was older than Mabel by at least ten years. In one hand, he held a walking stick with a round brass top and a bouquet of sombre-coloured dahlias in the crook of his arm. With his free hand, he swept off his hat, looked at Mabel and his eyebrows shot up.

'Why, Bridget, how you've changed!' he said, with such pretend innocence that Mabel giggled. 'Oh, there now' – he gave a nod – 'you can't be Bridget if you're laughing at one of my jokes.'

'No, sir, I'm not Bridget,' Mabel said, sobering up by reminding herself of the occasion. 'Please do come in.' As he did so, she added, 'I'm Mabel Canning from the Useful Women agency here to help Mrs Despard this afternoon.'

The man looked up the stairs as voices – Rosalind's and Bridget's – drifted down from above.

'It's good you're here, Miss Canning,' he said quietly. 'Our girl needs all the support she can get today. Difficult times, you know.'

'Cyril!' Rosalind called over the banister and then hurried down the stairs. She had changed into a mauve day dress that looked muted but still elegant on her slim form. She appeared to be in the best of spirits. 'I'm glad you're first.'

He turned his face to Mabel, and a sadder man she could not remember seeing. His shoulders sagged, his mouth turned down at the corners and his mournful eyes looked as if they might fill with tears at any moment.

Rosalind ignored this transformation. 'You've brought flowers,' she said, reaching out.

Cyril offered them up. 'I never was all that interested in flowers,' he told Mabel in a slow, sad voice, 'but then I planted a few seeds and they grew on me.' His mournful look vanished like magic, and a wide smile burst onto his face, his eyebrows lifted and his eyes danced. '*Boom-boom!*' he said, tapping his walking stick in time.

Mabel laughed before she could stop herself.

Rosalind smiled. 'This is Cyril Godfrey – Serious Cyril.'

'Pleased to meet you, Mr Godfrey,' Mabel said.

'Oh now, it's just Cyril, Miss Canning,' he said, his face on the verge of a smile, 'and the pleasure is all mine.'

'Cyril is the real music-hall star,' Rosalind said. 'He's at Collins now – it's a wonderful show.'

'It'll be better with you in it,' Cyril said.

'So you say,' Rosalind replied, laughing at what Mabel thought sounded like an old joke. 'But I'll leave the song and dance to you. Now, Mabel has come to help today.'

The bell was pulled again, and Rosalind's good cheer faltered.

'I'll stay down here to answer,' Mabel said.

Rosalind nodded, taking Cyril's arm.

Cyril dropped his walking stick into the umbrella stand. 'I'm sorry I won't be here for the entire afternoon,' he said, as they went up, 'but you know—'

'Yes,' Rosalind said with good cheer, 'you have a matinee.'

Mabel opened the door and there began a non-stop stream of arrivals. She repeated 'Hello, good afternoon, may I take your hat? Please continue up to the drawing room' until she knew no other words. The blue sky had hardened to a threatening grey, and she thought it fortunate no one wore overcoats or carried umbrellas because where would she have put them? The hats were enough to deal with. She hung them on every peg she could find, crowded them onto the entry table and then carried the rest into the dining room and set them on chairs and lined them out on the long table.

Not a single person introduced himself or herself, and so Mabel categorised them in her own way. There were businessmen in grey or dark blue suits with their boots polished to a high shine, and working-class men in well-worn, mismatched but clean suits. There were women of business in suits, too, and well-dressed women who didn't look as if they needed to worry about work. There were a few women whose attire carried a rather carefree air about it. All wore black armbands as if Guy Despard had only just died, instead of vanishing seven years ago.

When the arrivals slowed to a trickle and then stopped, Mabel took over from Bridget, and ferried platters of sandwiches up to the drawing room to offer to guests, while the maid took round glasses of sherry or whisky. As she worked, Mabel thought about how she had spent her first week with Useful Women.

She had collected and delivered orders from drapers and milliners, and helped with shopping. She had read aloud to an invalid with a penchant for romances and failed in spectacular fashion at being a fourth in bridge. Assisting at the wake of someone who may or may not have died seven years ago may not be as ordinary as taking shoes to the cobblers, but as one of Miss Kerr's Useful Women, she must be prepared for anything.

Mabel watched Rosalind circulate – smiling, taking offered hands and speaking with aplomb. But when Rosalind turned away from an exchange, the animation in her face was replaced with a tight, anxious look.

Mabel had just come up to three women discussing a charity for the families of blinded soldiers when one of the women gave a gasp and whirled round with an indignant look.

'Sandwich?' Mabel asked her, holding out the tray.

The other two women squealed and looked round in confusion, catching the attention of a wider circle. Then Mabel felt something brush her leg and spotted a disappearing form with rough fur and a dark saddle mark on her back.

'Gladys!'

The dog shot off and Mabel gave chase, shouting, 'Let me through!' The sea of people between her and Gladys parted as if Moses himself had raised his staff – still, Mabel managed to catch her foot on a chair leg. As she sailed through the air, she flung the platter away, but the sandwiches continued with their forward motion in Gladys's direction. The dog locked her eyes on one and, at just the right moment, leapt straight up, twisted her body to shift position and opened her mouth. The sandwich didn't stand a chance.

Two men had grabbed Mabel before she could hit the floor and after thanking them, she straightened herself and shook a finger at Gladys, who gazed up at her with innocent chestnut-brown eyes and licked her chops.

Bridget appeared at Mabel's elbow. 'I'll sort this out,' she said, and Mabel realised she must have been talking about the rest of the sandwiches that she now saw had landed on the floor, against a lampshade and on the chest of one of the charity women.

'Thank you,' Mabel whispered. 'Now, come along, you.' She hooked a finger through the dog's collar and led her to the door, feeling the eyes on her from a roomful of people there to pay their condolences on a death.

At the back stairs, Mabel let go of the dog and Gladys trotted on down so that she was already lying on the hearthrug in Bridget's room by the time Mabel got there. She examined the doorknob, an oval variety, and asked the dog, 'Was it not closed, or did you open it yourself?'

Gladys yawned.

'No matter,' Mabel said, giving the dog a scratch behind the ears. 'That's enough excitement for one day, isn't it?'

Mabel came back up the stairs from the kitchen to see one of the men in a dark blue suit hurrying up the steps to the drawing room. Had he gone out and returned? Then she heard voices in the front of the house – voices of several people talking furtively over each other, and at least one of them a woman. What was it that made them sound furtive, Mabel wondered, as if an argument were taking place, everyone straining to keep their voices low? She crept forward. She couldn't hear what was being said but did locate where the voices were coming from – the dining room. The door stood open and through the narrow opening between door and jamb, she saw three of the working-class men, one of them in a brown suit. She could tell nothing more other than one was tall and one shorter and she couldn't see the other one at all – and the back of a woman with black hair. Had the man in the dark blue suit been in there, too, before Mabel came up from the kitchen? When the black-haired woman moved towards the door, Mabel scurried off and up the stairs.

She made it to the drawing room just as there was a *tink-tink-tink* from someone tapping on a glass. Bridget motioned Mabel over to the far corner and handed her a glass of sherry. As the room quietened, motion at the door caught her attention. Mabel thought it was the group she had heard talking downstairs coming in, but the men had blended into the crowd too quickly for her to identify which ones they were, and only the woman with the black hair remained by the door. Then the blue-suited man she'd just seen on the stairs cleared his throat and began to speak.

'On behalf of Mrs Despard, I thank you all for coming. I am Thomas Hardcastle, Mr Guy Despard's solicitor in all his business pursuits. We've gathered today, as you all know, so that we can at last bid a farewell to Mr Despard, whose untimely...' The solicitor pressed his lips together as if the word that wanted to come out needed to be stifled. Mabel thought he should've practised his speech a few more times. 'Who did so much good for so many people during his life.' He raised his glass of whisky. 'Guy Despard.'

Glasses round the room were lifted. 'Guy Despard.'

But before anyone could take a drink, the doorbell was pulled – a shrill interruption, the sound seemed to rush up the stairs and circle round the quiet room. Everyone looked towards the drawing-room door – at least it seemed that way to Mabel, who stood by it. But before she could move to answer, there was a loud *thump*, as if something heavy had been thrown against the front door.

Now, Mabel hurried down the stairs and heard others following. She pulled open the door, and an enormous bundle of something rolled in, hit her legs and almost knocked her over. She grabbed hold of the door and staggered back, bumping into the wall as the bundle dropped at her feet. From behind her came screams and shouts, but the sounds were muffled in Mabel's ears as she looked down and saw a man in a greatcoat lying on his back. His face was a sickly pale, almost green, and he had one arm flung out, with the other inside his coat, as if he clutched at some hidden pain. He didn't move but stared up at her, his pale blue eyes unblinking and mouth open in a silent scream.

Mabel's wartime village nursing skills kicked in. She dropped to her knees and felt for a pulse at the man's neck. Nothing. Steeling herself, she tore open his shirt and recoiled. A massive dark purple mark spread like a starburst across his pale skin – it looked as if his heart had exploded inside his chest.

TWO

After a moment, one of the men called down, 'Is he dead?'

Mabel looked back to see that no one had set foot in the entry – instead, they were lined up the staircase and on the first-floor landing, staring down at her.

'Yes,' she replied. 'He's dead.'

Rosalind slipped between people down the stairs until she reached the entry. She came close to Mabel and leant forward, looking puzzled. 'Who is he?' she asked, but no one answered.

There was a thick silence until Mabel, exasperated at the inaction, said, 'Bridget, telephone for an ambulance. And for the police.' Because there were questions to be answered. Who was this dead man? Why had he come to Rosalind's door?

Bridget elbowed her way down to the telephone on the entry table and rang the exchange. While she talked, Thomas Hardcastle, the solicitor, said, 'We should bring him inside and close the door.'

It was only then that Mabel realised a light rain had begun, and she saw that water beaded the man's greatcoat and his dark red hair. She glanced out and across to the square to find it empty, wet and dreary.

Hardcastle directed two volunteers, who dragged the man's body across the doorstep and in far enough for the front door to be closed. The jostling loosed the hand that had been inside the greatcoat and it slid out, holding onto something.

'What's that in his hand?' a woman called out. 'Is it a letter? Is he the postman?'

Interest grew and fear receded. The crowd began to migrate down the stairs to get a better look.

Rosalind stepped up and peered closely, and when Thomas Hardcastle reached out to take the letter, she snapped it up first.

'Mrs Despard,' Hardcastle said, 'why don't you let me—'

Too late. Rosalind had seen what was written on the envelope, and her eyes had grown wide.

'It's mine,' she whispered. 'It's addressed to me and it's Guy's handwriting.' She looked up to Mabel, who stood directly across the body from her. 'My husband wrote me a letter!'

Hands seemed to come from all directions to try to take it away from her, but Rosalind turned her back on them and ripped open the envelope and dropped it as she pulled out the letter inside. Mabel picked the envelope up. There was no postmark, although the letter looked well-handled. It was addressed to 'Mrs Guy Despard' in a strong, bold hand, suggesting to Mabel a military march. She put it in her pocket.

'Wouldn't you like to sit down?' Mabel asked, and reached across the body to put a tentative hand on Rosalind's shoulder.

Rosalind didn't respond. She held the letter out to get the best light, and her eyes flew over the single page again and again as if trying to take it all in.

Mabel looked at the letter in Rosalind's hands and read it upside down.

23 *September*

My Dearest,

I left home in such haste, I didn't have time to write a message to you, and have arrived at the station only to find my train was delayed. It's finally readying to leave now and so I'm off. I am entrusting this letter to a fine young soldier I've had a chat with while waiting. I've offered him a position when he returns from the war. He has promised to put this letter in the post for me before he takes his own train. He's heading to the front, and we can only wish him – and all the others – the best.

As for me – I'm going only as far as Ireland. I need to have a word with Michael Shaughnessy – do you remember him? I won't be long – two or three days at the most. I will count the hours until I am with you again.

All my love,

Guy

'No, no, no,' Rosalind muttered. 'What is this? You didn't... you should never have... What good is it?'

Rosalind continued to ramble. Hardcastle came up to her side and read over her shoulder, then stepped back quickly and looked into the crowd of guests. Mabel looked too. Most of them appeared lost as to what to do, but there was a woman with black hair and a creamy complexion, who had pulled two or three men aside and was speaking to them in a rushed way. Mabel had seen that woman talking with the same men in the dining room earlier.

Rosalind clutched the letter to her chest. 'I thought he was alive,' she said to no one in particular. 'I thought this meant he'd forgiven—'

'Tea!'

It was Bridget and it was more of a command than an announcement. She made her way over to Rosalind and led her into the study, and Mabel, glad for something to do, said, 'Why don't the rest of the ladies follow? There's no need to stay out here.'

No one questioned her authority. She stood at the study door like a schoolteacher as they filed in. The woman with the black hair noticed Mabel watching and hurried over.

''Tis a dreadful thing to happen today of all days,' she murmured, and continued into the study without waiting for a response.

Mabel heard one of the women in the study say, 'Give her some air.' She looked in to see Rosalind sitting with her hands in her lap, worrying a lace hanky, and inundated with sympathy. She smiled weakly at Mabel.

Bridget had yet to come up from the kitchen when, only a few minutes later, there came a sharp rap at the door. The men had remained in the entry – no, perhaps not all of them. A few were missing, Mabel thought, and Thomas Hardcastle among them. But then he came out of the dining room and, with a glance at her, stood waiting.

Mabel opened the door to two men in dark suits and bowler hats. The older of the two took his hat off and said to her, 'I'm Inspector Tollerton, and this is Sergeant Lett from Scotland Yard. There was a call—'

At that point, Hardcastle came forward and took over, introducing himself and explaining what had happened. As the detectives and several uniformed constables poured into the entry, Mabel wondered at such a quick response with so many officers. Was it the name Despard that brought them?

The police went straight to the body, Hardcastle following and describing his duties as solicitor for Guy Despard's business. The constables told the men crowding forward to keep their distance, but what with the new arrivals and the body taking up so much space, there was very little distance to keep.

Mabel retreated to stay out of the fray. She could see out the open front door and across the road. Another constable stood in front where a small group of people had gathered despite the rain – a couple of men and the woman with the Scottie at her feet. The constable had stretched out his arms to discourage escape, although it didn't look as if anyone was trying to rush past. What had they seen?

Then something caught the eye of the constable across the road, and he shouted, 'Oi! You there, hold up!'

Everyone indoors froze. Footsteps slapped on the pavement, coming closer and closer, and then a man burst into the door-way. The constables on either side caught and held him. He shook them off long enough to push the round, framed glasses up the bridge of his nose and sweep the homburg off his head, dislodging a single curl that fell onto his forehead.

He took in the sight of the body just as Rosalind came out of the study, saying to a woman behind her, 'No, it's all right. I want to,' then turned to see the man at the door. 'Park!'

Park Winstone, Mabel thought – the brother. She watched as he locked eyes on his sister for a moment. Then his gaze flickered to Mabel, and lastly to the two detectives. No one moved, no one spoke.

Sergeant Lett glanced at the inspector, who gave the new arrival a grim look. But after an uneasy moment, as if conceding some unspoken point, Tollerton jerked his head. 'Let him in.' The constables released him, and Tollerton added, 'You watch yourself, Winstone.'

Winstone took what sounded like a threat in his stride, taking his glasses off and drying them with his handkerchief.

The senior detective knelt by the body, but when Rosalind drew close, he stood again and introduced himself. 'Mrs Despard. I'm Inspector Tollerton. You may not remember—'

'Yes, of course I do,' Rosalind replied, her voice devoid of emotion. 'You're an inspector now?' She didn't wait for an answer before asking another question. 'Who is he?'

'He isn't familiar to you?' Tollerton asked, and then looked round. 'To any of you?'

There were murmurings to the negative from the men and the few women who had drifted out of the study.

Tollerton nodded to Rosalind's hand, which still clutched the letter. 'What do you have there?'

'It's a letter from Guy!' Rosalind held it out. 'That's his handwriting. Guy wrote me a letter and that man' – she pointed to the corpse – 'was delivering it. And then he...'

The inspector's expression didn't change upon hearing that a dead man had written a letter. He held out his hand. 'I'll have to take that,' he said.

She snatched her hand away. 'It's mine.' She threw a panicked look to Winstone. In a shaky voice, she said, 'Park, he can't have it. It's mine.'

'Leave it for a bit, Tolly,' Winstone said.

'We don't know what's gone on here,' Tollerton replied. 'This could be evidence in a crime, and I want that letter in police hands.'

Winstone towered over the detective. 'For God's sake, she isn't going to run off with it.'

'Don't start this again,' Tollerton said, standing red-faced over the body and jabbing his finger at the man. 'It didn't do you any good the first time, and it won't do you any good now.'

'Have some compassion, sir!' Mabel's voice cut sharply through the raised voices, and both men turned. Her face heated up, but she continued. 'What harm could it do to let Mrs Despard hold onto the letter from her husband? She's been in this dreadful limbo for seven years.'

Tollerton narrowed his eyes at her. 'I'm sorry, ma'am,' he said. 'Who are you?'

'Miss Mabel Canning.' She was uncertain if she should add that she'd been sent from Useful Women because Miss Kerr might not think this the best time to spread the word of the agency. 'I'm the one who found the man. That is, we were all upstairs in the drawing room and the bell was pulled, and then there was a noise, a loud *thump*, and I was first down. I opened the door and he' – she nodded to the man's body – 'fell over the threshold.'

'Lett,' Tollerton said, and his sergeant pulled out a pocket-book and began writing. 'Now, Miss Canning, what is your position in the household?'

'She is a friend,' Rosalind said, taking Mabel's arm and giving it a squeeze.

Rosalind's hand felt cold, and Mabel covered it with hers. When questioned further, the declaration may not hold up, but Mabel wouldn't be the one to disprove it. Mabel noticed the scrutiny Winstone gave her, but she didn't meet his eye.

'Miss Canning—' Tollerton began.

'She's right,' Winstone said. 'Miss Canning is perfectly right. I'm sure Rosy won't mind you reading the letter, but don't take it away. Not yet.'

'All right, all right,' Tollerton said, as if swatting away a fly. 'But we'll need the fingerprint team here. Lett, get them over here. Mrs Despard, you can wait in the...'

'The study,' Winstone suggested.

'The study. We'll need to speak to each of you,' Tollerton announced to the guests. 'So, would the gentlemen please go in there' – he nodded towards the dining room – 'and the ladies—'

'Upstairs to the drawing room,' Park said.

Tollerton's jaw worked as if he were grinding his teeth.

The men and women separated to move to their desig-nated rooms, and Mabel saw that there were fewer men than there had been at the wake, but she wasn't sure who was missing. Those three men talking with the black-haired woman? But she had stayed behind. Had the solicitor gone? No, there he was still wittering on in one of the policemen's ears.

Tollerton saw Mabel hesitate. 'Miss Canning, upstairs, please.'

'I want Mabel with me,' Rosalind said, and, without waiting for permission, pulled her along into the study.

At that moment, Bridget appeared with the tea tray and followed them.

Tollerton took two long strides and reached the doorway, then pivoted, causing Winstone, who had been on his heels, to crash into him.

Tollerton stuck a finger up in Winstone's face. 'You are not a part of this investigation.'

'Park?' Rosalind called.

The inspector pulled himself up to his full height. 'You remember what I said.' He stood aside to let Winstone pass and then beckoned his sergeant over and the two spoke.

Rosalind and Mabel had settled on the sofa, and Bridget stood at the long table arranging cups and saucers. Winstone approached her.

'Where were you when that fellow landed on the doorstep?' the maid muttered to him.

'On my rounds,' he replied in a low, growling tone. 'But at the far side. I came round the corner just as this lot arrived.'

Tollerton had finished with Lett and stood in the doorway glaring at Winstone and the maid.

'Tea, Inspector?' Bridget asked. 'Milk and sugar?'

The afternoon wore on, becoming an endurance test. Tollerton came and went. Mabel looked out of the study occasionally and reported what she saw to Rosalind, whose emotions bounced from anxiety to misery to cheery helpfulness and back again. More policemen arrived and, for a while, the entry was lit in sudden bursts as photographs were taken of – it seemed to Mabel – everything. Eventually, the body was taken away.

Tollerton managed to get hold of the letter, but only with Winstone's help. The inspector left the room and Winstone spoke to Rosalind softly at first, but the two ended up bickering. Then Mabel heard Winstone mention 'Mum and Dad.' Eventually, Rosalind's resolve wore down, and she handed the letter to Winstone, who took it out to Tollerton.

'So, that's your brother?' Mabel asked Rosalind, when they were left alone.

'Yes – oh, I should've introduced you,' Rosalind said. 'I'm so sorry. What you must think of me.'

'Extenuating circumstances,' Mabel said. 'You've more important things to think about.'

Rosalind's gaze had followed the letter as it left her presence. 'If Guy asked that man to post the letter to me, why hadn't he?'

'Are you certain your husband wrote it?' Mabel asked.

'Yes, I'm certain.' Rosalind frowned. 'Do you believe he wrote it?'

How would Mabel know that? 'Well,' she said, drawing the envelope out of her pocket, 'do you have anything handy that you know for certain he wrote? Because we may be able to—'

'What's that?' Inspector Tollerton had materialised at the door. He nodded to the envelope. 'What do you have there, Miss Canning?'

Poor timing, Mabel thought.

'It's the envelope the letter came in. I put it in my pocket without thinking. Here' – she held it out – 'I suppose you need it, too, to see if there are any fingerprints on it.'

'Yours, for example?' Tollerton asked.

Mabel didn't answer, recognising the question for what it was – chastising her for her actions. At that moment, she saw Bridget with a tray heavy with tea and cake for the guests who were overstaying their welcome but not of their own accord.

'Shall I go and help Bridget?' Mabel asked Rosalind.

Rosalind absent-mindedly patted her hand and said, 'Yes, you go on.'

Bridget immediately relinquished the tray and sent Mabel up to the drawing room. There, she noticed that the different groups of women had mingled – charity workers with secretaries with women dressed with a bit more flamboyance – and were carrying on quiet conversations in mystified tones that included the oft-repeated phrase, 'I don't know, I just don't know.'

Mabel served tea, and then sat next to two women, one older and one younger than her. The older one introduced herself as Mrs Farraday – her chestnut hair was piled on top of her head in the style of a few years earlier – and then introduced her daughter, Miss Farraday, whose black hair sparkled when she turned it to the light.

Wanting to avoid the topic of the body downstairs, Mabel asked, 'How do you know Mrs Despard?' although she had a fair idea.

'Ma was at the Grand with her,' said Miss Farraday. 'That was before she married Mr Despard. Rosalind d'Ville she was then. I remember her. She was an evocative dancer and had such a lovely voice.'

'I was finished being on the stage about then,' Mrs Farraday said, 'and so it was quite convenient for me when Bridget left to come and work for the Despards. I took over looking after the young 'uns in the show, doing their sewing and the like. I do still – but the Grand closed, of course, so I'm at Collins now.'

'I'm in the chorus there,' Miss Farraday added. 'I started just last year.'

The mention of Collins caused Mabel to look towards the landing, her mind travelling as far as the study downstairs.

'I live near Collins in Islington,' Mabel remarked. She hadn't had the chance to say that to anyone yet. 'You must know Cyril. Have you seen him?'

'He left ages ago,' Mrs Farraday said. 'Before all this. He had a matinee. Cyril has never missed a performance – not in twenty years.'

'And he won't let anyone forget it either,' Miss Farraday added with a laugh. 'Weren't you brave back there, standing up to the police?'

'Oh, I don't know,' Mabel said. 'I spoke without thinking.'

Sergeant Lett, sitting in a far corner of the drawing room and conducting interviews, asked Mrs and Miss Faraday over, and Mabel stood to leave. She got as far as the landing, where she met Winstone, platter in hand.

'Did Inspector Tollerton give you permission to serve cake?' Mabel asked, but changed the subject when he gave her a hard look. 'Mr Winstone, there were several more men here earlier.' She described them as best she could.

'I'll ask Rosy, but I expect they'd worked for Guy. Probably still work for the business.'

'Winstone,' Tollerton said from the bottom of the stairs. 'Come on.' He glanced at Mabel. 'You, too, Miss Canning – your presence is requested.'

Mabel sat next to Rosalind on the sofa, with Winstone behind them and Tollerton in front. The letter had been set between two panes of glass and secured with clamps – it was as if the inspector was handing Rosalind a work of art. There was an entire Fingerprint Branch at Scotland Yard – Mabel had read an article about it in one of the London newspapers that her papa had delivered to Peasmarsh. Each person's fingertips were unique – it beggared belief, and Mabel would love to have asked questions about the process, but now was not the time.

'Mrs Despard,' the inspector said, 'are you certain your husband wrote this letter?'

'Yes,' Rosalind said, quick and sure. 'I didn't kill this man. In case that was your next question.'

'Rosy—' Winstone began, but Tollerton shook his head.

'No one can identify the dead man,' the inspector said, 'and he had no other papers on him. He had a key that could be to any one of a million flats or houses in London. We can't try every lock.'

The dead man was himself the key, Mabel thought. The key to what had happened to Guy Despard seven years ago, who – now it was confirmed – had meant to take a train. He had been travelling to Ireland. Had this man in the greatcoat done away with him? Why? How? Had Guy Despard been intercepted by someone he knew, someone he trusted? And wherever had this dead man come from? Mabel cut her eyes at Winstone and away. She thought of Rosalind's mercurial emotional shifts and wondered just how she and her husband had got along.

'Do you remember him, Mrs Despard?' Tollerton asked. 'This Michael Shaughnessy your husband mentioned?'

'No,' Rosalind said. She frowned. 'Yes, perhaps. I'm sorry, Inspector, I can't think straight. Thomas may remember him. Thomas Hardcastle, Guy's solicitor. He's with the other men, isn't he?'

Tollerton called his sergeant in and spoke for a moment. Lett went off and the rest of them waited without speaking, except for Rosalind, who reread the letter aloud, but quietly, to herself.

Sergeant Lett returned to report Thomas Hardcastle had gone.

'We'll leave it for the moment,' Tollerton said. 'I'll talk with Mr Hardcastle later, but please do try to recall anything you may know about this Michael Shaughnessy, Mrs Despard, and let me know if anything comes to you. For now, I'll need to take the letter with me.'

Rosalind spread her hand over the glass. 'No, it's mine,' she whispered, and took a ragged breath. 'You've had your way with it, now it's mine.'

'We are not equipped to lift fingerprints from paper here,' Tollerton explained. 'We need to take it in. Perhaps you could write out a copy and keep that.'

Rosalind made no move and Tollerton sighed.

'Winstone.'

'Rosy?' Winstone prompted, laying a hand on his sister's shoulder.

'Yes, yes, all right,' she said, and thrust the encased letter towards the inspector.

Tollerton took it but hesitated. 'I need to say, Mrs Despard, that the fingerprinting process on paper can result in some damage.'

'Damage?' Rosalind said, her voice shaking with anger. 'You mean, you'll destroy it – the last letter my husband wrote to me?'

'So you meant it when you suggested writing out a copy?' Mabel asked. 'I could write one out for Mrs Despard if she'd like. Could you leave it for a few more minutes, Inspector?'

'Yes, fine,' Tollerton said.

'Sir,' Lett said. 'We've finished with everyone – all right to let them go?'

'Before there isn't a tea leaf left in the house,' Bridget said from behind the sergeant. Lett jumped back to let Bridget in.

'Don't let them go yet – I want another look at them,' Tollerton said. 'Park, come along.'

When the inspector and Winstone had gone, leaving a constable just inside the door and Bridget collecting cups and saucers, Mabel asked, 'Would you like the copy to look like your husband's writing? I could try my best to imitate it.'

'That would be lovely,' Rosalind said, but in an absent-minded fashion.

With Bridget complaining about the mess that would be left

behind, Mabel sat at the desk, propped up the glass-encased letter and studied the firm hand before taking up a pen and writing.

In a short while, it was done, and she called Rosalind over, 'Would you like to see?'

Mabel held out the copied letter and Rosalind's face widened in surprise as she looked to the original in the glass and back to the copy.

'Your best is very good,' Rosalind said, and clasped the copy to her chest. 'Thank you.'

'You're welcome.'

'Right,' Tollerton said, entering the room. 'Now, we're finished.' He held out his hand. 'I'll need the letter please, Miss Canning.'

Mabel handed it over as Rosalind slipped the copy under a stack of letters.

'You,' Bridget said to Rosalind, 'you are going to bed. This minute.'

Rosalind blinked slowly, all at once looking as if she could fall asleep on the spot. She patted Mabel's hand and said, 'I'll see you soon.'

There was a general exodus. Bridget took Rosalind off, the guests departed with some haste, and the police and Winstone went upstairs. Mabel found herself alone in the entry. The sun dipped below the clouds and a shaft of late-afternoon light came through the side window of the front door and cast a swathe of gold across the floor, which vanished when a figure stepped up. Mabel opened the door to Cyril.

'Ah, Miss Canning. Have they all gone?' he asked.

'The police are still here,' Mabel said. 'Upstairs.'

'The police?' Cyril repeated. He pushed the brim of his hat

up with the end of his walking stick. 'What have I missed – did someone give stuffy old Thomas Hardcastle a pop?'

Mabel was too weary to explain. She called up to Winstone on the first-floor landing, and he came down.

'Park, what's all this?' Cyril asked him, dropping his walking stick in the umbrella stand.

'Come into the study, Cyril,' Winstone said. 'I'll explain.' He paused. 'Thank you, Miss Canning.'

Thank you, Miss Canning, you are dismissed.

Mabel felt as if all the air had been let out of her. In the course of the afternoon, she had become entangled in the mysterious disappearance of Guy Despard, had been drawn into Rosalind's desperate need to know what had happened to her husband and had been dropped into what looked to be the murder of a man no one recognised. A man who had fallen dead at her feet. Now, she was being sent on her way.

She opened her mouth to protest, but Winstone had already walked into the study and closed the door.

'Good evening,' she said, her voice echoing in the empty entry.

THREE

Mabel took her usual tram home to Islington. *Her usual* – after only a week in London, she felt as if she could say that, and she had the Reverend Ronald Herringay, the vicar in Peasmarsh, to thank for spurring her into action to fulfil her dream. Not that he wanted the credit.

Two years earlier, Edith, Ronald's wife and Mabel's dearest friend, had died. Everyone knows that a vicar needs a wife, and after an appropriate time for mourning had passed, Mabel had begun to see the looks thrown her way and knew that the village was talking about possibilities. She agreed that the vicar needed a wife, but it certainly wouldn't be her because Mabel would be moving to London and living as an independent woman, her lifelong dream.

She had plunged into planning and reading anything she could about today's independent woman in newspapers and magazines. In her research, she had come across an article in the *Gazette* about Useful Women, in which Miss Kerr espoused the fact that 'middle-aged women are among my most experienced and so most successful workers, meeting the needs of the gentlewomen of London'. It was as if Miss Kerr were speaking directly to Mabel.

She had immediately written away for details, and had received a letter, along with Useful Women booklet number eight, which listed the agency's services – all ninety-nine of them. Blithely, she vowed to herself to take on any job from repairing antique furniture to visiting the sick to training a mouse. *How does one train a mouse?* No matter, she had sent her letter of application by return post. At thirty-two, she was barely old enough to be middle-aged, and so in the letter, she had seized upon Miss Kerr's statement about experience. She'd written that her enthusiasm for the work was equal to her skill. Possibly greater, but she kept that to herself, and when Miss Kerr had extended the offer for Mabel to be added to the rolls of Useful Women, Mabel had leapt at the opportunity.

She'd lived her entire life in the company of other people, and so accustomed was she to having someone to talk with that the first night in her flat, she had fallen into a conversation with herself. Aloud. She had put an end to that abruptly and instead sat quietly over a cup of cocoa and stared out the window to the pavement below and the green just over the road, then wrote a cheery letter home to tell them about the jobs she'd carried out on her first day, which had included eating four servings of sticky toffee pudding as a judge in a children's cookery course – and needing a strong cup of tea with no milk or sugar directly afterwards – and repotting an aspidistra.

Now, Mabel walked the short distance from her tram stop to New River House as light began to fall and the gas street lamps were lit against the coming night. It would be Monday before Miss Kerr would get the full report of Mabel's assignment to help out at a wake. Perhaps by then Mabel's thoughts would've settled and she could speak about the wake, the dead man on the doorstep and the rest of the day in a coherent fashion. She didn't believe Miss Kerr would ever have had such a

Useful Women report before. Mabel wished she had more background details on the story. She wished she knew more about Guy Despard.

She pushed open the door of the building to find the porter in his office behind the counter – already a homely sight.

'Good evening, Mr Chigley,' she said.

Mr Chigley looked up from a cup of tea and lifted one side of his mouth in a smile. The other side, heavily scarred from a fire decades ago, didn't move, making it look as if he wore a mask on half his face.

'Miss Canning, good evening. End of your first week in London – won't your father be proud?'

'Yes, I'm sure he will be.'

'Let me get your post,' Mr Chigley said, moving over to the wall of pigeonholes.

Mabel knew her papa's pride would be tinged with concern – dare she say fear – for his baby girl, who had taken it upon herself to up sticks from their village and move to the Big Smoke, and it had been a hard sell to convince her father that today's woman had more freedom than ever before and could live on her own quite safely, even though Mabel had read him an article about it from the *West Sussex Gazette*.

He had reluctantly gone along with her plan, but trouble had come when Mabel pored over the advertisements for accommodations in London and had found the offerings dismal. There were serviced flats, but they were too costly for the budget she'd set herself, and she wouldn't squander her savings – the money her mother had left her. At the other extreme, she had found listings for bedsitters or flatlets. What was a flatlet but a sectioned off room and a cot?

Then Papa had remembered that his old friend Mr Chigley, with whom he had served in India, was now a porter at New River House, a proper block of flats in Islington, so near to the center of London. This arrangement had suited everyone concerned.

Mr Chigley handed over Mabel's post – a letter from Mrs Chandekar and one from the vicar – but she lingered by the porter's window as two women came down the stairs. Mabel had met them early on in her week. One, Miss Portjoy, was a bit shorter than Mabel. She had apple cheeks and wore a cloche, edged with silver beading and pulled down so far she needed to tilt her head back to see anything. The other, Miss Skeffington, was tall and wore trousers with a long coat. Her hair was cut quite short, and she had on a sort of tam with a narrow bill and a cigarette in her hand.

They all exchanged greetings and then Miss Skeffington asked, 'Good day, Miss Canning?'

Mabel had an impulse to tell them everything about the wake, Despard, the dead man on the doorstep. She caught herself just in time, remembering Mr Chigley was listening and he was her papa's eyes and ears in London, and so instead, she stumbled over a few words. 'Oh well... it was...'

Miss Portjoy put a hand on Mabel's arm. 'It's like that for all of us some days,' she said.

Mabel certainly hoped not.

'What about that drink we promised?' Miss Skeffington asked, and Mabel vaguely remembered the open invitation. 'Why don't you come up to ours later and we'll have a right chinwag?'

It was agreed.

Mabel ate cold chicken with piccalilli for her evening meal and finished with a jar of last year's pears. At about eight o'clock, she made her way up from her flat on the second floor to Miss Portjoy and Miss Skeffington's flat on the third and knocked.

'Here we are now,' Miss Portjoy said, opening the door wide. 'Do come in.'

The women's flat was no bigger than Mabel's – that is, it held a small sitting room, a separate bedroom and bathroom, and a kitchen that was more alcove than room. Still, they'd made it quite comfortable – its most prominent feature the many different styles of hats hanging on the backs of chairs, over small statuettes and on top of the bookcase.

'It's so kind of you to ask me up,' Mabel said. 'I forgot to say, Miss Portjoy, I admired the cloche you were wearing earlier.'

'Now none of this "Miss" business,' Miss Skeffington admonished from the kitchen. 'She's Cora and I'm Skeff.'

'And I'm Mabel. And here's some damson jam straight from Sussex,' she replied, offering a jar. 'Mrs Chandekar and I put it up just before I left.'

'Splendid,' Skeff said. 'A bit of the country in the city.'

'How've you managed your first week in London?' Cora asked, offering a place to sit on the sofa. 'I was eighteen when I arrived from Hollinsclough, and I tell you, it pretty near killed me.'

'Hollinsclough?' Mabel asked.

'Yes, it's in Staffordshire,' Cora said, bringing out her apple cheeks with a smile. 'Do you know it?'

'No, sorry, I don't.'

'You wouldn't, of course,' Cora said, nodding. 'It's quite small.'

Mabel's head was filled with a thousand questions she wanted to ask these women, but she didn't want to pry. Much.

'And you, Skeff?' she asked.

'Londoner – cockney, if you will,' Skeff said over her shoulder, as she muddled the contents of a tall jug. 'Born within the sound of Bow Bells. That's the thing about London – it brings us all together, doesn't it?' She poured out three tumblers, and handed them round. 'Cheers!'

Mabel raised the glass and breathed in the aroma of oranges and lemons and gin. She took a sip, and the liquid slid down her throat as if it knew the way.

'That's quite good,' she said, and gave a little cough.

'My grandfather's gin punch,' Skeff said. 'He taught me how to mix it before I was even in school.'

Mabel hadn't thought she was in much of a mood to talk, but somehow the gin punch helped her along. Skeff's grandfather's use of child labour notwithstanding, it was good stuff, and soon she was explaining how she had got on with Useful Women and the interesting jobs she'd had in her first week. She stopped just short of her assignment at Rosalind Despard's. She asked Cora and Skeff about their lives.

Cora worked at a milliner's.

'She's a designer, mind you,' Skeff said. 'She's done all these' – she swept her arm round the room – 'and she'll be selling her own hats before long. Women won't be able to get enough of the dramatic lines and creative shapes. You'll be all the rage.' Skeff put her hand on Cora's knee and leant towards Mabel as if to confess a secret. 'She's a true artist.'

Cora blushed and smiled. 'I say "change your hat and you can change your life." Skeff here works at a newspaper.'

'The *London Intelligencer*,' Skeff confirmed. 'We're just off Fleet Street on Shoe Lane. My uncle Pitt owns it, and I'm on staff.'

'She writes important articles about people's lives,' Cora said. 'Both men and women. Do you know the American Nellie Bly – the one who had herself sectioned to a mental hospital so that she could write about it? That's Skeff for you – she searches for the truth.'

'How did the two of you meet?' Mabel asked, getting a fair idea of Cora and Skeff's relationship, but still hoping she wasn't overstepping any bounds.

'On the bus,' Cora replied, her apple cheeks turning even

redder. 'There wasn't a seat to be had, and Skeff offered hers and I said, oh, no, you stay there, and then the bus came to a sudden halt and—'

'Cora fell into my lap,' Skeff said, and burst out laughing. 'I told her she could stay there if she liked.'

'I didn't, of course,' Cora said in a scandalised whisper and then giggled. 'Too many eyes.'

Mabel laughed too. She determined to take this arrangement in her stride because she lived in the city now and London was filled with all sorts of people, and it was none of her concern. Plus, she quite liked these two.

'And you, Mabel?' Skeff asked. 'Any man in your life?'

'No.' Mabel shook her head vehemently as Skeff refilled her tumbler.

Cora offered a sympathetic smile. 'Did you lose someone in the war?'

It was the obvious question – so many had.

'No,' Mabel replied. 'It's just I don't have time for that sort of thing now.'

'Ah, *now* you say. But there may have been one or two in the past,' Skeff said with a shrewd look.

'Well, one or two,' Mabel said, and took a drink. Three, actually – all offers of marriage. That had been before the war, and she'd turned them down because she had planned to move to London. Why had it taken her this long? 'But, you see, I want to concentrate on being an independent woman. And when I decide to do something, then I do it – you can ask my papa, or my Mrs Chandekar, or anyone.'

'You're in the vanguard, you know,' Skeff said. 'An unmarried woman moving to the city, living on her own. Quite different from the village life, I suppose.'

'Today certainly was,' Mabel remarked. She took a drink, unsure of what to say next.

A look of concern furrowed Cora's brow. 'What's happened?'

Well, why shouldn't she tell someone? It would be good practice for when she explained the day to Miss Kerr.

'I was engaged to help at a wake, you see,' Mabel began. 'It was at a house in Belgravia – lovely neighbourhood. But when I arrived, I found out that the wake wasn't for someone who had just died – it was for someone who went missing seven years ago and was now declared dead. His wife has no idea what happened to him. The police were involved at the time, but—'

Skeff paused with an unlit cigarette in one hand and a burning match in the other, until the match burnt through and she had to drop it onto the ashtray. 'I say, hang on.' Sticking the unlit cigarette between her lips, she went over and began riffling through a teetering stack of newspapers and magazines on a chair, pulled one out, searched through a few pages and then turned the paper out and flicked it with her finger. She handed it to Mabel. 'Is this your story?'

MR GUY DESPARD DISAPPEARANCE

Seven Years On

What Happened To Prominent Businessman?

Wife, Former Music Hall Entertainer, Questioned at the Time

Mabel's jaw dropped. 'This is it – how did you know?'

'Skeff has a nose for news,' Cora said, 'and a head full of facts. It's the newspaper life.'

Mabel read through the brief article. There was little of substance. Guy Despard had made his money in shipping. He had married Rosalind d'Ville, as she had been known on the stage, two years before his disappearance. Rosalind had been questioned – the article implied wives were always the first to be suspected of foul play – but nothing had come of the investigation, apart from some sort of row within the Metropolitan Police. Now, at the anniversary of Despard's disappearance and because seven years missing equalled legally dead, the story had been dredged up. The point was made that Rosalind would be in for a great deal of money.

'That's the *Daily Herald*,' Skeff said dismissively. 'Uncle Pitt won't give space to such stuff. I remember when it happened – just at the beginning of the war. The innuendoes thrown about were typical and atrocious. Where had the wife been, what did she stand to gain from his death – that sort of thing. And here they are dragging it all up again.'

'There's more to it than that,' Mabel said. 'Right in the middle of the wake, the doorbell was pulled and I went to answer, and when I opened the door—' and she told the rest of the story.

Cora was aghast. 'You opened the door and there he was dead at your feet?'

'And no one knew him, you say?' Skeff's voice held a fair bit of scepticism. 'Are you certain?'

'No one admitted to it,' Mabel replied. 'Although…'

'Ah,' Skeff said.

'It's only that there seemed to be some intense talking going on in quiet corners. Mrs Despard's – Rosalind's – brother showed up. The police knew him, but I'm not certain how.' Mabel frowned. 'What does the man in the greatcoat have to do with Guy Despard? It isn't fair to be handed a puzzle to solve and then have it snatched away from you again. Also, I liked Rosalind, but she's quite troubled and I wonder if others don't take advantage of that. But what does it all matter? On Monday, Miss Kerr will probably send me off to do someone's shopping.' She huffed.

Skeff lifted the jug and Mabel held her tumbler out.

'The nature of the agency, I suppose,' Skeff said, pouring more gin into their glasses. 'You never know what you may come across.'

The chat turned to more pleasant things, and at the end of the evening, Mabel thanked the women for their hospitality, stood to leave and then promptly lost her balance and fell back onto the sofa again. Skeff and Cora insisted on escorting her to the door of her flat, where she assured them she was quite fine and said good night.

Mabel woke the next morning fully clothed, lying on top of her bedcovers, and with such a head. Squinting into the sunlight that dared to stream through the window and trying to put the previous evening into focus, she realised that she didn't want to be known as someone who couldn't hold her drink, so she either needed not to drink or become more accustomed to it. By the time she'd washed and had tea and toast, she felt almost normal again.

Midmorning, she set off for Westminster Abbey with her Baedeker's. At least for this Sunday, being a tourist would replace attending service, although she wouldn't mention that in her letters to Papa.

In the afternoon, she ate chips in Trafalgar Square and sat on a bench feeding the ducks in St James's Park. Only then did her mind wander and she speculated on what sort of activity filled Rosalind Despard's Sunday. Perhaps the police were still in attendance. Maybe someone had recognised the dead man in the greatcoat. He must've known what had happened to Guy Despard all those years ago. Mabel would like to know how he died – either of them – but she'd been cut adrift from the investigation and so should concentrate on her second week as one of the Useful Women and making enough money to cover her living expenses.

On the way back to Islington, Mabel sat behind a woman with one of those new bob haircuts, which looked ever so smart with her beret. This reminded Mabel it was the night to wash her own waist-length hair. What a chore. It hadn't seemed that way in Peasmarsh, of course, because she and Mrs Chandekar would wash their hair on the same night and, banning Papa from the kitchen, the two women would stand in their shifts at the cooker, rubbing their wet hair with towels and chatting about who had said and done what in the village lately.

Mabel didn't have that luxury now, and as a modern woman, she should consider timesaving solutions to her problems.

Mabel had just opened the door to New River House when, behind her, she heard Skeff call, 'I say, Mabel!'

Cora and Skeff. How fortuitous, Mabel thought without examining why.

'Hello,' she said. 'Your hat's lovely, Cora.'

Cora wore a jaunty style Mabel had seen only since she'd arrived in London – the brim was turned up across the front, forming a point on either side.

'Thanks,' Cora said. 'Fashion's gone batty for the bicorn hat because of *The Three Musketeers* at the cinema.'

They stood in the foyer and Mabel glanced into the porter's office – the door to Mr Chigley's private quarters stood ajar and she could hear him humming.

Without thinking further, Mabel turned to Cora and Skeff. 'It's time I cut my hair,' she said as a sort of announcement.

'Oh yes, do,' Cora said. 'A bobbed cut – it would suit you.'

'You're right, Cora my love,' Skeff agreed. 'That's the ticket, Mabel – it would be a new you.'

'Yes, good,' Mabel said, at once regretting even mentioning the prospect. 'Perhaps you could recommend someone, and I could make an appointment next week.'

'As a matter of fact, I can recommend someone,' Skeff said. 'Cora. She's a dab hand with the shears. Cuts her own hair as well as mine. Are you free now? No time like the present.'

Mabel could feel her heart thumping in her chest. Had she really meant now? Yet, if she put it off, would she ever take action?

The two women waited for her to speak, Cora lifting her eyebrows, and Skeff taking a pull on her cigarette. *Carpe diem.*

Mabel swallowed hard. 'Yes, let's do it.'

The two women took Mabel straight to their flat and, as it happened, Cora was so careful and Skeff so good at distracting Mabel with idle chit-chat that the entire event passed without incident. Once she'd finished, Cora led her to a mirror on the wall beside the door, and Mabel was both shocked and pleased by what she saw. Her hair now ended just below her chin and, without the weight of its former length, curled of its own accord. *A new you indeed.*

FOUR

Monday morning, Mabel walked out of her flat and had reached the stairs just behind a young man in a narrow, fitted suit who swaggered down carrying a small case in one hand. She followed him at a distance until on his final few steps to the foyer, he turned back to her and clicked the side of his tongue at her as if he were calling a horse.

She raised an eyebrow and said, 'I beg your pardon?'

'All right there, Miss Canning,' Mr Chigley called, leaning out of his porter's window. She saw his eyes narrow when he spotted the young man. 'Good morning, Mr Jenks.'

The young man's Adam's apple bobbed and his face flushed scarlet. 'Yes... er... good morning, Mr Chigley.' He pulled the boater off his head and began inching his way to the door.

'Miss Canning,' the porter said, 'this is Mr Jenks, salesman of threads and embroidery floss.'

'And bobbins,' Mr Jenks added, his eyes flickering to Mabel and then away.

'And bobbins. He's in flat fourteen, so below you.'

Mabel flashed a smile at the young man. 'Pleased to meet you, Mr Jenks.'

'My pleasure entirely, Miss Canning,' Mr Jenks mumbled, then added, 'Good day,' and dashed out the door.

The cheek, Mabel thought. *Mr Jenks better keep his bobbins to himself.*

It was with a great deal of caution that Mabel walked into the Useful Women office at 48 Dover Street, just off Piccadilly. In her first week, she had found Miss Lillian Kerr, proprietress, demanded dedication from her employees, even those women who were working for only pin money. Mabel, who needed to earn her living or she'd be back in Peasmarsh with her tail between her legs, was unsure how Miss Kerr would take her report of Saturday's events.

Along with all of the Useful Women, Mabel had paid a consideration fee of two shillings and sixpence. Miss Kerr charged the clients according to the job. Collecting a dress from the drapers wouldn't run nearly as high as arranging a tour of the zoo for foreign visitors – that seemed obvious – and Mabel thought that helping at a wake would be on the high end, but she had no idea if having a murder victim fall at your feet would be extra or a discount.

Mabel arrived barely after nine o'clock, with Miss Kerr already on the telephone, just as she had been a week ago on Mabel's first morning as one of the Useful Women.

She had been winded that first day from hurrying up the two flights of stairs or – more likely – from the excitement on her first day as an independent woman. After a deep breath, she had obeyed the sign on the door that read 'Please Come In', and had stepped over the threshold.

The woman at the desk had been on the telephone. She looked perhaps in her late forties. Her dark hair was threaded with silver, matching the silver-framed spectacles that hung on a chain round her neck and rested on her peach crêpe de Chine dress. She had ended the conversation with, 'Yes, she will be arriving forthwith,' placed the earpiece back on its hook and looked up. 'Good morning.'

'Good morning,' Mabel had said, 'I'm—'

The telephone on the desk had jangled, and the woman had held up a finger. 'Excuse me for a moment, won't you?' She'd picked up the earpiece and leant forward to speak. 'Hello, good morning' – her tone was honeyed but businesslike – 'this is the Useful Women agency, and I am Miss Lillian Kerr. How can I help you?'

Mabel had waited just inside the door and looked round while Miss Kerr had taken the particulars of a job involving laundry starch. The office was large but sparsely furnished. Chairs lined the walls. In one back corner sat an oak filing cabinet and, in the other, a plain deal table with a Remington typewriter, as if the machine might not be in daily use. On Miss Kerr's desk, in addition to the candlestick telephone, was a ledger marked Jobs on the spine, a stack of folders and another record book labelled Register of Useful Women. Under the desk was laid a rectangular, floral-patterned Axminster rug doing its best to reduce the austerity of its surroundings.

When Miss Kerr had finished assigning the laundry starch job, she'd looked up at Mabel. 'Now, are you one of mine?' she'd asked.

'Yes – that is, I'm on your rolls. My name is Mabel Canning, and I wrote to say I'd be ready to begin today.'

'Miss Canning, of course.' Miss Kerr had reached for the register. She'd turned page after page, at last stopping and running her finger down a column. 'Here you are. Come, sit down, please. You're new to London?'

Mabel had taken the chair across the desk. 'I am, yes. Not to worry, though. I may be new, but I know my way round.'

She had arrived only the day before – Sunday afternoon – but already, on her first morning, had sorted out which tram to take from Islington to Piccadilly and how to walk from there to the Useful Women office in Dover Street. In addition, she had Bacon's pocket map of London in her bag and knew how to use it. What else could there be to learn?

Miss Kerr had murmured an unintelligible reply and turned the register back two pages, lifted the earpiece and asked the exchange for a number.

Mabel had sat straight in her chair but glanced across the desk and read upside down what Miss Kerr had written in the Jobs ledger: 'Shopping for silk at Liberty. Bed jacket.'

As one of the Useful Women, Mabel knew she must be ready to take on any assignment given to her, from shopping to serving tea to the more intellectual tasks, such as cataloguing a library. But, although she had heard of the shop Liberty, she had always relied on Mrs Chandekar for such things as selecting fabric and sewing clothes. Just as well to be passed over for this assignment.

When the job had been assigned, Miss Kerr had turned to Mabel. 'Now, shall we take a look at your details?' From the stack of folders on her desk, she'd pulled the one labelled 'Canning, Mabel.' Having her name on a folder gave Mabel a thrill. Miss Kerr had scanned the pages, murmuring in approving tones. 'I must say, you come with glowing references – one from your vicar and another from Giles Greenberry. A barrister, no less. I recognise his name from the newspapers.'

She'd expected the letter from Ronald, but didn't quite know how Papa had persuaded Mr Greenberry, who was a distant relative on her mother's side and had laid eyes on Mabel once, when she was five years old. Perhaps Mabel would look him up now she was living in London.

'And how were you of service to the Reverend Herringay?' Miss Kerr had asked.

'I took care of his correspondence.'

'Good, good,' Miss Kerr had said and wrote: *Works well with the Church.*

Mabel wouldn't have gone that far, but Miss Kerr seemed pleased, and so she'd said nothing.

'Your family is in Peasmarsh, Miss Canning?' Miss Kerr had asked.

'My father,' Mabel had replied. 'And Mrs Chandekar. She was my ayah when I was in the nursery. You see, we were living in India – Papa was with the Indian Army Service Corps. My mother died not long after I was born. Papa hired an ayah to accompany us on the voyage home, and she stayed with us and became our housekeeper. She's—'

The telephone had rung, and Miss Kerr had answered. Mabel had reminded herself not to talk too much.

When Miss Kerr had dispatched the new job to another of the Useful Women, she'd said, 'Well, Miss Canning, I don't expect you to wait here in the office all day. After all, that's what the telephone is for. I'm happy to ring you when an appropriate assignment arises.'

But Mabel had noticed how many pages of Useful Women were in the register. Each, like Mabel, had paid her two-and-sixpence fee and was also probably ready and willing to work. Mabel also knew that out of sight was out of mind and had decided the proper course of action was to be present and accounted for.

'No need, Miss Kerr,' she had said. 'I'll stay, it's no trouble at all. I'd much rather be on hand for whatever may come my way.'

Now, one week later and with Miss Kerr on the telephone, Mabel didn't hesitate to take up what had quickly become her usual position – the chair across the desk from her employer.

When Miss Kerr returned the earpiece to its hook and rested her forearms on the desk, she said, 'Good morning, Miss Canning. I see you've been taken by the new hairstyle – it quite suits you.'

'Thank you.' Mabel patted her short curls. She had felt a bit light-headed this morning but in a good way.

'And how was Saturday?' Miss Kerr asked.

'Not what either of us expected,' Mabel replied.

Miss Kerr straightened. 'You're not going to tell me Mr Guy Despard walked into his own wake?'

So, of course, Miss Kerr had known the Despard story. Could she not have mentioned it to Mabel?

'No, not Mr Despard. But there was an incident.'

She went through it again, glad she'd had the practice with Cora and Skeff. Miss Kerr was suitably shocked and made a note in her Jobs ledger that Mabel was unable to read, upside down or not, because Miss Kerr closed the cover too quickly.

'Well, Miss Canning, we'll wish the best for the Metropolitan Police and hope that they solve their case quickly for all concerned. For our part, we will hope for a less exciting week, won't we?'

No need to reply because the telephone jangled. Miss Kerr took a request for someone to read to an invalid in German. While Miss Kerr looked through her register of Useful Women, Mabel averted her eyes. Her German was *nicht gut*, and so she breathed a sigh of relief when the job passed her by. As Miss Kerr had said more than once in Mabel's first week, she prided herself in her ability to match job to worker.

Mabel admired the life Miss Kerr had made for herself. She had a no-nonsense attitude touched with sympathy, which seemed a good combination for both her clients and her employees. As attuned to her Useful Women as Miss Kerr said she was, Mabel had no doubt she would be given an easy job – perhaps discussing one of Mr Dickens's novels such as *Our Mutual Friend* with a kindly old lady in a cosy parlour.

. . .

'Useful Women, Miss Lillian Kerr speaking. How can I help you?'

It was afternoon. The morning had worn on, and then the office had closed for lunch. Mabel had eaten an apple in Green Park and then returned directly to take up her usual position just as the telephone had rung.

Miss Kerr listened, and her eyes grew wide.

'Why, Mrs Malling-Frobisher, how lovely to hear from you. Time again already? My, the school holidays flew by, didn't they?' While the voice on the other end of the line spoke, Miss Kerr opened the ledger and made a note. 'Oh yes, that's right, there was that day jaunt to the seaside as well. She's recovered quite nicely, thank you for asking, although I don't believe she's available today.' Miss Kerr reached for the register and ran her finger down page after page of names. 'Never fear, I have just the person for the job.' A pause. 'No, no' – she laughed, a tinkling, light-hearted sound – 'I'm sure there'll be no need for an ambulance to be called... Yes, I'll have someone to you with time to spare.'

Miss Kerr depressed the hook on the telephone for a moment before starting in. She asked the exchange for first one number, then another and another, but each time she got no further than 'The client is Mrs Malling-Frobisher' before the conversation was ended abruptly. At last, she set the receiver back on its hook and sighed.

'I'll do it,' Mabel said. 'I'll take Augustus to his train.'

Miss Kerr glanced down at what she'd written in the ledger and up at Mabel.

'No, Miss Canning, I would prefer to send a more seasoned worker on this particular venture.'

After doing nothing all morning, Mabel had realised she would prefer nearly any job. 'A little scamp, is he?' she asked. 'I'm quite accustomed to boys from my years teaching the infants' Sunday school.'

'I'm afraid this goes beyond Sunday school, and I wouldn't want to—'

'Please, Miss Kerr. I know I can do it.'

Miss Kerr drummed her fingers on the desk and then took a deep breath.

'Well, then, as you are eager to prove yourself, I will give you that opportunity.' She wrote on her notepad, tore off the page and handed it to Mabel. 'Eight year-old Augustus Malling-Frobisher III to be escorted to Victoria Station and put on the train – be very certain he is on it, please – that will take him to his grammar school. And may I suggest, Miss Canning, that you brook no quarter.'

To Mayfair she went. Miss Kerr had provided basic directions, and Mabel attempted to fill in with her Bacon's walking map of London but found details lacking there too. She walked too far and had to retrace her steps, all the while a clock in her head ticking off the seconds she was wasting. Little Augustus mustn't miss his train. Poor little fellow – eight years old and off to boarding school.

She found a police constable on his beat, and he walked her to the correct corner. Mabel hurried down a crescent and breathed a sigh of relief when she saw a taxi idling at the kerb outside the house she wanted. A curtain twitched as she approached, and a moment before she could pull the bell, the front door flew open to a red-faced maid clutching the arm of a small boy. 'Are you the one?' she asked.

Mabel wondered if this maid was related to Bridget, but thought it unlikely. Perhaps this attitude was the way of the new maid.

'Hello, I'm Mabel Canning from Useful Women. I'm here to escort Augustus to Victoria Station.'

The boy – dressed in short trousers, a school jacket, tie and billed cap – gave Mabel a shiny smile and said, 'Hello, Miss Canning. I'm Augustus. I'm very pleased to meet you.'

A woman wearing a floor-length dressing gown came rushing up from behind the maid, calling out, 'Wait, wait,' and waving a handkerchief. She knelt and took the boy in her arms. 'Dear Augustus, Mummy will miss you so. Do be a good boy for...' She looked up at Mabel with her eyebrows raised.

'Miss Canning,' Mabel said.

'Miss Canning,' Augustus's mother repeated. She straightened his tie and the cap, which her embrace had set askew.

'Yes, Mother,' Augustus said. He turned to Mabel. 'We'd best be off, don't you think?'

His mother stepped back. The maid handed Mabel the train ticket to Tunbridge Wells, told her the boy's trunk had preceded him that morning and said, 'He's ready.'

'Perhaps not quite,' Mabel replied, and in a swift move that any pickpocket would've admired, she swooped down and extracted a bent and flattened cigarette from Augustus's breast pocket.

The mother gasped. The boy grinned and shrugged.

Mabel handed the cigarette to the maid. If this was the worst of Augustus Malling-Frobisher III, then she could take it. It was nothing compared with some of the boys she'd taught at Sunday school in Peasmarsh.

On the taxi journey to the station, Mabel said, 'Holidays over, are they? Are you sad to leave home?'

'I like school,' Augustus said brightly.

'Well, then, you'll soon be on your train.'

'What time is it, please?' the boy asked.

'We've plenty of time,' Mabel replied. 'Fifteen minutes.'

The boy looked out the window of the taxi and muttered something Mabel didn't hear.

The cabbie, having already been paid at the house, drove off the second they were out of the vehicle. Mabel escorted

Augustus into the station, checked the departure board to find the platform had yet to be listed, and found room on a bench for them to wait.

'Won't be long now,' Mabel said.

She took a moment to glance over at the café across the way and wonder if she'd have time for a cup of tea after Augustus had departed.

The boy looked up at the clock almost directly overhead. Mabel followed his gaze and then checked the departure board again. The letters and numbers clicked into place, and Mabel stood.

'There we are,' she said, but when she turned, Augustus was gone.

Mabel looked in front, in back, and beneath the bench, then towards the platform.

'Augustus?' she called.

She scanned the vast open area of the station. People – not one of them the eight-year-old boy she sought – hurried across the black-and-white tiled floor, their paths criss-crossing as if they were dancers in a synchronised routine.

'Augustus!' she shouted.

No one gave her a second glance.

Had she lost him? How? He'd been beside her on the bench. For one second, she had looked away and—

He must've gone ahead to his train. Mabel ran, but they were stuttering steps because she paused and asked people along the way, 'Have you seen a small boy in a school uniform?' In return, she received blank looks and shaking heads.

At the platform, which looked a mile long, she spotted a porter standing alongside an open carriage door.

'Have you seen a small boy running past?'

'Have you lost one?' he said, in an entirely unhelpful manner.

Mabel grabbed the front of his jacket with such violence

that he nearly toppled over on her. 'Yes, I have,' she said, 'and I must find him.'

'Sorry, ma'am, no, I haven't seen one,' the man replied. 'But don't you worry, we'll locate the lad.'

He quickly called over two other porters, and Mabel apprised them of the situation. One of them led her onto the train – Augustus's train – because, they told her, perhaps the boy had boarded on his own. *Unlikely*, she thought, as she had his ticket in her handbag. Still, they searched from one end to the other.

Augustus was not on the train – not in a seat, in a compartment, between carriages, in the luggage car, or hiding in the toilet. At the engine, the driver had seen no one. As a last resort, one of the porters climbed up and looked into the coal car. This both frightened Mabel and angered her. Is this what the other Useful Women had dealt with – a vanishing Augustus?

Then a porter said that someone had seen a young boy alone get on the through train to Dover just before it pulled out. Dover! What was his plan? Steal away on a ferry and make it to France and... Mabel shook the silly idea out of her head, but still asked the porter if he could ring ahead to the next station.

Should she alert Miss Kerr?

No, not yet. Not until there was news from the Dover train. But she wouldn't sit idly by waiting. Instead, Mabel marched up and down each platform stopping to scrutinise any young boy in short trousers before passing on. She slowed as she neared the end of the last platform. It was empty. In the dim, dusty light, she could see a large wagon piled high with luggage, and beyond, the wide arched openings out into the city.

'Ma'am?'

It was one of the porters.

'No sign of him on the Dover train.' He pulled out a prodigious handkerchief, mopped his face and blew his nose. 'Have to send some of these young fellows back to school kicking and screaming. Might've run off back home, do you think?'

Unlikely was what Mabel thought. Augustus had been excited about school. Then why hadn't he got on the train? *If I were Augustus...*

'What's down there?' Mabel asked, nodding to the end of the platform.

'Unclaimed luggage,' the porter replied. 'Someone'll come and shift it at the end of the day. Now, ma'am, I've a constable waiting at the stationmaster's office – don't you want to report him missing?'

'Yes,' Mabel said, her voice weak in her own ears. 'Yes, I'll be along – you go ahead.' She heard the footsteps of the porter retreating as she continued to stare ahead, her vision blurred as her eyes filled with tears. Was this it – the end of her grand adventure?

All her life, she had made so much over moving to London and being an independent woman – and she'd done it at last. Or had she? Was she so unfit to be one of the Useful Women? When she'd read about Miss Kerr's business, it had seemed custom-fit for Mabel's plan but now, only a week later, she had fallen at the first hurdle.

A man dying on the doorstep at the wake was unfortunate, but it had not been her fault. Losing a child, on the other hand – would Miss Kerr keep her on the rolls? Mabel shook her head vehemently. No, she couldn't be struck off. Instead, she would make herself indispensable by taking on, with not a word of complaint, the most odious and unwanted assignments – those jobs that truly Useful Women wouldn't take because it would be too much like being in service. Mabel didn't care. She would scrub floors, beat rugs, clean out drains – anything to prove herself not entirely useless, if Miss Kerr would give her one more chance.

Her chin quivered. Mabel sniffed with self-pity and dug in

her bag for a handkerchief. She paused, put her nose in the air and sniffed again. A breeze had blown in from the arched openings and brought with it a scent of smoke – tobacco smoke.

Mabel stood stock-still for a moment, peering into the dim light. Then she stole down the platform, not letting her heels touch the floor lest they make a sound, until she was standing at the wagon of unclaimed baggage. From behind it, she saw a thin ribbon of smoke rise. Mabel bent over, looked under and saw knobby knees.

'Not gone to Dover then?' she asked.

Augustus scrambled out, threw his cigarette away and made a break for it, but she caught him by the collar. When he squealed, she let him go, but not before giving him a little shake.

'Oh, do be quiet, Augustus. What are you playing at? I thought you wanted to go back to school.'

'I do, miss. I like it there better than at home.' His shoulders drooped, and he dropped his gaze to the ground. 'I'm sorry I missed my train. I suppose I'll have to go on the next one.'

'You will, and I'll put you on it myself.'

Augustus needed no coaxing, but skipped away and checked the departure board himself. 'Platform six!' he shouted gaily and dashed off – Mabel on his heels – darting among the crowd of people getting on board and leaping up to look in every window as he passed.

Then, up ahead, a small boy leant practically his entire body out the window of one of the compartments. When he spotted Augustus, he waved his school cap and shouted, 'Gussie! Gussie! Here I am!'

'Walter!' Augustus shouted and waved back. He leapt aboard, disappeared for only a moment, and reappeared at the same window.

'Is that what this was about?' Mabel asked, as she handed the boy his ticket. 'You wanted to be on the same train as your friend?'

'No one listens when I say what I want to do,' Augustus replied, in a triumphant voice and with his shiny grin back in place. 'So I do it anyway.'

There was a burst of steam, and the train creaked and lurched into motion. Mabel stood where she was, but called out, 'It's a pity you didn't say from the start that you wanted to take a later train. We could've gone for ice cream while we waited.'

As the train pulled away, Mabel took pleasure in seeing that shiny grin on Augustus's face begin to melt.

Her triumph was short-lived. Mabel turned away from the departing train and stood for a moment amid the hustle and bustle of the station considering her failure. Augustus had not taken the train he should've, and although he was on his way now, someone at his school, or waiting for him at the station in Tunbridge Wells, would already have noticed he was missing. They had most likely rung his mother, who no doubt had immediately reported the incident to Miss Kerr, who would be waiting at the Useful Women office for an explanation.

Mabel mustered her courage and walked into the station-master's office, where the police constable waited.

'All's well,' she said. 'Just a boy with high spirits.' *The little blighter.*

Then, because the office would be closed before she could arrive back, Mabel rang Miss Kerr and gave her report in as few words as possible.

Miss Kerr responded likewise. 'I see,' she said. 'And he's on the train now?'

'Yes, I'm certain of it.'

'Well, Miss Canning, we'll discuss this further tomorrow.'

Mabel did not look forward to it.

Dragging herself up the stairs at New River House, Mabel paused on the first-floor landing. Mr Chigley had told her the flat nearest the landing was vacant, but that apparently was no longer the case because Mabel heard a piano. *An étude*, she thought. She stood on the landing and listened.

Yes, Chopin, for certain – one of his easier études, if that could ever be said about Chopin. She'd played that same piece, although not as well as this.

There was another noise too. Mabel took a step towards the door and cocked her head. The piano stopped, a man spoke a few words, and then the door opened.

'Gladys!' she exclaimed as the dog wriggled her way out and licked Mabel's proffered hand. She looked up and froze. There before her stood Park Winstone.

FIVE

Park Winstone, Rosalind Despard's brother with that errant curl on his forehead and the light reflecting off his glasses, was standing before Mabel. There was no mistaking the man. He had been at the wake and had irritated Inspector Tollerton. He and Rosalind seemed to get on well, although he acted as if she needed protecting. From the police? Every bit of knowledge Mabel had about the man sorted itself into a small, neat pile, but it didn't help make sense of this.

'Gladys,' he said, pulling the dog back inside.

'What are you doing here?' Mabel asked.

'What?' he asked. 'I live here.'

'Since when?'

'Since... this morning,' he said, avoiding her gaze.

A sick feeling came over Mabel. 'Are you following me?'

'Certainly not,' Winstone replied.

'I don't believe you. We met on Saturday under... unusual circumstances – and two days later, you've moved into the same building I live in? That can't be a coincidence. I want to know why you are here.' It was a demand, her voice coming out louder than she'd expected.

'Quiet!' Winstone said, keeping his voice low and glancing down the stairs. He grabbed her wrist. 'Come in here.'

Mabel jerked her wrist free and shouted, '*Let go of me!*'

Winstone released her as if his hands had touched fire.

'I want to know how it is that you have moved into New River House. Are you following me – trailing me or tracking me, whatever it's called? And if so, for what purpose?' she pressed.

'I can explain,' Winstone muttered.

'Go on then.' Mabel took one step back and stood her ground, tense and ready to run if he tried anything.

'Everything all right, Miss Canning?'

She hadn't heard Mr Chigley come out from behind his counter, but here he was halfway up the stairs.

Gladys, apparently happy to hear another friend's voice, gave a happy *woof* and wagged her back end.

'Yes, fine, thank you, Mr Chigley,' she said, smiling as if nothing were amiss. Mabel didn't need the porter giving her papa the idea that she had a man following her.

'I didn't realise you and Mr Winstone had met,' the porter said.

'As it happens,' Mabel replied, 'I am friends with Mr Winstone's sister. I've stopped at his door and offered to take Gladys for a walk. Mr Winstone is just getting her lead.' She narrowed her eyes at Winstone, daring him to contradict her.

'She won't go with you,' Winstone whispered. 'She doesn't care for strangers.'

'Gladys,' Mabel said, bending over and putting her hand under the dog's chin. 'Walkies?'

Gladys wriggled all over, looking from her master to Mabel and back. Mabel held her hand out, palm up, and after a moment, Winstone took the dog's lead from a peg by the door and handed it over.

Mabel marched down the stairs, pausing only to let Mr Chigley give Gladys a pat.

'We'll be on the green, Mr Winstone,' Mabel called up to him. 'I trust we'll see you there.'

Mabel was glad for a walk on the green to clear her head, and Gladys seemed happy for the walk, too, trotting along, tugging at her lead, then suddenly stopping to inspect a particular blade of grass.

The green was shaped in a long triangular fashion and lined with plane trees. The far corner had been allowed to grow into a thicket while the rest of the space had trimmed shrubs and lawn. Gladys showed great interest in the scruffy, overgrown corner, but once Mabel had allowed herself to be drawn in, she realised it was difficult to see beyond the branches, so she persuaded Gladys to come out.

They'd already made two turns round by the time Winstone came striding up. Mabel noticed his hair remained untidy, so he hadn't spent any time on grooming.

The dog dashed towards him, pulling Mabel along with her.

'I hope she hasn't been any trouble,' Winstone said, bending to stroke the dog's head.

'She's very sweet,' Mabel replied. 'I thought she was Bridget's dog, but now I realise Bridget was looking after Gladys for you. While you were... just what were you doing?'

Winstone did not pick up on the opportunity to explain himself.

Gladys pulled on the lead, and they began to walk, the dog zigzagging ahead of them.

Winstone cleared his throat. 'Miss Canning, I apologise for my behaviour just now. It was rude and... forward of me to speak to you in that way. To...'

'Take hold of me and try to force me into your flat?' Mabel offered.

'I didn't!' His face turned scarlet. 'No, yes, I did, and I'm terribly sorry, but, as you can imagine, this is a delicate matter. I beg your forgiveness and your discretion.'

Mabel was glad to see him flustered and thought it spoke well of him. Still. 'I hope you're ready to give me an explanation for arriving on my doorstep.'

'Not exactly your doorstep,' Winstone said, taking off his glasses and cleaning them with his handkerchief. 'Couldn't it be that I needed a flat and just happened to find a vacancy here at New River House?'

'No, it couldn't,' Mabel replied. 'It's too convenient. You seem to be everywhere, Mr Winstone. I saw you in the square across from Mrs Despard's when I arrived Saturday morning before the wake, didn't I? When that man died on the doorstep and the police arrived, you came rushing in. Why weren't you attending the wake for your brother-in-law?'

'I wanted to see who came and went.'

'Except you missed the man in the greatcoat and whoever did that to him.' Mabel frowned. 'How did he die?'

'Massive blow to the chest,' Winstone said. 'Traumatic injury to his heart.'

'Who told you that?' Mabel asked. 'I can't imagine it was Inspector Tollerton – he didn't seem all that happy to see you.'

'That isn't the point of this conversation.'

'Then what is the point?' Mabel asked.

Winstone lifted an eyebrow. 'I want to know who you are, Miss Canning.'

Mabel stopped. 'You what? *You* want to know who *I* am?' Mabel couldn't believe what she'd heard, but when she opened her mouth to throw the accusation back at him, she realised he had a point. Even after spending only one day with Rosalind, Mabel could see that the woman was fragile. From Winstone's vantage point, it could easily look as if Mabel had all-too-quickly insinuated herself into the situation for her own benefit.

'I was sent to do a job – to assist at the wake,' she said with some pride.

Winstone made a noise as if he didn't believe Mabel.

'My skills for Useful Women are beyond number, Mr Winstone,' she continued. 'Why, in only a week I've written out luncheon invitations, mended the handle on a majolica jug and lost a little boy at Victoria Station.'

He grinned. 'Was that the assignment – to lose him?'

'Of course it wasn't,' Mabel said. 'And it was only temporary. I tracked him down behind the unclaimed-luggage cart, smoking.'

They came to a bench away from the foot traffic and, with a mutual but unspoken agreement, sat. Gladys plopped down on the ground between them. Mabel reached down to stroke the dog so as not to be fixated on that loose curl on Winstone's forehead.

'Why do you feel the need to protect Rosalind?' she asked. 'And how far would you go to do so?'

Winstone stared ahead of him and then threw a quick glance at Mabel. 'This is a difficult time for my sister,' he said. 'She's vulnerable and could easily fall prey to someone trying to take advantage of her – a journalist or a treasure seeker posing as a friend. You think it hasn't been tried before?'

'I am not a treasure seeker,' Mabel said. 'Would you like the same references I gave Miss Kerr at Useful Women, Mr Winstone? I'd be happy to provide them.'

The corner of his mouth twitched. 'Not at the moment.'

'And now, I have a question,' Mabel said. 'How did the police know you? Inspector Tollerton wasn't all that happy to see you.'

Winstone snorted.

'But neither did he send you away,' she continued. 'Are you actually with the police?'

Mabel waited as Winstone looked round the green and at the few people hurrying through.

'I am not police,' he said without looking at her. 'Although I was at one time.'

'When Mr Despard went missing?'

'Yes.'

So, Mabel thought, Winstone had run afoul of his superiors – hadn't Tollerton alluded to that? – and had been booted out of the Met. Mabel recalled the newspaper article about the anniversary of Guy's disappearance.

'There was a row inside the Metropolitan Police at the time of the investigation,' Mabel said.

Winstone gave her a sharp look. 'So you do know more than you've let on?'

'Only what was in the papers,' Mabel replied. 'Now, Mr Winstone, back to why you've moved into New River House. We met on Saturday at Rosalind's and in the blink of an eye, you're living in the first-floor flat at New River House. To keep an eye on my nefarious doings?'

'I've seen nothing nefarious... as yet.'

'You made your move quickly,' she said. 'From wherever you were lodging before.'

'We travel light,' Winstone said, scratching Gladys behind the ears. 'Just a couple of cases.'

'But your piano,' she said. 'That took effort.'

'My piano is a portable.'

'A portable?' Mabel sighed, at once distracted by music. 'That would be a lovely thing to have.'

They were quiet for a moment. A yellowed leaf, set loose from its branch in the plane tree above, languidly rocked its way to the ground.

'Have you seen her today? How is Rosalind?' Mabel asked.

'She says she's just fine and to stop treating her with kid

gloves,' Winstone said. 'She's always been good at putting on a brave face under any circumstance.'

'She did well when a man died on her doorstep.'

Winstone cut his eyes at her. 'She held on, as did you, Miss Canning. You were very good at keeping your head.'

Mabel agreed but was not one to blow her own trumpet. 'Has he been identified yet? Do you think he had something to do with what happened to Guy? What about this Michael Shaughnessy?'

'Shaughnessy probably...' Winstone turned a puzzled look on Mabel. 'Why is this of interest to you, Miss Canning? Why are you so curious?'

She'd showed her hand too early, allowing Winstone to become suspicious again. 'Here's why, Mr Winstone. Despite the fact that I was employed by your sister for only one afternoon, you have seen fit to move into New River House to keep an eye on me. That tells me you believe Rosalind may want to see me again. Apart from the circumstances, I enjoyed meeting her and I believe she could use a friend. If she seeks support from me, I will give it.'

He appeared mollified. Mabel hadn't lied – she had liked Rosalind and thought it possible they could become friends. It seemed quite obvious that she needed someone on her side – not only a brother who might go to any length to protect his sister. If she could help ease Rosalind's troubled mind by finding the truth behind the dead man in the greatcoat and if that led to discovering what had happened to Guy Despard all those years ago, Mabel would've accomplished great things. It was certainly better than mending lace or returning library books. Too bad it wouldn't pay her bills.

Winstone had not spoken but was giving Mabel an appraising look – possibly approving, probably not. Even so, Mabel felt her face heat up at his gaze.

'Do you believe he's alive?' she asked. 'Guy.'

There was a pause.

'No.'

Gladys sat up, put her head on Winstone's knee and gave him a look as sorrowful as one of Cyril's.

'It's time for her tea,' Winstone said.

'Then we'd best be off,' Mabel said. She handed Gladys's lead over. They rose and walked through the green to the road. She gave the dog a pat. 'Well, Mr Winstone, I daresay our paths will be crossing often. Good afternoon.'

The traffic had cleared and before he could reply, Mabel walked off over the road with Winstone and Gladys in her wake.

SIX

Mabel boiled an egg for her evening meal and had tea with no milk, all the while wishing she had a plateful of Mrs Chandekar's samosas – a fried bit of heaven that never failed to comfort Mabel even at her lowest. Her head swirled with images from the wake and the dead man at her feet, along with Augustus waving goodbye on his train and Winstone and Gladys – and the portable piano – one floor below.

After her meal, she stood at the open window. A fog had descended, and despite the gas street lamps blazing, she could make out only those people walking along the pavement below. Across the road, Islington Green was full of tall, ghostly shadows. Up at the top of the green, obscured by the tree canopy, was Collins Music Hall where Cyril performed. That would be a treat, wouldn't it? Depending on the price of a ticket, of course. What could she afford?

Mabel went to bed but didn't sleep. Instead, she lay staring at the ceiling adding up the pennies she put in the gas heater, the thruppence tram fare, the pint of milk and half loaf of bread she bought every couple of days. If a seat in the music hall was a shilling, that would be all right, but a half-crown? All the while light poured into her bedroom through the window. It had surprised her to find that night in London wasn't actually dark. Finally, when the city outside her window at last grew quiet, Mabel drifted off into an uneasy sleep.

Morning brought a new day and a return of Mabel's usual confidence. She would apologise to Miss Kerr – after all, Augustus did make it to school, no harm done.

She stopped at the porter's window on her way out, glancing up the stairs to be certain no one was coming down. Then she said in a low voice, 'And so, Mr Winstone has taken the vacant flat on the landing.'

'Walked in yesterday morning and asked if we had a vacancy,' Mr Chigley replied as he sorted the morning post. 'I said we did and showed it to him. He paid on the spot and returned in the afternoon in a taxi with luggage, the portable piano and the dog.' The porter looked up. 'Quite a surprise that you knew him.'

'Yes, wasn't it,' Mabel said.

'He isn't being a nuisance, is he?'

'Not at all,' Mabel replied. 'I love dogs, and I envy him his piano, even if it isn't a full keyboard.' She paused. 'Did he say much about himself?'

'Not a word. He asked if I'd got this in the war' – with his thumb, Mr Chigley pointed towards his scarred face – 'and I told him I got it when I was with the service corps in India. Not fighting, I explained, just a fire in the stores. But his question did make me think he might be ex-army, although I don't think he'd've seen any action wearing spectacles.'

'Perhaps his poor eyesight was caused by action,' Mabel suggested. The damages of war were many and not always as apparent as a lost limb. Had Winstone joined up after leaving Scotland Yard in 1914?

'Could be,' Mr Chigley said. 'He seems a nice enough sort. Just the same, I don't want you being bothered, and so I'll be sure to keep an eye on him.'

Mabel walked out of New River House and paused on the doorstep, inhaling deeply just as a passing motorcar belched a dark cloud from its tailpipe. Mabel coughed and then stepped out onto the pavement, only to be knocked into by a man hurrying by. He didn't stop but did raise his hat as he passed and called back, 'Sorry.' Mabel retreated onto the doorstep. She watched as the heaving crowd rushed by and shot out into the foot traffic when a gap appeared.

When Mabel alighted from the tram at Piccadilly, she was swept along down the pavement, pausing briefly to drop sixpence into the tin cup of a soldier with only one leg who sat in a doorway. She entered the amount into her accounts notebook and continued.

But the closer she got to Dover Street, the slower her steps, and by the time she'd reached the door to number 48, she had nearly stopped forward motion altogether. She huffed and took herself to task – *Buck up, Mabel* – and marched in and up the stairs.

'Ah, Miss Canning, good morning,' Miss Kerr said, looking up from the Jobs ledger and back down again.

Mabel stood halfway in the door at the Useful Women office, reading Miss Kerr as best she could. She had heard no tone of recrimination or impending doom in her employer's voice and so returned the 'Good morning' and slipped into her seat across the desk.

'About yesterday afternoon, Miss Canning.'

Now she was for it.

But the telephone rang, and Miss Kerr raised a finger to pause the conversation. After a brief exchange, she made a note in the register: 'Away until Monday.'

When the call ended, Mabel gathered her nerve. 'About yesterday afternoon,' she said.

'Yes,' Miss Kerr said mildly, 'little Augustus—'

The telephone rang again, and Mabel sat on pins and needles as Miss Kerr spoke with a client and wrote in the ledger: 'Trousseau to be chosen for European honeymoon.' At the end of the call, she promptly rang one of her Useful Women – more useful than Mabel – and assigned the task.

'Now, Miss Canning,' Miss Kerr began, 'I want to say not everyone who signs on here at Useful Women is up to the task, but I pride myself in understanding the qualities of my workers and being able to match them with the proper jobs and the proper clients. It's true that sometimes that isn't possible.'

Was this about more than Augustus – was it about the wake and the dead man too? Did Miss Kerr believe that Mabel attracted disasters? That certainly wouldn't be good for business.

'It's entirely my fault about Augustus,' Mabel said. 'I'm terribly sorry I let you down, Miss Kerr, but I do hope you will give me another chance to—'

'You are the fourth of my Useful Women I have sent to meet Augustus to escort him to his train,' Miss Kerr continued, talking over Mabel. 'And so, I want to say to you, Miss Canning – well done.'

In the next moment of silence, Mabel let those words ring in her ears. *Well done.*

'But, Miss Kerr, Augustus got away from me and hid behind the unclaimed baggage and smoked and missed his train and had to take the next one – which, as it turned out, was his intention all along. That must've worried the school or whoever was waiting for him at the station. Or his mother at home.'

Miss Kerr inclined her head in a non-committal way. 'I'm sure you wonder why I persevere with such a challenging situation. Why not decline the request? Here is why – a happy client is not only a repeat client, but also one who will recommend Useful Women to her friends. We want to be the first solution that comes into the minds of the gentlewomen of London when faced with any manner of predicament. Mrs Malling-Frobisher is well connected, and she is pleased with how we have carried out the assignment.'

'Because there was no need for an ambulance?' Mabel asked.

'Indeed. By the way, how did you manage to find him?'

'Well,' Mabel said, 'I admit I was about to give up hope.' But she wouldn't admit she had been near to tears. 'I'd been dashing about the station, but when I stopped and stood still, that's when I realised where he was hiding. Perhaps, in that moment, I was thinking like Augustus.'

'There's a chilling thought,' Miss Kerr said.

Miss Kerr spent a busy morning on the telephone, receiving and assigning jobs. Mabel waited, her only activity paying five pence for tea and a bun from Mrs Fritt, who pushed her trolley up and down the corridor twice a day. While she waited, she kept an eye on job details Miss Kerr wrote in her ledger. Mabel could read upside down – a useful talent she had acquired years ago – and disguised her impatience as best she could. She could have collected and delivered the birthday cake Mrs Longlake had ordered. She could've attended the autumn horticultural show for Lady Hacknall and written a report. Mabel was keenly aware that it was Tuesday and before she knew it, Friday would arrive.

The previous Friday, at the end of her first week, Mabel had arrived to find a queue of Useful Women that had nearly reached the door. Friday was payday. She had joined the queue and while she waited, she'd glanced round at the office. Miss Kerr's desk remained at the centre of the room, with an Axminster rug underneath. The plain deal table that sat in the corner had been pulled away from the wall and the typewriter it had held no longer sat atop the filing cabinet, replaced by a box of envelopes and a ledger. Behind the table, a woman with black hair and one grey streak that swept up and under her hat had been doling out pay packets in exchange for a signature.

When her turn came, Mabel had identified herself to the woman.

'Ah, you're a new one, aren't you?' the woman had asked, looking through the envelopes. 'I'm Effie Grint.'

Miss Kerr had heard the exchange. 'Mrs Grint does accounts for me,' she had told Mabel. 'She can spot a wrong number from ten foot away.'

'I was a bookkeeper for my late husband's business,' Mrs Grint explained. 'He was in jams – strawberry and raspberry. Our son has carried it on, but he thought it looked mean to put his mum to work. But I like to work, and so I came here.'

'Mrs Grint has a special skill,' Miss Kerr had said.

Mabel had skills, but perhaps they weren't as special as Mrs Grint's bookkeeping. She had signed the ledger, taken her envelope and thanked Mrs Grint. Surreptitiously, she had felt the envelope's bulk before dropping it in her bag – a pound note and a florin, she'd thought. Slim pickings, as they say, and not enough to pay for her lodgings, but, as she'd told herself, it was early days yet.

Now, Miss Kerr's voice cut through Mabel's reverie. 'Miss Canning, how are you at restringing pearls?'

'Oh, I'm quite good at that!' Mabel couldn't believe it. Here was a task she had actually done, even if it had been ages ago. When she'd turned eighteen, her father had given her a strand of pearls that had belonged to her mother. The strand had broken on her first wearing, but Mrs Chandekar had dried Mabel's tears and, together, they'd restrung them.

Mabel set out from the Useful Women office and walked

only two streets on the other side of Piccadilly before she came to her destination. There, she found that the client, an older lady, had all the necessary equipment – clasp, number 2 silk thread, threading needles and the bowl of pearls – waiting on a table in the drawing room. Once Mabel took a moment to study what lay before her, she had no trouble remembering what to do.

For lunch, Mabel ate her usual apple in Green Park, happily doing the sums in her head and speculating that if she could carry out six such brief and easy jobs a day, she might make up to three pounds. She didn't waste any time returning to the office after lunch, eager for her next assignment.

Once there, Mabel found what amounted to a crowd – four Useful Women appeared to be waiting for jobs and one of them had appropriated Mabel's chair across the desk from Miss Kerr. Taking the high road, Mabel sat patiently in a seat along the wall, ostensibly reading over Useful Women booklet number eight, which she already knew by heart. Each time the telephone jangled, the general chatter in the room quieted, and so Mabel had no trouble picking up the gist of the next conversation.

'Yes, that is certainly possible,' Miss Kerr said into the speaker. 'We have several Useful Women who are quite accomplished when it comes to... Oh, yes, of course you may.' Miss Kerr's eyes flicked to Mabel and away. 'I feel certain she's available and can be there within the hour. Thank you so much for ringing Useful Women for your needs. Good day.' Miss Kerr rang off, rested her forearms on the desk and said, 'Miss Canning, how are you at flower arranging?'

Rosalind met her at the door with a smile that could light up a room.

'Mabel,' she said, taking Mabel's hand and drawing her in.

'I'm so glad you were free today – do you think Miss Kerr minded I asked for you specifically?'

'She didn't mind a bit and I was quite happy you did,' Mabel replied, glad to see Rosalind in such good spirits but, at the same time, worried that she was overly cheerful. Some of Winstone's concern must've rubbed off on her. 'How are you today?'

Rosalind shrugged and laughed and frowned all at the same time. 'We must soldier on, mustn't we? Oh, how silly! I sound like my mother during the war. Let's not talk about it now. Come on – flowers.'

At the back of the house, instead of going down the stairs on the left that led to the kitchen and Bridget's rooms, they went through a door on the right and into the scullery. It had a deep metal sink and shelves lined with cleaners and brushes and a fair amount of old crockery and a broom closet that stood partly open on the far side. A window looked out onto a small garden – more of a yard, really, as there was little green, apart from ivy covering the walls and a tangle of shrubs in the back corner. A table took up most of the open space and held a riot of colour from pails of dahlias, China asters, daisies, chrysanthemums and even roses, all in shades of autumn. It looked as if the entire florist's shop had been emptied.

The telephone jangled, but Rosalind paid it no mind and ran her hand lightly over the blooms. 'I'm so glad they had roses.'

'I say' – Mabel nodded towards the entry – 'the telephone?'

It was as if Rosalind hadn't heard the ringing until that moment. 'Oh, the telephone! Bridget usually answers. She was a bit under the weather this morning, you see, and I told her to stay in bed, not that she ever pays any attention to what I say. I'll see to it.'

'And I'll get to work. The vases?' Mabel asked.

'The vases, yes.' Rosalind looked round the scullery. 'Would you mind collecting them? They're in the rooms and on the landings, and' – she dashed out, calling back – 'you know, here and there.'

Mabel shuttled vases with flowers that had looked fresh enough on Saturday, but now had given up the ghost, as her papa would say, and had a difficult time with the rasping stems of dried daisies, which caught in her curls. Rosalind sat next to the entry table, where the telephone was, talking with what seemed like a variety of people about a charity event. Every time Mabel passed through the entry, Rosalind would wave and Mabel would smile and, arms full of vases, waggle a finger at her in return.

She ended up at the top of the house, where she found Rosalind's bedroom, which was bigger than Mabel's entire flat. She paused to take in the grandeur. At the near end of the room were a fireplace, a four-poster bed and two dressing tables. One obviously was Rosalind's. It held a mirror in a gilt frame and a large vase of dahlias that had dropped most of their petals onto the various boxes and bottles below. The dressing table next to it was most definitely masculine and, although pristine in condition, gave off an air of disuse. Guy Despard's, of course, and it touched Mabel that Rosalind would keep her husband's silver-backed brushes and combs and a velvet-lined case opened to display an elegant shave set with a bone-handled straight razor. As if, all these long years, she had expected him to walk back in the door. Or knew he wouldn't and couldn't accept it.

On the mantel above the other fireplace at the far end of the room was another tall vase, along with a line-up of photographs. Mabel, conscious of the fact she was working, took the vase and resisted lingering over the photographs. For now.

As she reached the ground floor, the doorbell was pulled. Rosalind was no longer in the chair by the entry table, and there was no sound of someone rushing to answer, so Mabel thought she had best do it. Then she considered just how. She had a large vase in each arm and no place to leave them – Rosalind had left behind an open diary on the table – and so, Mabel kept hold of a vase in each arm and just managed to open the door. She peered between a forest of dead flower stems to see Cyril.

He squinted and dodged back and forth as if trying to get a good look at her.

'Miss Canning, is it you?' he asked, his smile causing a sunburst of fine lines from the corners of his eyes. 'Have you disguised yourself as a walking thorn bush for any particular reason?'

Mabel laughed. 'I'm doing the flowers. Please come in, Mr —' Oh dear, what was his surname? She shouldn't call him Cyril because he was older than her and they weren't exactly friends and—

'Cyril, Miss Canning, only Cyril,' he said, stepping in and relieving her of one of the vases. 'Now, where are we off to with these fine botanical specimens?'

'We're tipping them onto the rubbish heap in the yard,' Mabel said, 'so that I can begin again. Follow me.'

'I confess to being flummoxed by a flower that is as big as a cricket ball,' Cyril said, holding a deep red chrysanthemum at arm's length. 'Is it intended to intimidate the little asters and daisies?'

'We'll set the dahlias to defend them,' Mabel replied, draping a strand of ivy over the edge of a vase. 'What do you think?'

'I think that's a fine strategy,' he said, and they went back to filling the vases.

Rosalind looked in briefly to say hello and explain that she must finish her telephoning because Bridget was up and about and would be bringing up the tea soon. Cyril insisted on staying to help Mabel, although she found him better at emptying vases rather than refilling and best at standing aside, chatting and dropping in the occasional joke.

'... So I motioned to the conductor and said, "I say, I say, I say, does this bus stop at the Embankment?" And he says to me, "It had better, sir, or there will be a big splash." *Boom-boom!*' he said, tapping his hand on the table in time.

Mabel laughed as she reached for the large shears to cut the stems off the roses and noticed Park Winstone standing in the door of the scullery. Her laughter faltered and her face heated up.

'Mr Winstone,' she said. 'Hello.'

'Miss Canning,' he replied, and she could hear the unspoken question. *What are you doing here?*

'Your sister rang Miss Kerr at Useful Women,' Mabel answered. 'She needed someone to arrange the flowers.'

'And you just happened to be free?'

'No,' Mabel said, annoyance overcoming apprehension. 'She asked for me in particular.' She just barely kept herself from putting a hand on her hip as if she were addressing Augustus Malling-Frobisher.

Gladys scooted past Winstone and went directly to Mabel.

'Hello, girl,' she said. 'How are you?' She gave the dog a scratch behind the ears, and Gladys responded by sitting on Mabel's feet and leaning against her legs.

Mabel looked up at Winstone and he held her gaze until footsteps were heard coming up the back stairs and Bridget appeared with a large tray and took in the scene.

'I won't serve tea in the scullery, if that's what you're thinking,' the maid said. 'Herself'll be in the drawing room. She's been looking for you,' she addressed Winstone. 'And you' – she nodded to Cyril – 'don't you go sneaking one of those squirting flowers into a vase.'

Cyril saluted her with a chrysanthemum and Bridget

pressed her lips together, although Mabel saw a bit of a smile escape as the maid walked on with Winstone in her wake.

'*Herself will be waiting for us,*' Cyril said in a passable imitation of Bridget's Irish accent. 'Tell me, Miss Canning, how do you think *herself* is doing?'

Here was someone who thought it was fitting for Mabel to have an opinion on Rosalind's state of mind – it was refreshing.

'Well, of course, I only just met Rosalind on Saturday,' she said. 'Even so, I can see she does seem to have wide swings of emotions, but at least she has you and her brother to watch out for her.'

Cyril glanced out towards the entry and back. 'Do you have brothers and sisters, Miss Canning?'

'No.'

'Neither do I,' Cyril said. 'So you and I may not understand, but Park has always taken the job of being protective of his sister to the extreme. To the point he punched out one of those reporters who hung about all those years ago. Scotland Yard didn't look kindly on that.'

Although true that she was an only child, Mabel understood the closeness of siblings. All her life, she and her friend Edith had been like sisters in every way except for being related. Mabel would've done just about anything to keep Edith safe, but Mabel and Edith's husband, the vicar, had been helpless against the Spanish flu. Edith had died two years earlier, but Mabel could still occasionally catch herself thinking 'Oh I must tell Edith' before being hit by a deep pang of grief.

She pulled herself away from those thoughts. 'I wish I could've seen Rosalind on stage,' Mabel said.

Cyril smiled. 'She was born for the music hall,' he said. 'Perhaps you'll get the chance one of these days.'

'But not at the Grand. It closed, is that right?'

A cloud passed over Cyril's face. 'It did, along with far too many others. Some say the music hall is finished, what with the cinema and all, but don't you believe it. Not when we still have the likes of Harry Lauder and Ida Barr. We will prevail. Now, tea.'

Mabel begged off tea until she finished her job and sent Cyril off. She set out fresh arrangements in the entry, dining room and study, and then took a small vase in one arm and a much bigger one in the other and began the climb to the second floor. She paused on the first-floor landing, attempting to push a dahlia away with her chin and blow a curl of her hair out of her line of sight. Suddenly, there was Winstone.

'Give me one of those,' he said.

Mabel turned away from him. 'I've got them, Mr Winstone,' she said, although that was debatable.

'Do you regularly refuse an offer of help?'

She was about to object, but instead laughed. 'You sound like my papa.' She handed over the larger of the two vases and added, 'Thank you. Although I'm sorry to take you away from your tea.' And yet glad she may get the chance to ask about the dead man on the doorstep.

Winstone gave a dismissive nod. 'They're reliving the time a performer named Maude Mainwaring used a live goat for her shepherdess number and the goat ate half her dress before she realised it.' A burst of laughter came from the drawing room. 'It was funny the first ten times I heard it,' he added. 'Lead on.'

In Rosalind's room, Mabel said, 'Yours goes on the end of the mantel.' She set the smaller vase on Rosalind's dressing table and fussed with the arrangement before turning to view the large vase from a distance. Winstone stood resting his elbow on the mantel and didn't move when Mabel crossed the room and reached up to adjust a few dahlia stems. When she finished, she didn't move either.

'Go on,' she said, 'accuse me of something. You know you want to.'

She saw amusement in the eyes, undisguised by his glasses.

'Give me a minute,' he said. 'I'll think of something.'

Mabel clicked her tongue and looked away, her gaze falling on the row of photos on the mantel.

Here was a framed photograph of Rosalind and Guy in bathing costumes and up to their knees in the sea. Next to that was an older photo of parents and a baby wearing a long christening gown, with a young boy leaning against his mother. Mabel picked up the photograph closest to her. It showed a girl wearing a rough tunic tied with rope with a pillow stuck under it to make her appear round. An older boy stood with her. He wore a short tunic and held a child-sized bow and arrow. The boy had an errant curl escaping from under a peaked cap.

'Well, Mr Winstone,' Mabel said, turning the photo to him. 'I had no idea Robin Hood was your true identity.'

'Look at those children,' Winstone said with a grin. 'School play. Rosy insisted on being the friar – she's always enjoyed comedy.'

'We did Robin Hood when I was in school,' Mabel said. 'I was Much the Miller's Son – not a terribly exciting role.'

'Would you rather have been Maid Marian?' Winstone asked.

'Only if I had my own bow and arrow,' Mabel replied.

'Would Robin allow that?'

'Would Marian ask permission?' Mabel retorted.

'The flowers look lovely,' Rosalind said from the doorway, and both Mabel and Winstone jumped.

SEVEN

Mabel replaced the photo on the mantel. 'Thank you.'

Rosalind smiled at her brother, and Mabel caught him frowning back.

'Has your brother told you how he likes living at New River House?' Mabel asked brightly. 'I was quite surprised to find he'd moved into a flat in my same building.'

Rosalind might've staggered back, she looked so shocked. 'Park!' she cried. 'You haven't!'

Winstone narrowed his eyes at Mabel.

Ah-ha, she thought, *caught you out*. It had occurred to Mabel that because Rosalind hadn't enquired about her brother moving into New River House, she might not know about it. And Mabel had been right. She stifled the urge to crow and only raised her eyebrows at his vexation.

'I had to find a place in a hurry,' Winstone said to his sister.

'I don't believe that,' Rosalind replied. 'You seemed quite happy with your... lodgings.' She drew out the word and her voice took on a teasing note. 'With the wife of a friend from the service, wasn't it?'

What sort of arrangement had that been? Her thoughts began to turn a dark corner, and she pulled them back.

Winstone's face turned the colour of beetroot. 'It wasn't convenient,' he said. 'What with Gladys and the piano.'

Mabel thought Gladys and the portable piano were two of Winstone's greatest assets.

Winstone didn't dally, but left with his sister, and so Mabel finished with the flowers and was in the scullery cleaning off the table when Rosalind came in.

'They're gone now – Cyril and Park.' She shook her head. 'You mustn't mind them. They both believe I need protecting. I know they mean well, but I often feel nearly smothered with their efforts.'

Mabel brushed bits of stem and leaf into her hand. 'You mentioned your brother was in the service. Was this during the war? Was he with the territorials?'

'Diplomatic service,' Rosalind replied. 'He says he spent most of the war sitting behind a desk in Paris. He's adjunct now, he says.' She took Mabel's hands. 'You were so kind on Saturday and really kept your wits about you with all that happened, but the way things went, we never had a minute to talk. Won't you stay a bit longer?'

Such a simple heartfelt request caused Mabel's eyes to prick with tears.

'Of course I will stay.'

Rosalind led her into the dining room, where there was a small table and comfortable chairs in the oriel window that looked out onto the road and the square beyond. Mabel had experienced the Despard house full of guests and then, after the man fell dead on the doorstep, full of police too. Now, it felt more like a home.

'I don't eat dinner in here,' Rosalind said, glancing over her shoulder at the dining table that could easily seat twenty. 'It's a bit much for one, so I usually have a tray in the study. But for tea, this is a lovely, bright place. Now, you sit here, and I'll go down to the kitchen. Bridget's taking a rest, but I won't be long.'

Mabel didn't have the chance to sit because the doorbell rang and as she was the only one near, she went to answer as if she were a part of the household.

A young man wearing a newsboy cap held out a parcel wrapped in brown paper.

'For Mrs Guy Despard,' he said, and pulled a receipt book from his pocket. 'Sign here, please.'

Mabel signed, took the parcel and closed the door. Under the wrapping, she could feel a box. Weighty for its size – possibly heavy enough to be a large book. She held it out when Rosalind came up the stairs, tray in hand.

'A delivery for you,' Mabel said.

'Oh, that's all right,' Rosalind said. 'I was afraid it was one of those reporters. Bring it along, why don't you?'

Once settled at the table, Rosalind took the parcel, pulled the twine and the paper off and removed the lid on the box. She drew her hands away and stared at the contents, twirling the thin gold band round her ring finger. Mabel could see what had stopped her – the parcel was a supply of writing paper and envelopes with a heavy black border. Mourning stationery. Rosalind replaced the lid, took the box over to the dining table and put it down gently, as if it contained an adder about to strike.

She came back to Mabel and poured the tea. Gesturing to the slices of buttered tea bread studded with sultanas, she said, 'This is barmbrack. It's Irish. Bridget baked it yesterday. She's a fine hand with cakes too. I don't know what I would've done without her all these years. For cakes and... and everything else.' The brief spurt of talk seemed to have exhausted Rosalind, and she looked down into her cup of tea.

'Do you know anything more about the man who died?' Mabel asked. 'Have the police told you anything?'

'No, they haven't,' Rosalind said with force, jutting out her chin. 'No one tells me anything. I've half a mind to ring Sergeant Tollerton – no, Inspector now – and demand to be kept informed.'

Mabel wasn't sure how her question would be taken, but she hadn't expected this fiery response. It emboldened her.

'And your brother?'

'I'm not sure Park hasn't annoyed the police enough for one lifetime, and even if he learnt something, I doubt he'd tell me.'

'But this man's death could have something to do with what happened to your husband.'

'It must,' Rosalind said heatedly. 'But Park won't tell me what he knows because he worries any news will put me over the edge... again,' she added in a quiet voice, and tapped a finger on her teacup. 'I wasn't well after Guy went missing and the police carried out their enquiry. After it was finished, I went to Mum and Dad's for a few months.'

'Aren't they here in London?'

'No, when Guy and I married, he bought them a cottage in Shanklin on the Isle of Wight.' A wan smile emerged. 'It's a lovely place.'

'I don't see what harm there could be in someone asking a few questions,' Mabel said, almost to herself. 'Staying out of the way of the police, of course.' A few answers might go a long way to settling Rosalind's mind. 'I wouldn't mind doing that for you.'

'Is that the sort of work you do at Useful Women?' Rosalind asked.

'No,' Mabel said. 'At least I haven't done yet. I've run errands and played bridge quite badly and washed a dog. And arranged flowers. But I believe you deserve to know what happened and I am happy to help in any way I can.'

'Then please do,' Rosalind said. 'Do you know someone to ask?'

'I might.'

'Good day?' Mr Chigley asked, when Mabel walked into New River House.

'Very good,' Mabel replied. 'And you?'

'Warm and dry and well fed,' he replied, 'nothing to complain about.' He reached behind him to the wall of letter boxes. 'Letter from your father here and two others.'

Letters from home. Mabel clasped them to her breast for a moment before she looked through them. Papa had written, and here was a letter from Mrs Chandekar and one from Ronald – the Reverend Herringay. She tucked them in her pocket to read later.

'Mr Chigley, do you know if Cora and Skeff are at home?'

'They are not, Miss Canning,' the porter said, checking the clock on the wall. 'I often see them returning about six o'clock, so not long now. Shall I tell them you asked after them?'

'Yes, why not. Thanks.'

Mabel ate her evening meal early – potted meat on toast and applesauce – as she read her post. Papa's letter was filled with anecdotes of the villagers who came into his greengrocer's shop. Mrs Chandekar passed along news that the niece of Mrs Pickering – housekeeper at the vicarage – was due for a visit. Ronald had created for himself the role of Mabel's guardian even though he was only five years older. He wrote to say – and not for the first time – how worried he was about Mabel living alone in such a place as London. She wrote back to each of them. She told her father how many interesting jobs she'd carried out and how her pay packet was sure to grow each week. She described

Rosalind's house to Mrs Chandekar. She reminded Ronald that Mr Chigley was keeping an eye on her.

She had just set the kettle on the gas ring when Skeff and Cora arrived. She asked them in and gestured to the sofa. If all three of them tried to sit at the table, they'd knock knees.

'It's good of you to stop by,' she said. 'Oh Cora, your hat is stunning.'

Today's creation had a rounded crown and wide brim that drooped on either side of Cora's face. 'It's a picture hat, you see,' she said, and patted the cluster of fake purple grapes that adorned one side. 'It would be lovely on you, Mabel, accentuating your curls.'

'Well, Mabel,' Skeff said, 'I suppose you've seen this?' She reached into the deep pocket of her coat and handed over a copy of the *Daily Mail*.

Man Dies at Wake for Missing Businessman Guy Despard

'Oh dear,' Mabel said.

'They're fairly even-handed, the *Mail*,' Skeff proclaimed, 'but there are reporters on every paper assigned to the death lists, and they take what they can get. Doesn't look like they knew much about this fellow – not even a name.'

'He still has no name, as far as I know,' Mabel told them. 'Although the police aren't telling Rosalind much.' She scanned the brief article, and then brought over tea and a plate of digestives. 'I'm sorry I can't offer you a proper drink.'

'I'd never say no to biscuits and tea,' Cora said.

'It's quite distressing for Rosalind,' Mabel said, as she poured. 'The dead man is obviously a link to her husband, and he could even have been the cause of Guy Despard's disappearance, yet there is no trail to follow. She needs peace of mind, and so I've decided...' Mabel cleared her throat. 'I've decided to help her find out who this man was and perhaps that will lead to learning what happened to her husband.'

When neither woman spoke, she asked, 'Do you think it's a good idea?'

'Rather,' Skeff said. 'You show true initiative.'

'I'm glad you think so because I could use your help,' Mabel said.

Cora nodded. 'Of course. A newspaperwoman has a great many contacts.'

'It's my job,' Skeff said with some modesty.

'And here's something. Do you remember during the police enquiry into Guy Despard's disappearance, there was an internal row at Scotland Yard?' Mabel asked.

'Indeed I do,' Skeff said.

'It concerned Rosalind's brother who was with the police at the time, but he left the Met, I believe because he thought they were treating his sister unfairly. Well, that's who is living here in the flat on the first-floor landing.'

'Oh, Mr Winstone, isn't it?' Cora asked. 'And his sweet dog.'

'Gladys,' Mabel said. 'Yes, that's right. I believe he doesn't trust me and has set himself a watch. I can take care of him, so you won't, you know, try to get anything out of him, will you? It'll only annoy him.'

'Skeff isn't that sort of reporter,' Cora said, and gave Mabel a reassuring pat.

Skeff herself had kept silent but was giving Mabel an appraising look. 'Yes,' she said now, 'perhaps we will leave Mr Winstone to you.'

'What did he look like, Mabel?' Cora asked. 'If you can give Skeff a good description of this dead man, it'll help her research.'

'Cora, my dear,' Skeff said, wagging an unlit cigarette at her, 'you're brilliant. What about it, Mabel?'

'Oh, I don't know. It's all such a blur.'

'Try.'

Mabel grew quiet as she turned her thoughts to the previous Saturday afternoon at the Despard house. She put herself back in that moment upstairs in the drawing room when, as Thomas Hardcastle gave his toast to Guy, a *thud* had been heard at the front door. In her mind, she ran down the stairs and opened the front door and something large and heavy fell against her, almost knocking her over. The dead man lay on his back, looking up at her with unseeing eyes.

'He wore a greatcoat,' she began.

'A soldier?' Cora asked.

'Perhaps,' Skeff said. 'Perhaps not.'

'Dark hair,' Mabel continued, as she stared off into the middle distance, seeing the man once again. 'Dark red. His face was pale. Blue eyes.' She swallowed. 'They were open.'

'What about his clothes?' Skeff asked.

Mabel squinted at the image. 'Nothing fancy, but in fair condition. Shirt, braces, trousers. Boots that had seen some use. His hands,' she said, holding her own up. 'They were rough – working man's hands.'

'How tall?' Skeff asked.

Mabel frowned. She hadn't seen the man standing upright. She gestured to the floor. 'I'm not sure because he was there.'

Cora popped up. 'Here now,' she said, and lay down on the hearthrug. 'What do you think? As tall as I am?'

Mabel studied Cora's form. 'Taller,' she said.

'C'mon, Skeff,' Cora said, rising. 'Your turn.'

Skeff took Cora's place.

'Yes,' Mabel said. 'You're more his length— height. He was bigger than you, of course. Neither thin nor fat either. Average.' She shook her head in exasperation. 'It's not much.'

'But it's more than you thought you remembered, isn't it?' Skeff asked.

And it was.

. . .

Mabel managed only one short job before lunch the next day –
returning books to the London Library. In the afternoon, she
walked into the office as Miss Kerr, with a perplexed look, ran
her finger down the list of names in the Useful Women register.
She glanced at Mabel, then went back to her work, but then
looked up again.

'Miss Canning, one of your references was from the vicar in
your village. He mentioned your kind help with correspondence for the church – was it by hand?'

'Some of it,' Mabel said. 'But also by typewriting.' She was
shaky on Pitman's shorthand, and so didn't mention it.

'Lady Bellecourt needs assistance writing out luncheon
invitations. She is an exacting client, and I don't want to send
her someone who may not be up to her standards.'

'My penmanship is quite good,' Mabel said.

'I'm glad to hear it,' Miss Kerr replied. 'And I know you will
take the utmost care. Each client is important to Useful
Women, but Lady Bellecourt has a great deal of influence. Best
of luck.'

Lady Bellecourt 'exacting'? Barely in the door and Mabel
could've added a few other descriptions – unbending, dictator-
ial, imperious. The maid had answered and quickly transferred
her to the client, who started in on the failings of staff, the qualities of writing paper and the weather as she led the way to a
writing desk by a window.

'Sit.'

Mabel sat.

'You must write carefully and legibly,' Lady Bellecourt said,
as if she were speaking to someone in the next room. 'I won't
stand for a single blotch, do you understand?'

'Is this yours?' Mabel asked, holding up a sheet of writing paper with the luncheon invitation on it. 'You've a lovely cursive hand. The scrolls and the way the words flow along the line remind me of a waltz.'

Lady Bellecourt puffed up. 'I've always been proud of my hand. I can't expect anyone to come close, but I do require—'

'Shall I give it a go?' Mabel interrupted. 'I'll use yours as a sample and write one out. Then you can check my work.'

'Yes, go on then.'

Lady Bellecourt hovered near her shoulder as Mabel wondered how she could politely be rid of the woman. She was saved from the effort when the maid called her mistress away. Then Mabel set to studying Lady Bellecourt's writing but found she could not settle to work, because her mind wandered to the envelope she'd held in her hand on Saturday that had held a letter purportedly written by Guy Despard to his wife seven years ago that had never been delivered. Rosalind had sworn it was her husband's hand. If that was the case, he'd had a bold style that had called to Mabel's mind a military march.

Had the police discovered the identity of the dead man in the greatcoat? Did thoughts of Guy and the dead man fill Rosalind's head this afternoon? Wouldn't Inspector Tollerton want to talk with Mabel further? If he did, perhaps she could find out more about—

'Miss Canning,' Lady Bellecourt called from the doorway, 'how are you progressing?'

'It's coming along just fine,' Mabel said. Sweeping away thoughts of the Despards, she took up a clean sheet of writing paper and the fountain pen. And, with a waltz playing in her mind, she set to work.

When Lady Bellecourt returned, and Mabel handed the invitation to her, the woman flew into a rage.

'I don't want to see my own work!' She thrust the invitation back at Mabel. 'I want to see yours.'

'That is mine,' Mabel said, and handed her the original. 'Here is yours.'

The woman took the invitations and peered at one and then the other. Her eyes widened. 'I can barely see a difference. My goodness, that's quite a dangerous talent you have there.'

Mabel smiled. 'A well-honed skill and used only for good, I assure you. I thought your friends would want to see the invitations in your own hand.' Lady Bellecourt's writing had been easy to imitate.

'Well, Miss Canning,' Lady Bellecourt said, 'if that is the case, you may carry on.'

EIGHT

Mabel returned to the Useful Women office in time for the afternoon run of Mrs Fritt's tea-and-bun trolley and settled in the chair across the desk with her light repast while Miss Kerr complimented her on the work for Lady Bellecourt – apparently, the client had already telephoned to say she appreciated Mabel's 'special skill'.

'That's kind of her to say,' Mabel said, 'but it's just something I can do. I look at a handwriting, and it's as if I can hear music and with the music playing in my head, I'm able to... write in the manner of the... originator.' Mabel strove to avoid the word 'forge' because that sounded illegal. 'It began with my papa's writing. His letters are upright and no-nonsense and have always reminded me of a brass band parading down the pier in Brighton, and so I—' Mabel stopped abruptly. Miss Kerr appeared not to notice.

'You are learning, Miss Canning,' Miss Kerr said, 'that not every job is as easy as a journey to the drapers or as difficult as little Augustus, but even the most tiresome jobs give us an opportunity to show our skills and aplomb. Doing that furthers the image of a woman's place in the world.'

Mabel straightened in her chair. She was a middle-aged, independent woman living in London, and she would continue to represent Useful Women in whatever task given.

'Now, how are you with dogs?' Miss Kerr asked.

'I love dogs,' Mabel said. 'We had Wiggles when I was small, and after that—'

'That's fine,' Miss Kerr said, handing her a slip of paper. 'Mrs Seabrook's gardener's rheumatism is acting up, and her dog needs a bath by teatime.'

Mabel paused. 'What sort of dog is it?'

'The sort with four legs and a tail, I presume. Mrs Seabrook is a gentlewoman fallen on hard times and doesn't get round too well herself these days, so do take care.'

When Mabel arrived at Mrs Seabrook's, she was greeted by a housemaid who looked barely old enough to be out of school.

'Hello, I'm Mabel Canning from Useful Women.' The girl kept her head down and didn't reply, and so Mabel added, 'About giving the dog a bath?'

The girl looked up. 'Oh yes, ma'am. Very good. This way, please.'

She turned and hurried off, and Mabel followed her through the house and out into the yard. There, she found a large washtub and, sitting in the mud next to the tub, an even larger Irish wolfhound.

Mabel smiled at the dog. The dog yawned.

'You'll be able to lend a hand?' Mabel asked the young maid.

'Oh, no, ma'am,' she said, backing away towards the house. 'I must see to the mistress's lunch. The soap's just here' – she nodded to a cake on the windowsill – 'and you're welcome to wear the gardener's tunic and his boots. Frederick's a good dog, he is. Aren't you, boy?'

At the question, the dog rose and wagged his tail.

The maid retreated into the house and shut the door.

'Well, Frederick,' Mabel said, 'shall we get to it?'

No one on the tram would sit next to Mabel on her way home, and for good reason. Although the tunic and rubber boots had done what they could, the bottom half of her skirt and her stockings were covered with a thick coat of mud from diving after a frolicking Frederick. She'd taken off her hat and left it in the kitchen for safety, but that only resulted in her face splattered in mud and new bob cut weighted down with it. And then it had begun to rain.

Mabel dragged herself into the foyer of New River House. The porter's office was empty, although she could hear Mr Chigley humming through the open door that led to his own quarters. She sneaked past.

Upstairs in her flat, she stripped, hung her dress above the gas heater and fed every penny she had into the slot. These were her best daily clothes, and she would need to dry them and then brush them clean.

She had a wash and then, while rinsing her stockings out for the second time, glanced out the small window in the bathroom and across the green to Collins. When the gas heater clicked off, it spurred Mabel into action. She pulled on her second-best dress and stockings and headed out the door to the music hall.

But deciding she – a woman on her own – would go into a music hall was one thing and actually doing it something entirely different. Her steps slowed as she drew near to Collins until she stood in the vestibule-like area outside the doors. She watched men alone, women in pairs and couples walk up to the lighted ticket booth, buy their tickets and go in, casual as you please. They looked like reasonable people and acted as if this were the most natural thing in the world. Perhaps she could attach herself to those two women she'd just spotted so it wouldn't look as if she were alone. But Mabel hesitated, and the opportunity was lost.

The woman in the ticket booth motioned her over.

'I see you ginning up your nerve to come in,' she said with a toothy smile. 'Just wanted you to know you're all right on your own.'

'How did you know I wasn't waiting for someone?' Mabel asked.

'If you was waiting for someone, you'd've been looking out to see who was coming across the green or down the pavement. Instead, you was looking this way to see who was buying a ticket and going in.'

Mabel wanted to tell the woman she had good observation skills, but a queue had formed behind her, and so she found her purse, paid her shilling and walked in.

The lobby smelt of beer and smoke. There was a bar off to one side where an enormous kettle sat at the ready, steam drifting out of its spout, and a young woman was busy setting out rows of cups and saucers while she chatted with a man who gestured with a glass of beer in his hand. Heavy red curtains hung at the three doorways off the lobby and were held open by thick, gold braided rope. Although the room was lit well, it felt dark and close.

This was worlds away from the stage in the church hall in Peasmarsh, where, for several years, Edith and Mabel had put on a pantomime show for the Christmas festivities. Decidedly an amateur affair, they had written their own sketches and songs and made certain to cast as many of the children in the parish as possible in order to bring in their parents to make up a goodly sized audience. Performances were entertaining, because even the gaffes were memorable, such as the time the front half of the horse – Ronald – had lost its head.

Mabel marched forward, handed over her ticket and was

directed upstairs to the gallery, where she took a moment to survey the landscape, debating which of the single seats would be best. There was one near her at the end of a row, but she would need to sit next to a man. Another empty seat in the middle would put her near two other women, but she'd cause a disruption getting there.

The lights began to dim, making the decision for her. She dived in, excusing herself as the men in the row stood to let her pass. The theatre darkened as she sank into her seat, exhaling in a rush and spent from the effort of being an independent woman.

The moment the curtain rose and the lights came up on the stage, Mabel was dazzled – the song and dance and comedy, all accompanied by a small orchestra in the pit. The acts were of a wide variety – there were little dogs that wore skirts and danced on their hind legs, and a group of young men called the Daft Boys who, in an attempt to give a girl some flowers, tripped over one another in a series of silly blunders. Two women told funny stories about their husbands, ending every one with 'God love 'em,' and the audience roared with laughter. That was followed by one of the women singing a ballad about a lost love, and Mabel felt tears prick her eyes.

When a line of eight women dressed in exotic robes danced in a serpentine fashion onto the stage, Mabel recognised Miss Farraday, whom she'd met at the wake. Next, a man sang a few songs, ending with a number everyone in the hall sang along with at the top of their lungs. 'Knees up, Mother Brown, knees up, Mother Brown, under the table you must go, ee-aye, ee-aye, ee-aye-oh!' The chorus was repeated so many times, Mabel was able to join in by the end and clapped along with the rest of the audience.

Then there was Cyril. He came out holding his usual walking stick and looking as sad as the day is long. The house grew quiet, and Mabel noticed a few people prod their neighbours and smile. Serious Cyril launched into a story about a man who couldn't find his hat that ended with 'Mind you don't sit on it!'

'*Boom-boom!*' the audience shouted, and Cyril tapped his walking stick in time.

Then a young woman came out to join him. She wore a dress with a bustle and held a parasol like a walking stick. When she moved, she shimmered. The dress looked like the one Rosalind had been wearing in the photo of her music-hall days.

Cyril and the young woman sang together, and after that, Cyril danced up and down the stage.

And all at once, the show was over. The curtain dropped, the theatre lights came up and people rose and shuffled down to the lobby.

Well, that was grand, Mabel thought, and wanted to tell Cyril so, but she wasn't sure how to find him. She asked the woman behind the bar in the lobby, who told her to go out and round to the stage door.

Mabel followed her directions and came to a narrow, empty passageway between the music hall and the next building. She saw a lighted Stage sign halfway down marking the door. Would she wait here on the pavement or go and ask for him?

While she waffled, a young woman wearing a violet cotton day dress and thick lisle stockings came out, walked past Mabel, and looked up and down the road and across to the green.

This was the young woman who sang with Cyril.

'Hello,' Mabel said, and the woman glanced over for a moment.

'Oh, hiya.'

'I enjoyed your number.'

That drew the woman's attention briefly. 'Thanks.'

'Will Cyril be coming out?' Mabel asked.

'Dunno.'

Mabel would give it one more try.

'I'm Mabel Canning. It's only that, Cyril and I have a mutual friend, and I wanted to tell him I was here.'

The woman tore herself away from watching people and said, 'Pleased to meet you. I'm Florrie. Florrie Hart. Sorry, but I'm expecting my fellow to stop by.' Florrie shook her head and looked down at her feet. 'I don't know where he's got to.'

Neither did Mabel, so she changed the subject.

'The dress you wore was lovely.'

'Did you like it?' Florrie asked, turning her full attention to Mabel. 'It's a bit tight on me and I asked the dresser if it could be let out, and you wouldn't believe the commotion!'

'She didn't want to?'

'She said she had to keep her hands off it and that I should slim down. Still,' Florrie said, 'I won't pass up a chance to be in a duet instead of just one of the chorus. If you're looking for Cyril, you should ask Bert' – she jerked a thumb over her shoulder – 'he's the stage-door manager and signs us all in and out.'

'I will, thanks,' Mabel said. 'I hope your fellow shows up.'

'It isn't looking good,' Florrie replied glumly.

Bert sat just inside the door on a stool behind a tall table that held a ledger. He had glasses perched on the tip of his nose and wore a flat cap, braces and no coat. Once he noticed Mabel, he hopped off his stool, ground his cigarette out into a chipped bit of crockery and took the coat from a nearby wall hook and pulled it on.

'Ma'am,' he said, and nodded.

'Good afternoon. I'm Miss Mabel Canning. Is Cyril inside?'

'Gone, Miss Canning,' Bert replied, glancing down at the ledger on the high table in front of him. 'Fair near shoots out of here after a matinee, he does. Was he expecting you?'

'No, he wasn't. It's just that I've met him before, and this was my first time to see him on stage. I only wanted to say how much I enjoyed the show.'

'Your first time?' Bert said. A few young men bumped Mabel as they emerged from the theatre into the light of day. 'Oi – you lot! Manners.'

The men mumbled apologies, called out 'Seeya, Bert' and went on their way. The stage manager pointed at each of the retreating figures and mumbled, 'Martin, Bullen, Smith, Lanford,' and jotted something down in the ledger. 'Martin!' he called. 'Cyril find you?'

One of the young men stopped, turned back and said, 'He did, Bert.' He gave Mabel a nod and a wink, and she half expected him to click his tongue at her as Mr Jenks had. Bert saw the wink.

'Here now, Martin. Is that how you are with ladies?'

'No, Bert,' Martin said, hanging his head. 'Begging your pardon, ma'am.' He scurried off.

'Young men these days,' Bert said to Mabel. He sat back down and entered something in his book. It reminded Mabel of a teacher's attendance ledger at school.

'Do you keep track of everyone in the theatre?'

'Everyone backstage,' Bert said, 'I sign 'em in, I sign 'em out. Been at the job for thirty-six years and seven different music halls, and I've kept all the ledgers to prove it.'

'Sounds as if you've got the makings of a museum display,' Mabel said.

'Yeah, that's what we'll be good for before long. They keep closing them, you see – the music halls. You come back before the second show and you'll catch Cyril.'

'Yes,' Mabel said, 'because he hasn't missed a show in twenty years.'

Bert laughed. 'So they say.'

. . .

Mabel and Rosalind stood over the desk in the study where a heap of letters lay.

'This isn't all from this morning's post, is it?' Mabel asked.

'No,' Rosalind said. She studied the disarray. 'They've been coming in for a while now. I've started to answer one or two, but I don't get far. I'm afraid I don't have the heart for it. And so, I need your assistance.'

It was the next morning and Mabel had no more arrived at the Useful Women office than Miss Kerr had sent her off, saying, 'You are to see to Mrs Despard's correspondence, Miss Canning. I will expect you to be free for another assignment after lunch.'

'Do you want me to open and read them?' Mabel asked Rosalind. 'Won't some of them be private?'

'You may read them all,' Rosalind said. 'The private ones don't hurt – the notes from friends. The letters that come from other quarters are a different matter.'

Mabel picked up one of Rosalind's unfinished replies, looked at her handwriting and smiled at its jaunty tone. It reminded her of one of the war tunes that aimed to make everyone happy about life – 'Pack Up Your Troubles in Your Old Kit Bag' and the others. She noticed that the tails of Rosalind's cursive Gs didn't loop but went down to a point and then off to the side in an arc, like a dancer's kick.

'I can't think of what to write,' Rosalind said glumly.

'The words are token,' Mabel said. 'It's that they want to hear back from you personally.'

'I suppose,' Rosalind said. 'Although the thought of writing the words out over and over again makes me want to go and lie down.'

The doorbell was pulled.

'Leave this with me,' Mabel said, giving the heap of letters a pat. 'Do you have something more you've written I could take a look at?'

Rosalind didn't question the request but rummaged round in the cubbyholes of the desk before finding a report for a charity called Backstage Benevolence. 'Will this do?'

The bell rang again.

'Where has Bridget got to?' Rosalind asked, checking her wristwatch. 'We'll need coffee in a while.'

'Why don't you go and find her and I'll answer?'

The gentleman on the doorstep wore a slim-cut, dark-blue double-breasted suit with faint stripes to the fabric and polished, pointed-toe boots. He had his eyes on his wristwatch while, at the same time, holding out his hat to her. 'Mrs Despard is expecting me,' he said.

Mabel cleared her throat, and only then did he look up. He pulled his hat away as if she'd been trying to snatch it from him.

This was Thomas Hardcastle, Guy Despard's solicitor. Mabel remembered him from the wake.

'Who are you?' he asked.

Mabel responded to his dreadful manners with aplomb. 'Good morning. I'm Mabel Canning from the Useful Women agency. I was here on Saturday. Please do come in.'

Hardcastle did so, keeping hold of his hat as he eyed the entry.

'Mrs Despard has just gone down to ask Bridget if she would like to bring coffee up.'

Hardcastle grunted. 'I often wonder who runs this house,' he muttered, but certainly loud enough for Mabel to hear.

'Thomas!' Rosalind called, as she appeared at the top of the kitchen stairs. When she reached him, she took his hat and put it on the entry table. 'Mabel, this is Mr Hardcastle, my solicitor. Thomas, Mabel is helping me with my correspondence.'

Hardcastle nodded his head. 'How do you do?'

'Pleased to meet you,' Mabel said.

A shadow fell across the frosted privacy glass panel beside the door, and the bell was pulled. Rosalind answered to a small woman wearing a cloche with a green band that matched her suit. She looked a few years older than Mabel with startlingly blue eyes and her black hair brushed lightly at the temples with grey.

'Gabrielle, come in,' Rosalind said. 'This is Mabel Canning. Mabel, Gabrielle Roche was Guy's secretary, and she has carried on in that position with the business.'

'Pleased to meet you, Miss Canning,' the secretary said, a light Irish lilt to her voice.

'Well, shall we begin?' Rosalind said, and set off for the study, pausing in the doorway to let Hardcastle and Miss Roche go ahead, and then giving Mabel a nod to follow.

'Mabel will be working at my desk while we talk,' Rosalind said, as she sat at a large library table that held a stack of ledgers at one end.

Hardcastle remained standing behind a chair at the table. 'I'd hate to disturb Miss Canning,' he said. 'Perhaps we should go up to the drawing room?'

'No, Thomas,' Rosalind replied, 'I'm sure we'll be no bother to her, and so we'll stay here.'

Mabel crossed the room and settled at the desk in the study while the three at the table spoke casually of the weather, and Rosalind enquired after the solicitor's ceramic collection. Mabel found that she could observe what went on at the library table by turning her head ever so slightly and looking out the corner of her eye.

'Thank you both for meeting with me today,' Rosalind said. 'I'm eager to learn all about Guy's business interests so that I can take over making decisions the way he would have. Thomas, I appreciate you sending the account books over for me to look through. I do have questions, but perhaps you could give me a general description of what has gone on.'

Rosalind's hands must've been tied until Guy had been declared legally dead. Now she wanted to take charge. *Good for you*, Mabel thought. But from the heavy moment of silence, it seemed that neither the solicitor nor the secretary had expected this.

Hardcastle cleared his throat. 'Yes, well, of course.'

He began to talk of investments and shipments of goods to and from various ports around Great Britain. This went on even during the war with minimal loss at sea from German attacks. Guy's interests were spread far and wide, and it sounded as if he'd been quite successful and had set the business up so that it could continue without him. Had he thought that a possibility?

Mabel's interest in the discussion drifted and she attended to the correspondence. The postmarks were various – not only from London boroughs, but also from cities and towns round the country and several from Ireland. Their tone ranged wildly. There were sweet personal notes signed by Sadie, and Letty and Jolly Jack, who remembered Rosalind fondly from their music-hall days together and wrote that if she ever needed anything at all to let them know. Mabel left these alone because Rosalind might want to answer them herself.

Others spoke more formally, offering 'condolences on your loss' and anticipating Rosalind now would begin the usual mourning period. Hadn't she already locked herself away for seven years?

Some letters asked for money, cloaking their coercion in veiled ways. 'Mr Despard had promised to help me, I'm sure you will want to uphold his wishes.' Mabel wanted to throw these in the fire but set them aside in case there was any connection between one of them and the dead man.

In general, to notes with any compassion, she replied, 'Thank you for your kind words and sharing your memories of Guy.'

'I've been going through the Irish accounts, and there seems to be a discrepancy.'

Rosalind's statement cut into Mabel's attention. She sneaked a look and saw Hardcastle frown, while Miss Roche kept her eyes down and held quite still.

'Two thousand pounds,' Rosalind said. She slid the accounts ledger across the table to the other two. 'I realise I haven't had time to look at every line, but this discrepancy is repeated, as far as I can tell, every six months. The money is received, but then seems to vanish.'

Miss Roche leant over the book and ran her finger down first one column and then another. 'Oh yes, let me see now. It's probably that the money is logged separately. Mr Despard liked to keep each ship's records separately, so it could be from the *Lady of Duncormick* or the *Enniscorthy* or the *Ballinacash* or one of the others. Don't you have those details, Mr Hardcastle?'

'Do I?' The solicitor began a methodical look through a sheaf of papers. 'Dear me, how did I overlook that?' He lifted one of the ledgers and looked underneath it as if hoping to discover the elusive details.

'Perhaps you'll deliver them to Mrs Despard tomorrow,' Miss Roche said, sounding more than a bit like a schoolteacher, although Mr Hardcastle didn't seem to notice. 'I would like to talk about the matter of restoring the Irish shipping out of Ballygeary.'

'I don't see how I can consider that until we get this matter cleared up,' Rosalind said. 'Guy didn't create a successful business by allowing two thousand pounds twice a year to leak through his fingers.'

'Yes, yes, of course,' Miss Roche replied, and Mabel heard the scratch of a pen nib across paper.

'There's something else I'd like to talk with the two of you about,' Rosalind said. 'Michael Shaughnessy.'

A heavy silence ensued. Were Hardcastle and Miss Roche waiting each other out?

'Guy mentioned him in the letter he wrote to me – the one the man who died had. I'm sure the police asked you about him.'

'Yes, certainly,' Hardcastle said. 'But, as I told the inspector, I have no recollection of a Michael Shaughnessy. Mr Despard did like to conduct some of his business in a rather offhand manner, and not all were on the books. Casual labour, you know. Here and in Ireland.'

'It's true that Mr Despard gave work to men who needed it,' Miss Roche said in a steely tone, her Irish lilt growing thicker. 'He was a man who understood how hard life can be and, yes, many of those men he employed casually were Irish. They're no less worthy of a decent life than you or me.'

'Please, Miss Roche,' Hardcastle said with exasperation, 'must you drag this up again? I am not disparaging the Irish and just because our political views differ is no reason for you to attack me in such a manner.'

'Politics,' Miss Roche said, as if tasting sour milk.

'And so, Thomas,' Rosalind cut in, 'you're saying you have never heard of Michael Shaughnessy?'

'Inspector Tollerton has already sent someone to look through our employee records, Mrs Despard,' Hardcastle said, 'and there's no sign of the man.'

'Gabrielle?'

'If Mr Despard ever wrote to this Michael Shaughnessy, it will be on file because I have always made a carbon copy of letters. I will look through our files.'

'Thank you, both,' Rosalind said. 'Thomas, please send over the employee ledgers as well so that I can take a look.' Hardcastle looked as if he were about to speak, but Rosalind hurried on. 'Why don't we leave it at that for today – look, here's Bridget with the coffee.'

While Bridget poured and set out a plate of seed cake, Rosalind went to Mabel and picked up one of the letters.

'You've done it again!' she exclaimed. 'That's quite a hand you have. I don't think even I could tell they weren't written by me.' She laughed. 'That doesn't make sense, does it?'

'I've left you to sign them, and I haven't answered them all yet,' Mabel replied. 'I didn't reply to those' – she nodded to the stack of the personal notes, the top one signed, 'With Much Love, Bessie Barker'.

'You've earned your pay this morning,' Rosalind said, 'and I'll be sure to tell Miss Kerr. Come over and join us.'

Mabel sat at the table, and the four of them carried on a conversation that skimmed across topics, including the price of coal and how many people turned out to see Charlie Chaplin on his recent visit to London. 'Thousands,' Hardcastle said. 'You'd have thought it was the king passing by.'

As they finished, the telephone rang. 'I'd better see to that,' Rosalind said.

When she left, Miss Roche rose, and so did Mabel. Hardcastle followed suit.

With a glance out towards the entry, the solicitor said, 'Good of you to help out, Miss Canning, in your capacity as...'

Mabel thought she might stamp on his foot if he tried calling her a maid-of-all-work, but instead, the end of the sentence dangled in the air. *Let him wonder.*

Hardcastle bade them good day and left, but Miss Roche remained, slowly pulling on her gloves. 'Such a terrible thing to happen on Saturday. Do you know, Miss Canning, have they learnt anything about the poor man?'

'I've no idea,' Mabel said.

When Bridget came in for the tray, Miss Roche smiled. 'That was lovely cake, Breej,' she said. 'Was there marmalade in it?'

'A melted spoonful stirred into the batter,' Bridget replied, gathering the cups and saucers. 'My mam's recipe.'

Miss Roche looked over at Mabel as if answering a question. 'Breej is spelt b-r-i-d with a fada, what you would call an accent mark, over the *I*. Bríd is Irish – Bridget is just the English way of pronouncing the name.'

'Is it?' Mabel said.

'Well, good day, Miss Canning. Bríd.'

Bridget stopped what she was doing and watched the woman go. Mabel heard Rosalind talking with Miss Roche, and then the front door close. Only then did Bridget say, 'I was christened Bridget, and saying my name the way she thinks it should be said can't make me more Irish than I already am.' She picked up the tray and walked out.

Rosalind came back into the study. 'I'm awfully glad that's done for now.'

'Perhaps I shouldn't have been within earshot,' Mabel said.

'No, that was the point,' Rosalind replied. 'It's true there's missing money and if that means either Thomas or Gabrielle had anything to do with that man who died on the doorstep or Michael Shaughnessy or... Guy... then I want to know. Do you think you've heard anything useful?'

'It's what I didn't hear that might be useful,' Mabel said. 'You asked them if they knew Michael Shaughnessy and neither of them answered the question.'

NINE

Rosalind dropped into the chair by the desk. 'If Gabrielle or Thomas were involved in Guy's disappearance, what does it say of me that for all these years, I may have harboured someone who would—'

At that moment, Bridget came thundering up the stairs from below shouting what sounded like threats and curses, even though the exact words were unintelligible. She shot past the study doorway with a broom in hand and headed for the front door. Mabel ran after her out onto the pavement, where the maid continued to shout and brandish her broom at the figure of a man in flight to the corner of the square and beyond.

'What is it?' Mabel asked. 'Who was it?'

'Coward,' Bridget shouted after the retreating figure. She turned to Mabel. 'He was here first thing this morning, pulling the bell and asking such questions. And just now I saw him from the basement window, out here on the pavement waiting. I won't have it!'

'It's starting all over again, isn't it?' Rosalind asked. She'd come as far as the front door and stood just inside, her hand on the doorpost. 'Was he asking if I did it – if I killed this man too?'

'Newspapers?' Mabel asked. 'Did he say which one?'

Bridget growled. 'The *Eye of London* or the *Ear of London* or the... I don't know! Could've been the *Backside of London* for all I care.'

'You should tell Inspector Tollerton,' Mabel said.

'What's the use?' Rosalind asked, her face washed of colour. 'They'll print what they like.'

Bridget whacked the side of the railing with her broomstick. 'If I ever get hold of one of 'em, there'll be the devil to pay.'

'Oh, Bridget, don't,' Rosalind said. 'Let's not dwell on it. Why don't we go in? Mabel, will you stay?'

'I can't. Miss Kerr expects me. But I have someone looking into missing persons and anyone who might fit the description of the dead man from Saturday.' Not that Mabel's description would do Skeff much good.

'Isn't that what police do?' Rosalind asked.

'And would they tell you anything about it if they did?' Bridget asked. 'They didn't before. It's good you've got your brother and Miss Canning here to put a shoulder to the wheel.'

Mabel, ever so pleased at Bridget's approval, tried to appear humble. 'Thank you, Bridget. Well, that's me away.' But she stopped herself. 'I forgot to mention – I went to Collins yesterday.'

That brought the smile back to Rosalind's face. 'Did you enjoy yourself?'

'I loved it,' Mabel said. 'There was so much to see, I'm sure I'll need to go back again soon. Would you tell Cyril for me?'

Rosalind locked arms with Mabel. 'I will. He'll be delighted.'

Mabel walked back to Piccadilly. It was just time for lunch, but she didn't believe the apple she had in her bag would do any good. She felt unsettled and needed something more than coffee and cake in her, and so, without a second thought, she walked past Dover Street and straight into the Lyons Corner House. Just inside the door, she paused, the novelty of her action hitting her – a woman on her own in a restaurant. She scanned the vast room and relaxed when she saw several other women without escorts. It's the way of the world, she told herself, and, hoping she looked as if she did this every day, she sat at a table and ordered devilled kippers on toast and entered the cost – nine pence – into her accounts book.

During the meal, Mabel reviewed what she'd done thus far, the sum total of which was that she'd set Skeff to work looking for missing persons. But now, Rosalind had entrusted her with the knowledge there could be problems with the books for Guy's business. Two thousand pounds disappearing every six months – was it going into someone's pockets? Did it have something to do with Michael Shaughnessy, who surely must have something to do with the dead man? How far would someone go to protect his – or her – theft? The Despard accounts needed going over with a fine-tooth comb.

Miss Kerr filled Mabel's afternoon with a series of menial and forgettable tasks – apart from breaking up an argument between a mistress and her daily about a missing glove that had fallen behind an Italian credenza in the front hall.

Once released from work, Mabel made her way home humming 'Knees Up, Mother Brown' and wishing she had a piano to pick out the tune on. In her flat, she poked around in her stores for a suitable evening meal and realised her lunch at the Corner House had been a good idea. She had eaten her way through most of the food she and her papa had hauled up from Peasmarsh. No matter. She had left an opened bottle of milk sitting in a pan of cool water in the dark cupboard, so there would be tea.

A knock came at her door. It was the first time anyone had knocked on Mabel's door, and with a flutter of nerves, she hurried over and opened it.

'Mr Winstone,' she said.

'Miss Canning.' He nodded, and that errant curl fell forward.

In a flash of optimism, Mabel thought perhaps he had news about the enquiry to share.

'Would you like to come in?'

Winstone hesitated, glancing down the short end of the corridor.

Mabel looked too. Should she worry what people might think – she, a single woman allowing a man in her flat? Nonsense, this was London.

He walked in and over to the fireplace, which held the gas heater.

'My sister showed me your handiwork,' he said. 'The copy you made of Guy's letter and the condolence replies you wrote.'

He wanted to talk about her skill at cursive writing?

'Do you often take up another person's style?' he asked. 'Is it a talent you use on a regular basis?'

Mabel closed the door but remained where she stood. 'Rosalind was happy for me to write those replies,' she said. 'The past seven years must have been terribly difficult for her, but no less difficult than it is now to publicly acknowledge her husband's death. Some of those letters were dreadful.'

Behind Winstone's round glasses, his look softened. 'She's borne up well. See here, Miss Canning, I wasn't taking exception to your willingness to help, only remarking on the skill with which you imitated her hand.'

Mabel thought for a moment, and then made a decision.

'My mother died in India when I was only a baby, Mr Winstone.'

'I'm sorry for your loss,' he said. Before he could ask what that had to do with the cost of tea in China, Mabel continued.

'My papa hired an ayah to accompany us on the voyage home, and she stayed and, over the years, became our house-keeper. Mrs Chandekar is a wonderful woman, and the only semblance of a mother I've ever known. When I was twelve, I was overcome with the fanciful idea that Mrs Chandekar truly was my mother. I told no one about this, except my friend, Edith, who knew me well enough not to argue the point. I set about proving my idea. I decided that one way I would do this would involve learning how to imitate my papa's handwriting. In doing that, I discovered I had quite a knack for such a thing. That I could, with care and attention to detail, imitate almost anyone's hand. When I look at cursive writing, in my head I see each style associated with a kind of music.'

Winstone looked perplexed at this explanation.

Mabel shrugged. 'I don't know how it works. But, with this skill in hand, so to speak, I wrote a letter to Somerset House pretending to be my papa and asking for a copy of my birth records.'

'But Miss Canning—' Winstone began.

'Ah, you see the error of my ways. The records are open. Why would government officials at Somerset House care if it was Papa who had penned the letter? But, to my young mind, it seemed necessary for the letter to be convincing. After I sent it off, I lay in wait so that I could intercept our postman before he delivered the answer – before Papa saw it. When the answer came, and I saw my mother's name listed as Margaret Addison Canning, I had to face the fact that Mrs Chandekar was my former ayah, a wonderful housekeeper and a dear woman. There' – Mabel nodded to a photo on the mantel behind Winstone – 'is my mother.'

He picked up the photo of a young woman with hair that

could've been the same as Mabel's golden brown and with a determined look and a sparkle in her eye.

'I thought this was a photograph of you,' he said.

Mabel smiled at his inability to recognise that women's fashions had changed since the 1880s. 'Yes, I look just like her – everyone has always said that. I've had that photo near me my entire life, and yet when I was caught up in my fantasy, the plain truth made no difference. And so, what I learnt from the whole matter was that even when you are faced with incontrovertible evidence, if you don't want to believe something, you won't.'

Winstone was silent. He set the photo back on the mantel, took off his glasses and polished them with his handkerchief. He cleared his throat and at last said, 'That shows a great deal of wisdom for a girl of twelve.'

'At first, I was mortified that I had done such a disservice to both my mother and Mrs Chandekar – she was the one who cottoned on to my wild fantasy, and she was ever so kind about it. The wisdom came much later.'

'Do you see that here?' Winstone asked. 'Do you believe there is evidence being ignored?'

This took Mabel aback. She had told the story to explain how she could imitate other people's writing, but Winstone applied it to the problem at hand and was asking her opinion. Would it be safe to share it with him?

'Well, Mr Winstone. I do have a few thoughts. Would you care for a cup of tea? I'm sorry I've nothing stronger.'

If he were disappointed in the offering, he hid it well. 'Yes, a cup of tea.'

'Please sit down.' Mabel went to her kitchen, filled the kettle and lit the gas ring on the stove. To entertain properly, she should really have something stronger than tea to offer her guests. Tomorrow, she would go out and buy a bottle of sherry. No, on second thought, she'd ask Mr Chigley to buy it for her.

Winstone perched on the edge of the sofa, while Mabel collected the cups and saucers, sugar bowl and milk.

'First, Mr Winstone, will you tell me what the police know about the dead man?'

A knock came at the door. Two visitors in one evening seemed a bounty to Mabel.

She crossed the room and opened the door. Waiting in the corridor and holding a carton overflowing with carrots and apples and an entire cabbage stood the vicar from Peasmarsh.

'Ronald!'

Ronald, tall and lanky, cradled the carton in his arms and leant back to balance the weight. Despite his heavy load, he smiled at Mabel.

'Hello. Are you surprised?'

'I am, yes. Come in, come in,' Mabel said, so pleased to see him that she laughed. 'Have you brought half of Papa's shop with you?'

'It certainly feels as if I have,' Ronald said, stepping over the threshold as he looked back at her. 'I hope you don't mind me pitching up on your doorstep, but Father has arranged a dinner for me here in London with the bishop and—' He stopped dead at the sight of Winstone. 'Oh.'

'Ronald, this is Mr Park Winstone,' Mabel said. 'Mr Winstone, this is the Reverend Ronald Herringay from Peasmarsh.'

'How do you do, sir?' Winstone asked, offering his hand and then withdrawing it when he realised Ronald was not free to shake. 'Can I help you with that?'

'Pleased to meet you, Mr Winstone. No, thank you, I'm all right.'

'Come, set the carton on the table,' Mabel said. 'It's really lovely to see you, Ronald.' Lovely, and a bit disconcerting to have two men in her flat, even if neither of them could be considered gentlemen callers.

Ronald deposited the carton and then brushed off his coat and straightened his already straight clerical collar.

'You came up on the train with all this?' Mabel asked.

'Just a few things your father and Mrs Chandekar wanted you to have.' He remained by the table fidgeting. Winstone hovered near the mantel, hands in his pockets. Mabel stood in the middle of the room thinking how to explain to Ronald who this strange man was. Meanwhile, the kettle rattled as it heated.

'I hope you have time to stay for tea,' she said to Ronald.

His gaze darted from Mabel to Winstone and back again. 'As it happens, I don't. Terribly sorry, but the bishop, you know. Mr Winstone.'

Ronald made a break for the door and got past Mabel before she could stop him.

'I'll just be a moment,' she said to Winstone, and chased after Ronald, catching him on the first-floor landing. 'Must you leave so soon?'

Ronald thrust his chin in the air. 'I certainly have no intention of getting in the way of your... your...' He breathed hard and frowned.

'My what?' Mabel asked sharply.

'Your romantic... whatever. I have no wish to be part of a... a triangle.'

Mabel stamped her foot. It was either that or laugh.

'Romantic triangle? I'll have you know Mr Winstone is the brother of one of my clients from Useful Women. There are no romantic notions between him and me, just as there are no romantic notions between you and me. And, unless I am very much mistaken, there are no romantic notions between you and Mr Winstone.'

'Mabel!'

'So, there is no triangle.' Mabel prodded him gently with her elbow. 'Come back and have a cup of tea. Please.'

After a moment, Ronald's head bobbed back and forth, which Mabel recognised as a sign of concession. 'Oh, all right,' he said.

He followed her back, and they met Winstone coming out of Mabel's flat. He made a show of checking his wristwatch.

'Sorry, I've got to be somewhere,' he said. 'Your kettle just boiled.'

'Goodbye, Mr Winstone,' Mabel called to him, as he vanished down the stairs. 'Well.'

'I didn't drive him off, did I?' Ronald asked with a hint of hope in his voice.

'No, Ronald, I'm sure you didn't. He probably needs to take Gladys for a walk. Come on – tea.'

They sat at the small dining table up against the wall by the kitchen, and as the pot brewed, Mabel brought out a tin from the carton and popped the lid.

'Jumbles!' she exclaimed. Jumbles, sweet dough rolled out, tied in a knot then baked, were a fine biscuit for dunking in tea. Whereas other biscuits went hard as they grew old, jumbles started out hard, so their age didn't matter.

Mabel poured the tea, and the first thing she did was dunk her jumble.

'Now, I want to hear all the news. Mrs Chandekar wrote to say that Mrs Pickering's niece has arrived, and she's helping you with your correspondence. It's Lucy, isn't it?'

'Lucy Edgerley.'

Mabel waited for more, but when it didn't come, she asked, 'What's she like?'

'I don't know anything about her, really,' Ronald said.

'Mrs Chandekar says she knows Pitman's – that must be a great help to you when you're dictating letters.'

Ronald squirmed in his chair. 'I don't speak fast enough to

make Pitman's worthwhile,' he said. 'It makes me rather nervous, the way she sits there waiting for me to say something, her pencil hovering over her notebook. And I feel as if everyone is talking behind our backs.'

Hopes were that Mrs Pickering's niece would become the new wife of the vicar – Mabel knew this to be true because she had encouraged the talk before she'd left for London. She had met Lucy and remembered her as a pleasant sort who got along with everyone.

'They wish the best for you,' Mabel said. 'As do I.'

'How are you getting on?' Ronald asked.

'I've had all manner of interesting work,' Mabel replied. 'I've been to the London Library, and I seem to be quite good at settling disputes.' She would leave out the murder.

'Edith always said you were a keen observer of human nature – not in the way Mrs Drinkwell is, of course.'

Mabel laughed. Mrs Drinkwell was the village nosy parker. 'Thank goodness for that. Edith and I once spied on Mrs Drinkwell eavesdropping on a conversation between that fellow who owned the garage out on the London Road and his married lady friend. Took about two minutes before the entire village knew of the affair – and they didn't hear it from us.'

Ronald warmed to his subject. 'Edith also said you would not be taken in by a person's... a person's... pretence.' He frowned and shook his head. 'No, that's not how she said it. What was it? It was some phrase she'd read in a magazine. A person's...' His face crumpled. 'I can't remember. I can't remember what she said.'

'Ronald—'

'Please come home, Mabel,' he blurted, his voice thick. 'You're all I have left of her.'

Mabel knew the feeling and it made her heart hurt. But she had promised Edith that she would be strong for Ronald. 'Just because you live your life doesn't mean you'll forget her,' Mabel said. 'You can't be miserable forever.'

'Yes, yes, I know.'

'What would Edith say?'

He sniffed and shuddered and threw back his shoulders. 'She would say, "Ronald, don't be a silly ass."'

Mabel laughed and so did Ronald.

'Good,' she said, and gave his arm a squeeze. 'Now, let me see what else you've got for me.' She stood and continued to rummage round in the carton. Amid the jars and fresh fruit and veg was a clear bottle full of purple liquid. Mabel held it up with delight. 'Sloe gin! This must be the end of last year's batch. I can entertain properly now.' She put her arms round the carton and gave it a hug. 'Such a bounty – I'd better see where I can put all of it.'

She stuck an apple in her mouth, picked up two jars of pears and went into her kitchen. The space comprised the cooker with two gas rings, a sink, one shelf, a plate rack and a small cupboard with room for nothing else. While she stood contemplating the storage possibilities, there was a knock at the door.

Mabel took the apple out of her mouth and nodded to Ronald. 'Would you?'

When he opened the door, she could see across the room and past him to Skeff, who squinted through the smoke of the cigarette in her mouth.

'Good God,' she said, and then called over her shoulder, 'Cora, come look. Mabel's got a vicar in her flat.'

TEN

Ronald looked to Mabel, who covered a snigger as she rushed to the door.

Cora, wearing a bronze turban with her hair showing all round the edges like a curly fringe, joined Skeff.

After introductions were made, Mabel said, 'Do please come in.'

'Delighted to meet you, ladies. Mabel, I must go.'

'Ronald's having dinner with the bishop of London,' Mabel said. 'You'll give Papa and Mrs Chandekar a good report, won't you?' She tilted her head and gave him a kiss on the cheek. 'Take care.'

Ronald coloured slightly, bobbed his head and left.

Skeff watched as Ronald disappeared down the stairs at the far end of the corridor. 'Herringay, Herringay.'

'Yes,' Mabel said. 'Lord and Lady Fellbridge's second son.'

Cora fiddled with a curl peeking from under her turban. 'I must say, Mabel, you have hidden depths.'

'Come in, you two,' Mabel said.

'Sorry, can't,' Skeff replied. 'We're off to a lecture, only wanted to stop and tell you what I've turned up about your unidentified man.'

'What have you found?' Mabel asked, eager with anticipation.

'Not a sausage,' Skeff replied. 'No one even close to his description has been reported missing in the past fortnight.'

The man, the only link to Michael Shaughnessy and what happened to Guy Despard, was not only dead, but also a dead end.

As she lay in bed that night, Mabel thought about the official enquiry into the death of the man on the doorstep. Was Winstone involved with the police? Would he be willing to tell her what he knew? Unlikely, she decided.

Mabel considered the different avenues that she would pursue if she were in charge. One: learn his identity through searching missing persons notices. She would leave Skeff on it. Two: find this Michael Shaughnessy. This meant further research into Thomas Hardcastle and Gabrielle Roche, who were both cagey when answering Rosalind's questions. Three: look into the dodgy accounting for Guy Despard's business.

That required expertise Mabel did not possess, but as she thought about it, a solution began to form in Mabel's mind – a vision, as it were, of Effie Grint sitting behind the plain deal table in the Useful Women office and handing out pay packets. She heard Miss Kerr's voice say, 'Mrs Grint knows a thing or two about bookkeeping.'

Tomorrow was Friday. Mrs Grint would be in the Useful Women office handing out pay packets, and Mabel would be there to collect hers. Perfect.

.   .   .

The pay-packet queue at the Useful Women office ran out the door and into the corridor. Mabel joined it, chatting with the woman ahead of her who had spent one entire afternoon spraying a client's pelargoniums for whitefly and had followed that up with demonstrating how to use a steam cooker to a client who had lost her cook and had never herself even put the kettle on to boil.

'I daresay you've earned your pay this week,' Mabel said, happy to commiserate and even happier to have escaped the whitefly assignment.

At last, she worked her way up to the plain deal table set beside Miss Kerr's desk.

'Hello, good morning, Effie,' Mabel said. She nodded to Miss Kerr, who was on the telephone and nodded back.

''Morning, Mabel,' Effie replied, and she shuffled through the box of envelopes. 'Here you are, just sign your name.'

As Mabel did so, she said, 'Tell me, in addition to doing bookkeeping for Miss Kerr, do you take other assignments?'

Miss Kerr's head shot up as she replaced the earpiece on its hook.

'That is, I mean,' Mabel hurried on, 'as one of the Useful Women, of course.'

'I do as my time allows,' Mrs Grint replied.

Mabel felt the press of women in the queue behind her and so took her packet and moved to the other side of Miss Kerr's desk. She leant in and spoke quietly.

'Miss Kerr, I believe Mrs Despard may be in need of Mrs Grint's services.'

Miss Kerr turned her Jobs ledger to a previous page. Mabel glanced down and saw Rosalind's name and telephone number.

'If she is, Miss Canning,' Miss Kerr said, 'then I would be happy to receive a request from her. I'm not in the habit of telephoning clients to solicit services.'

'No, of course not.'

The trouble with a good idea is that it begs immediate fulfillment. Mabel squeezed her pay packet to gauge its thickness – better than her first week – and put it away in her bag as she walked out into the corridor to think. She would dash over to Belgravia and tell Rosalind to ring Miss Kerr and book Effie Grint for as soon as possible.

From the far end of the corridor came Mrs Fritt and her tea-and-bun trolley. As she neared, Mabel took note of the teetering stack of buns.

'Fridays I always put on more,' Mrs Fritt said, 'for Miss Kerr's Useful Women.'

'A fine business move, Mrs Fritt,' Mabel replied. 'I'll have mine in just a moment, but can you tell me, is there a telephone nearby I could use? It's only that Miss Kerr is so busy at the moment.'

There was. Mrs Fritt introduced her to the secretary in the architects' office at the end of the corridor, who graciously allowed Mabel to use the telephone after Mabel offered to buy her a bun. As Mrs Fritt and the secretary chatted, Mabel asked the exchange for the number in Belgravia.

She didn't think anyone would ever answer, but at last Bridget did and once convinced it really was Mabel on the telephone, the maid went off to find Rosalind, who finally came on the line.

Mabel explained briefly, and Rosalind said, 'Brilliant' and that was that. When Mabel returned to the Useful Women office, Miss Kerr was on the telephone, but raised an eyebrow at her.

The office had mostly cleared and only a few pay packets were left in Effie's box when Miss Kerr said to Mabel, 'You'll be happy to know, Miss Canning, that Mrs Grint's bookkeeping services have been requested by a client.'

'Tomorrow,' Effie said. 'Good to have a piece of work on a Saturday.'

'It is, isn't it?' Mabel said. *See you there.*

'Now, Miss Canning,' Miss Kerr said. 'I have two assignments, if you're willing and able.'

Both willing and able, Mabel thought, as long as neither assignment included whitefly.

Mabel spent an hour mediating a dispute between a Lady Parfay's cook and the butcher about an order that had never been received. Mabel eventually pinned the trouble down to the fact that although the cook had written out the order for the butcher, she had put it in an envelope addressed to the wine merchant, who took the request for a four-pound-weight rib roast as a joke. Tempers ran high on all sides until Mabel reminded the businessmen of the value of keeping Lady Parfay's custom. The butcher had the roast wrapped for the cook in the blink of an eye, and the wine merchant offered a bottle of port gratis.

Off Mabel went to Mrs Ackerley, who needed a trunkfull of moth-eaten fur collars and muffs to be sorted through. She had inherited them from an old aunt some years ago. Mabel sighed inwardly but made no complaint because where would complaining get her except moved to the bottom of Miss Kerr's list of Useful Women?

Mrs Ackerley took Mabel up to the third floor, down a passageway and around a corner to a low door that stood open, revealing worn treads on a twisty, steep staircase.

'The trunk is in the attic, just up there,' she said. 'I've had my butler pull it out for you.' As she turned to go, she added, 'You can let me know if there is anything worth keeping.'

Mabel peered up the narrow staircase. Dust motes floated in the dim grey light from above. She sighed, hitched up her skirt, and climbed until she reached the vast upper space, where everything – floor, cartons, sheets thrown over furniture – was covered in a thick layer of dust. The air was close and warm. She took off her hat and coat and hung them on a nearby bedpost.

When she flipped the latches on the fur trunk and opened the lid, a cloud of moths rose up in her face. Mabel cried out and jumped back into a stack of chairs as the moths fluttered away. She straightened herself and looked down at the contents of the trunk – a dreary mass of fur bits in reddish brown, deep chestnut and something blondish. Mabel shuddered.

Picking up a fur collar between thumb and forefinger, she gave it a preliminary shake. Tiny white worms flew through the air and landed on her chest. With a garbled shout, she dropped the collar and danced a jig as she knocked the things off her.

She ran the back of her hand across her sweaty forehead, breathed in the thick, hot air, sneezed and got to work. Two hours later, the results were one large pile of fur pieces with no hope of redemption and one quite small pile in slightly better condition. She wiped the sweat off her brow and sought out Mrs Ackerley, who didn't care to see the results of Mabel's work and only instructed her to take the good pile to the furrier. 'The rest will need to be taken out to the yard and burnt.'

Mabel felt quite ill at the thought of carrying the maggoty mess in her arms down three flights of stairs, and instead, packed the redeemable furs in a small carton she found, left the attic and went all the way down to the basement and found the butler.

'Hello,' she said, 'I've finished going through the trunk of fur pieces, and I'm taking the best to the furrier. Mrs Ackerley wants the discarded furs in the attic taken out to the back and burnt.' She smiled. 'Good day.'

Once rid of the furs, Mabel took a deep breath of cleanish London air, which had a decided chill to it. She walked all the way to a kiosk at the end of Hyde Park across from the Wellington Arch and drank a cup of tea straight down in hopes of washing away the dust that coated her throat. The effort was met with limited success.

Mabel went to Belgravia ostensibly to talk further with Rosalind about Effie Grint, but really to avoid any further maggot-related job assignments. She didn't want a reputation.

Bridget greeted her offhandedly and pointed her up towards the drawing room. As Mabel climbed the stairs, she heard the piano. Someone was playing a sprightly tune. And was that Rosalind singing? It sounded like a music-hall tune. Mabel thought Cyril must have arrived, but when she looked in the drawing room, she saw Rosalind singing and Winstone playing.

'Daddy wouldn't buy me a bow-wow,' she sang.

'Bow-wow,' Winstone repeated.

'I've got a little cat, and I'm very fond of that, but I'd rather have a bow-wow.'

'Wow, wow, wow, wow,' they sang almost together.

'You're too slow on that last line, Park,' Rosalind said, as he finished playing with a flourish.

'I'm not,' he replied, 'you're too quick.'

'You always think you're right, don't you? Did you sing this twice a day for years?' she asked.

'It isn't my fault you learnt it wrong.'

Gladys was the first to notice Mabel. The dog popped up from behind the bench, trotted over and greeted her.

'Oh, Mabel, lovely,' Rosalind said. 'You caught our piece?'

'Yes, quite fine,' she replied, giving Gladys a pat.

'Thank you, Miss Canning,' Winstone said, rising and playing a few chords with his left hand.

'Park thinks he needs to keep me in good spirits, or I'll fall apart,' Rosalind remarked. 'He's a good brother but can be a bit annoying at times.'

Mabel saw past Rosalind's jolly attitude to the strained look on the woman's face, and knew that although 'cheering up' was needed, it was only putting a plaster on the problem.

'Let me see if Bridget will bring us coffee,' Rosalind said. She walked out and called over the banister but got no response.

'Isn't there a bell?' Mabel asked.

'A servant's bell?' Winstone asked with a laugh. 'For Bridget?'

Rosalind called again and then came back in. 'She must've gone down to the kitchen – I'll just go and see.'

Mabel moved closer to the fire, and Winstone approached, peering at her hair. Had he not noticed her new cut until now?

'I'm terribly sorry, Miss Canning,' he said, leaning closer and lifting his hand to her hair. 'You seem to have— Wait, don't move.'

Mabel held still as his fingers combed through her curls, and a tingle went down her spine.

'Please don't be alarmed,' he said. He pulled his hand away, and Mabel saw a small white worm wriggling in his palm.

Mabel made a choking noise. 'You little monster,' she said. 'Give it here.' She held her hand out, and Winstone, his brows lifted, turned the worm out onto her palm.

She marched over to the fireplace and tossed the thing into the embers, nodding in satisfaction when she heard a tiny *pop*. Then she ran her fingers through her hair. Nothing fell out, but to be certain, she turned to Winstone and bent her head.

'Do you see any more?'

'Er, no,' he said.

She *humphed*. 'I spent half the morning going through a trunk of maggoty furs,' she explained, brushing herself off as if to be rid of the experience. 'That fellow must've thought he could get a free ride.'

'Well,' Winstone said with a grin, 'he learnt his lesson, didn't he?'

Mabel glanced out to the landing, where Rosalind kept calling for Bridget, and then back at Winstone. 'You're hoping to lift her spirits, aren't you?'

Winstone gave a sharp nod. 'She plays along. But what happened on Saturday, just when she thought she could lay Guy to rest – it's hit her harder than she'll admit.'

'Is there news about the enquiry, Mr Winstone? Wouldn't knowing progress was being made help settle her mind?'

'You forget I'm not police,' he said.

'Are you telling me your friend Inspector Tollerton has told you nothing?'

Rosalind came back in. 'Coffee coming up,' she said. 'And Dundee cake as well.'

After coffee, Mabel reluctantly readied to leave. She stood at the door as Rosalind went to fetch her hat from wherever Bridget had left it, when there was a shadow on the privacy window beside the door, followed by the bell being pulled.

Mabel opened the door to Thomas Hardcastle, who clutched at least five ledgers in his arms and looked startled to see her.

'Oh, Miss... Canning, isn't it? Yes.'

'Yes, good morning, Mr Hardcastle.'

She stood back, and the solicitor stepped in, where, lacking any further direction, he stopped.

'Mrs Despard is talking with Bridget,' Mabel informed him. 'I'm sure she won't be long. Would you like to go through to the study?'

But before he did, Rosalind came up with Mabel's hat.

'Thomas, there you are. Are these the employee records?'

'I... er... no. You asked for the Irish books?'

'Yes, but I also want to see the employee records, remember?'

'I'm terribly sorry,' Hardcastle said, cutting his eyes at Mabel.

Mabel didn't care if she was unwanted and stayed where she was, noticing that the solicitor had developed a tic at the corner of his right eye. When the tic jumped, he blinked in a startled fashion.

'If I can be of service in explaining anything—' Hardcastle began.

'No, Thomas,' Rosalind said, taking the ledgers from him. 'That's fine.'

Winstone came down the stairs at that moment, greeted Hardcastle and turned to Rosalind.

'What's all that about?' he asked, nodding to the books.

Rosalind held the books close and gave her brother a bland look. 'Nothing. It's only that I thought I'd look over things. I told you I was going through the accounts, don't you remember?' She headed for the study with Winstone following. 'Thomas, would you like coffee?'

The solicitor trailed after them.

The telephone rang and Mabel didn't think twice about answering.

'Hello, Mrs Despard's house.'

'Who is this?'

Mabel bit her tongue to keep from telling the man he had deplorable manners. He was as bad as Winstone.

'This is Mabel Canning.'

'Miss Canning? You were there on Saturday. Mrs Despard's friend?'

Ah, the inspector.

'Who may I say is telephoning?' Mabel asked. Someone had to maintain a sense of etiquette.

'Inspector Tollerton. Is Winstone there?'

'Yes, he is,' Mabel said. 'If you'll wait, I'll fetch him.'

'No, don't. Just tell him I'll see him at the Gardeners Arms in twenty minutes and he'd better be there because I won't wait.'

The inspector rang off before Mabel could say another word.

Winstone reappeared from the study.

'You've just missed the inspector,' Mabel told him. She gave him the message and then asked, 'So, are you meeting him about the dead man?'

Winstone looked wary. 'Couldn't I just be meeting an old friend for a pint?'

'Not likely. Where is this Gardeners Arms?' Mabel asked.

'The street two over and down at the...' Winstone eyed her. 'Why? Are you thinking of coming along?'

'I would do if I thought the inspector would allow it.'

'He barely allows me,' Winstone said. 'But the fact that you're willing to listen to the morbid autopsy details, Miss Canning – you show pluck.'

'Pluck? You make me sound like a girl with my hair in plaits.'

'I never said that, I only meant...' Winstone swallowed his next words and grumbled. He looked up the stairs. 'Gladys?'

The dog appeared on the first-floor landing, trotted down and shook herself.

'I might have some information related to the enquiry,' Mabel said.

'About the dead man?' Winstone asked, frowning.

'I'd rather not say anything further at the moment,' she replied, flushed with how mysterious that sounded. 'Perhaps I'll see you later.'

ELEVEN

Mabel had a thought to follow Winstone to the Gardeners Arms and invite herself to his meeting with Tollerton, but didn't believe the inspector would look kindly on her. Instead, she returned to the Useful Women office, but as she sat and waited for a job, Mabel thought about Rosalind and Guy, his business, the dead man, Michael Shaughnessy and... the list went on. So, she begged off work the rest of the afternoon – alluding to the possibility that she carried a few more maggots about her person as an excuse – and took the tram back to Islington where she walked straight past New River House.

She made instead for the top of the green towards Collins. She had realised that an excellent source for at least some background material was at her fingertips. Hadn't Cyril known Rosalind for donkey's years? He would remember Guy, too, and seemed on familiar standing with Hardcastle and, by extension, Miss Roche. Mabel looked at her wristwatch. The matinee would be just ending and perhaps she could catch him.

People were drifting out the door of Collins as Mabel approached, but she walked past and made directly for the side passage that led to the stage-door entrance. There, once again, she encountered Florrie Hart standing on the pavement, scanning the crowd of people walking by.

'Hello,' Mabel said. 'Florrie, isn't it?'

Florrie turned to Mabel, her chin quivering. 'Yes, hello. You're Mabel, I remember.'

'Is it your fellow?' Mabel asked gently. 'Did he not show?'

A tear trickled down Florrie's cheek, still quite a bright red from her stage make-up. 'I don't know whatever could have happened. They all say I was just a passing fancy, and he's forgotten all about me, but I don't believe that.' Her voice came out high and wobbly, as if she feared it was true.

'Here now,' Mabel said, forgetting why she'd come this way in the first place. She drew a handkerchief from her bag and handed it over.

'Miss Canning,' Cyril said, as he came out of the passage.

'Hello,' Mabel replied. 'I was hoping to see you before you left.'

'I'm flattered,' he said. 'You came all this way for me.'

'I'm not terribly far, actually. I live just over the green in New River House.'

Cyril put his hand up as if to shade his eyes from the sun and peer off into the far distance. 'Well now, if that's the case, I'll expect you at three shows a week.' He turned back to her and smiled.

'I would do,' Mabel said. 'I enjoyed my first so very much.'

Florrie stood silent, dabbing her eyes, but now Cyril put a hand on her elbow.

'Ah girl, what's this now?'

Florrie sniffed.

'Do you two know each other?' he asked.

'I met Florrie when I came round looking for you after the show on Wednesday,' Mabel said.

Cyril looked from one to the other and he nodded to himself. 'Florrie,' he said, 'would you do me a favour? Would you go back and tell Bert I'll need a new bottle of whisky in my dressing room? Only I forgot to mention it.'

'Yeah, all right,' Florrie said, and went off.

When she was out of earshot, Cyril said, 'Miss Canning, you wouldn't have the time to be a good Samaritan, would you?'

'With Florrie?'

'Only the girl's got a broken heart and I hate to see it. I would ask her about it, but she doesn't want to be talking with an old fellow like me. She has friends her own age, of course, but an older-sister type like you could comfort and give her advice all in one. Would you mind?'

'That's good of you to want to help,' Mabel said.

Cyril waved away the compliment. 'I'm a selfish old sod – I can't have her breaking into tears in the middle of our number, now can I?'

Mabel liked his modesty and she liked that he looked after the younger performers. 'I'd be happy to,' she said, and put off her questions for Cyril to another day.

When Florrie returned, Mabel made the offer.

'There's a place over by the Underground station I've noticed, but I haven't tried it yet. Let's go have a cup of tea and we can have a chat?'

Cyril reached in his pocket and handed over a few coins. 'And a slice of cake too.'

'Yeah, all right. Thanks,' Florrie said, wiping her eyes and giving her nose a good blow, and stuffed Mabel's handkerchief in her pocket.

'And you remember, Florrie,' Cyril said, 'I'm the only one allowed to show a sad face on stage.'

Florrie gave him a smile. 'That you are, Cyril.'

'That's better,' he said. 'Off you go now.'

Mabel led the way, and when they got to the corner, she looked back to see Cyril watching. He put his hat on his walking stick and waved it round at them, then turned to go.

. . .

'Do you enjoy dancing with Cyril?' Mabel asked, as they settled at a table by the window.

'Yeah, he's a decent man,' Florrie said. 'He doesn't try anything with any of the girls.' She looked round them and leant over the table and whispered, '*Or the boys, if you know what I mean.* And he can put in a good word for you with the show manager, so none of us mind making him a cup of tea or brushing his hat or delivering messages for him.'

Florrie ordered a jam roly-poly and Mabel asked for toast. When their order arrived, Florrie added three spoonfuls of sugar to her tea and stirred, then stared at the swirling liquid.

'What's your fellow's name, Florrie?'

The young woman looked up. 'His name's Claude. It's a fine name, isn't it?'

'It is,' Mabel said. 'Where did you and Claude meet?'

'We met outside the stage door, just as you and I did' – she giggled – 'except, of course, he wasn't looking for Cyril as you were, he was waiting for me. Said he'd seen five shows before he ginned up his nerve to say something to me.'

'*Five?* Claude must know all the songs by now.'

'He's been a bit lonely, see, and just happened in one day,' Florrie said, becoming quite animated. 'He came up to London in the summer – his poor dear mum was ill, and then she died a few weeks ago. That's just before I met him. Died of a broken heart, he said. Isn't that sad?'

'Yes, it is.'

'And so he had time on his hands and was walking by Collins and just came in for no reason, he said.'

'He lives nearby?' Mabel asked.

'Well,' Florrie said, and cast her gaze out the window, 'I dunno really. Camden Town, I think he said.' She ate a spoonful of her roly-poly and washed it down with tea. 'It's only that Martin said he'd seen Claude yesterday, walking across the green.'

'Martin?'

'He's one of the Daft Boys,' Florrie said. 'I dunno – probably just Martin having me on.'

Mabel recalled the Daft Boys and their antics in the show.

'How did you start on the stage?' Mabel asked, and received from Florrie an earful of stories about music-hall life and its vagaries.

'But you're set now, aren't you?' Mabel asked. 'You've Cyril as a partner.'

'That's only temporary,' Florrie said, 'but even so, good for me.'

'Still, you'd like to find out where Claude has got to, wouldn't you?' Mabel asked gently.

'I would,' Florrie said.

'Why don't you ask that Martin from the Daft Boys about seeing Claude? Which way was he walking? Was he alone? Did he speak to anyone?'

Florrie looked at her with a blank expression.

Mabel persisted. 'There might be a clue, you see. And wherever Claude is, the least he can do is tell you why he stopped coming round.'

'Blimey, you're like one of them detectives,' Florrie remarked.

Mabel smiled and watched the young woman scrape up the last bits of cake from her plate.

When she'd finished, she said, 'Thanks, Mabel. I do go on a bit, but I feel ever so much better now.'

They walked up the high street as far as New River House, where Mabel said, 'This is me,' and Florrie headed back to Collins.

In the foyer, Mabel chatted with Mr Chigley, gathered her

post and started up the stairs, meeting Winstone and Gladys on their way down.

Mabel had half a mind to block the stairs until he agreed to talk with her, but before she got up the nerve, Winstone nodded at her and said, 'Miss Canning, might we have a few words together?'

Relieved, she said, 'Yes, Mr Winstone, that's a very good idea.'

They both fell silent. Mabel, for one, wondered just where these few words would be spoken – certainly not on the staircase. Absent-mindedly, she reached down and gave Gladys a scratch behind the ears.

'You wouldn't want to come into my flat?' Winstone asked.

Mabel gave a fleeting thought to his portable piano. 'No,' she said, 'perhaps not.'

'We could go out for a meal.' It sounded more a statement than an invitation.

'Where?' Mabel asked. She hadn't noticed any restaurants, only the tea shop she'd just come from. 'Not a pub, I hope.'

'No, certainly not,' Winstone said, but she heard disappointment in his voice.

'I tell you what,' she said, 'why don't you come to my flat? You've already been there once, so...'

'A precedent has been set,' Winstone said. 'I wouldn't want to put you out.'

'It's no trouble because it won't be fancy – in fact, it'll probably be the sort of meal you'd find at your pub. Apart from the beer.'

'I am grateful for any food set before me,' Winstone stated. 'I'll be up directly after Gladys and I take a stroll through the green. Then I'll leave her in my flat.'

'No, please bring Gladys with you.'

'You heard that, girl?' he asked, stroking the dog's head. 'You can play the gooseberry.' Barely a second of stunned silence passed before Winstone looked up and, with a red face said, 'No, I'm sorry, I didn't mean... that is, I...'

The warmth that had rushed through Mabel at his first words chilled in an instant.

'Quite all right, Mr Winstone,' she said in a breezy manner. 'It was a little joke. I understand. No chaperone necessary. You're safe.'

In her flat, Mabel flung her hat away, filled the kettle and lit the gas ring. She swept the breakfast crumbs from the table into her hand and tossed them into the sink. She looked at herself in the little round mirror that hung in the bathroom, pinched her cheeks, patted her hair and then waved her hand. 'Don't be silly,' she said to her reflection.

When Winstone knocked, she was entirely back to her normal self.

'Come in, please.' Mabel held the door open and watched as her guests entered. Winstone stopped at the end of the sofa, but Gladys set about sniffing the perimeter of the room before settling on the hearthrug.

There was barely enough room for one person to eat at the small table next to the kitchen alcove, let alone two, and so by the time Mabel had set out the few things for their meal – ham and a wedge of cheese, a fresh loaf along with butter, a few small apples and a jar of piccalilli – it now gave the appearance of a feast. She poured the tea, and they tucked in.

By some unspoken agreement, conversation was sparse as they both applied themselves to the business of eating.

He reached once again for the piccalilli, and the spoon clinked against the sides of the almost-empty jar. 'Sorry. I seem to be finishing it off.'

'Go right ahead – there's more,' Mabel said. 'Mrs Chandekar and I put it in all seasons, and use whatever's to hand.

This was a summer recipe, but she'll be cooking another batch soon. Perhaps Ronald will bring a few jars next time he comes up to London to dine with the bishop.'

'Ronald, yes,' Winstone said. 'Your vicar.'

'He isn't my vicar,' Mabel said. 'Well, yes, he is in the sense that he's the vicar at the church in Peasmarsh. Ronald is a friend because he was married to a dear friend of mine. I usually think of him as Edith's husband.'

'Was?' Winstone asked, laying his knife and fork down.

'Edith died two years ago April,' Mabel said. 'Spanish influenza.'

'We had it from all sides, didn't we?' Winstone remarked. 'The war, the 'flu. You must miss her.'

Gladys had come over to the table, and so Mabel offered her a wedge of apple. The dog took it carefully between her teeth and returned to the hearthrug. 'Yes, I do.'

Mabel came back to the moment and plowed on.

'You're here to tell me what Inspector Tollerton told you about the dead man, aren't you?'

'Am I?'

'Yes, you are,' she said with pique. 'Are there further details on how he died?'

Winstone pushed his plate away and rested his forearms on the table. 'Nothing more, just that he was hit with great force in his chest. It was such a shock to the heart that after a brief struggle, it stopped altogether.'

Mabel put a hand to her own chest and took a slow breath. 'Did it happen right there in front of the house? Didn't anyone see?'

'No witnesses,' Winstone replied, 'or so they say. It could've happened at the end of the terrace and around the corner – fewer people walking by and fewer windows. He could've stumbled as far as the door.'

'And still no idea who he is?'

'No. There's no match for his fingerprints in the system, but that tells us only that he hadn't been suspected in any past criminal activity.'

'And no missing person has been reported with his description,' Mabel said.

Winstone gave her a sharp look. 'How do you know that?'

'He came to Rosalind to deliver that letter,' Mabel said, pretending she hadn't heard the question, 'and someone tried to stop him. Stopped him for good in the end. Guy had offered this fellow work, so why would the soldier kill him? If he did kill Guy, why wait seven years to claim the offer? The war has been over for nearly three years – what had the fellow been doing?'

'Guy may have offered him work, but with him gone, I don't know that Rosy could've hired the fellow,' Winstone said. 'She could do only so much with the money during Guy's missing years. She was taken care of, but it was Thomas Hardcastle who kept the business going – Guy's right-hand man. Things have been going along much the same these years.'

'Miss Roche had an easy answer to it, saying that the money went through a different account.' Mabel thought about Miss Roche. 'Did Guy have an Irish connection?'

'His parents came over during the famine,' Winstone said. 'He was supportive of Irish independence, but I don't believe he would involve himself in the cause.'

'Perhaps someone wanted very much for him to be involved, and when Guy said no, he was murdered.'

'At the time,' Winstone said, 'that theory was ignored by the Yard.'

Mabel changed tack. 'What if the dead man had nothing to do with Guy? What if he came across the letter accidentally and was delivering it out of the goodness of his heart.'

'Came across it where? And why would someone kill him for his kindness?' Winstone asked.

'It's back to money then?' Mabel asked. 'Rosalind told you she's noticed money missing from Guy's business?'

Winstone nodded. 'She's always had a good head for numbers.'

'Here's one thing for certain – the accounts need a thorough examining.'

'That they do,' Winstone said. 'By someone discreet and independent from the matter.'

'A bookkeeper with a sharp eye,' Mabel said.

'And who knows how to keep his mouth shut.'

'Or hers.'

'Ah,' Winstone said. 'Your Mrs Grint?'

'You knew?' Mabel asked. 'Why didn't you just say?'

'And spoil your moment?' Winstone asked with a grin. 'Rosy told me.'

Mabel clicked her tongue in annoyance and then rose from the table. 'Would you like a drink? I have sloe gin.'

She poured out a small glass for each of them. When she took a sip, it brought back thoughts of home, and she heard a little voice inside her head that asked what her papa would say if he knew she was drinking alone in her flat with a man. She ignored the voice.

'Did you like him?' she asked Winstone. 'Your brother-in-law?'

Winstone downed his drink before answering. 'No,' he said. 'Not at first.'

She poured them out a bit more gin and waited.

'Guy was well known for a string of brief attachments before Rosy caught his eye,' Winstone said, 'and the other women were all from the stage too.'

'He had an eye for a show girl?' Mabel said.

'Yes, and so it seemed obvious to the rest of us that's what he was up to again, but Rosy couldn't be persuaded to believe that it was only a fling for Guy – she held fast, telling us she knew what he had been like, but he was no longer.'

'And?'

'And she was right, apparently. What had lasted a few weeks with each of those women went on for a year with Rosy before they married. It beggared belief, but Guy Despard settled down.'

'Could one of those other women have wanted revenge?'

'Now there's a line of enquiry no policeman would say no to carrying out,' Winstone said. 'Think of all the show girls to be interviewed. But nothing came of it – too much time had passed.' He held up his glass to the lamp so that the purple liquid glowed. 'This is properly good.'

'Thank you. Tell me, Mr Winstone, what did the Yard do wrong in the investigation into Guy's death in 1914?'

Winstone gave her a grim smile. 'I don't fault Tolly for toeing the line – we were both just detective sergeants and we had to do what we were told. It was a bad time for such an investigation – Guy went missing in September, only a month after war had been declared, and men were leaving the Yard to join up. But Rosy was mistreated, and then the case got pushed aside – there's no justice in that.'

'Certainly not. So, how did you and Scotland Yard part ways?'

'Detective Inspector Burge was a bully, and I decided I wouldn't stand for it, so I walked out, but not without sharing my thoughts with him first. Burning my bridges, as it were. If it weren't for Tolly, I'd probably have been arrested for anything Burge could think to pin on me. Rosy went down to the Isle of Wight, to our parents', for a while. She was done in after all that, her nerves were shattered.'

'Where did you spend the war?' Mabel asked.

'I did my part.'

Mabel kept quiet and listened for more, but it did not come.

'Where does Michael Shaughnessy come into all this?' she asked.

'Perhaps your Mrs Grint will find out. I vaguely remember the name. I'd say look to Miss Roche. Perhaps she's handed the money over to the Irish Brotherhood.'

'What?'

'In 1914, the Irish Volunteers were active – supported by the Brotherhood and other groups. There were cases of gunrunning in July that year, just two months before Guy went missing in September. There could've been other activity planned that they tried to get Guy involved in. Or pay for. Even now, while the talks are going on about Irish independence and there's a ceasefire, the violence hasn't truly stopped. And any war effort needs to be funded.'

'Guy's disappearance could be the result of his business dealings with Ireland,' Mabel suggested, trying to make sense of the idea. 'He might've been killed and his death covered up on purpose so that his money could continue to be siphoned off. Perhaps he had suspected fraud or embezzlement—'

'Or both,' Winstone interjected.

'Or both,' Mabel added. 'Perhaps Guy had suspected it and thought that this Michael Shaughnessy had information for him. Now that Shaughnessy's name is on all our minds – he can't be happy about that. Is Inspector Tollerton looking for the man?'

'He is.' Winstone tapped his empty glass on the table. 'And so am I.'

'Where do you even begin?' Mabel asked.

'I've been sniffing round St Katharine Docks – that's the working end of the business. The offices are in Holborn.'

'I've seen very little of the Thames since I've moved to London,' Mabel said as an observation.

'What if this letter was a ruse?' Winstone asked. 'Rosy is

certain Guy wrote it, but what if he didn't? There are more than you who have the skill to imitate handwriting.'

'I'm sure there are, but what would be the point? If it's a fake, when was it meant to be delivered – when Guy went missing, or now, seven years later? Was this soldier killed because he had the letter? If so, why didn't the person who killed him take the letter too?' Mabel covered her eyes. 'How do police do this? It's making my head spin.'

'We look at one thing at a time. Accounts.'

'Right – tomorrow.' Mabel looked at her empty glass but decided against another round.

'Good thing Bridget came along with Rosalind when she left the music hall,' Mabel said.

'Bridget's a force unto herself,' Winstone replied. 'She's the reason I felt it was safe to leave Rosy on her own these years. Even our mother approves of Bridget.'

'Mr Winstone, I asked you before, but I'll ask again: is Rosalind in danger? If Guy's business affairs have been running along under their own steam in the years since he disappeared, would they still do so if something happened to Rosalind?'

'Guy had a will,' Winstone said, 'and he made it quite clear Rosy inherits everything. She has a will, too, but she'll have to change it now that her assets are more clearly defined. It's possible someone is getting nervous about Rosy taking control and finding out what's been going on.'

'The murderer didn't consider she might have a head for business,' Mabel speculated. 'Just because she had been in the music hall?'

Gladys rose from the hearthrug, stretched and yawned.

'C'mon, girl, it's time to go.' Winstone stood and, keeping his eyes on the dog, said, 'I'm glad you're here, Miss Canning. For Rosy's sake and for mine.'

Mabel had but a second to bask in that statement before a knock came at the door.

'That isn't your vicar, is it?' Winstone asked.

'I told you, he isn't *my* vicar,' Mabel said. 'Of course it isn't Ronald – what would he be doing out and about in London at...' She glanced at her watch. 'Is it really past ten o'clock?'

Mabel crossed to the door and opened it. There stood Cora wearing a floppy tam-o'-shanter made from what looked like burgundy-coloured braided straw and holding in her hand another brimless hat with beadwork all across the front. Skeff was beside her, cigarette between her lips and hands plunged deep in the pockets of her coat.

'Evening,' she said, and her gaze shifted over Mabel's shoulder to Winstone. 'Terribly sorry to disturb.'

'You aren't disturbing,' Mabel said, but she blushed, nonetheless. 'Have you and Cora met Mr Winstone?' She proceeded with introductions.

'Pleased to meet you both,' Winstone said. 'Now, if you'll excuse me, I'll be on my way.'

'Don't leave on our account,' Cora said. 'I only wanted to offer Mabel this toque hat to give a try.'

'It isn't you, it's Gladys,' Winstone replied, nodding to the dog. 'It's time for her walk.'

'How do you do, Gladys,' Skeff said. Gladys accepted a head scratch from Cora.

'Evening, ladies,' Winstone said, and he and the dog went on their way.

The three of them watched Winstone and Gladys disappear down the stairs and when they were gone, Skeff said, 'I say, Mabel, a vicar, a former detective with Scotland Yard. Who will we find in your flat next – the prime minister?'

Only a few minutes later, Mabel had cleaned up after the simple evening meal. She sat on the sofa, took off her shoes and was contemplating a bath when there was a quiet knock at her door. She froze. Had Cora and Skeff returned? It seemed awfully late.

Mabel struggled to get her shoes back on, calling out, 'Yes?' and hearing the quiet reply, 'Miss Canning? Mr Chigley here.'

She answered the door, and there was the porter looking perplexed.

'A young woman has come calling for you, Miss Canning. She didn't know which flat you were in, and so I thought it best to come and speak to you first. Her name is Miss Florrie Hart.'

TWELVE

Florrie Hart stood in the middle of the foyer wringing her hands.

'Hello, Florrie.' Mabel turned to the porter, who had taken up his post behind the counter. 'Mr Chigley, Florrie is in the show at Collins.'

'Ah,' Mr Chigley said. This seemed explanation enough for him for her appearance because although Florrie was dressed in street clothes, her face was thick with make-up, and her lashes were painted on in a sunburst around her eyes that gave her the look of a startled hare.

'Pleased to meet you, sir,' Florrie said in a breathy voice. 'Mabel, I'm awfully sorry to disturb you so late. I wanted to have a word.'

'Of course,' Mabel said. She and Florrie had had tea only that afternoon – what could've happened in those few hours? Had Claude come back and they'd had an argument? 'Let's go up to my flat, why don't we? Would you like cocoa?' She spoke in a calm voice, sensing that at the least sudden movement, Florrie would bolt. 'Unless, of course, you have to be back to the show.'

'Just finished my song with Cyril,' she replied, 'and I asked one of the free girls to fill in for me on the last chorus number.'

'Good,' Mabel said. 'Here we go now.' She linked arms with the young woman and led her to the stairs, calling over her shoulder, 'Thank you, Mr Chigley.'

Florrie got no further than just inside the door of Mabel's flat, where she stopped, gazed round and said, 'Is all this yours?'

Mabel thought how her entire flat could fit in Rosalind's bedroom with space to spare. It's all a matter of perspective. 'It is all mine. Where do you live?'

'In a boarding house,' Florrie said. 'I share a room with two other girls.'

Mabel put the milk on to heat and then coaxed Florrie over to the table. 'Have a seat.' The young woman obviously had something to say or ask. Mabel didn't want to push, but when she'd stirred in the chocolate, poured out the cocoa and set the cups on the table, and Florrie hadn't spoken, Mabel realised she might need prodding. She pushed the sugar bowl across the table. 'There we are now.'

Florrie added four spoonfuls of sugar and stirred. Mabel added two and did likewise.

After drinking about half the cup down, the young woman sighed. 'That's awfully good.'

'Nothing like cocoa to lift your spirits,' Mabel said.

Florrie worked her mouth this way and that, and then burst out with, 'I did like you said. I asked Martin about seeing Claude. He was ever so vague about it that I don't think he saw him at all.'

'Why would Martin lie about it?'

'Dunno,' Florrie said. 'Anne says he's jealous. But I don't know anything more about Claude now than I did before. And, well, you've been so kind, thinking of things I could do to find Claude, instead of just fret about him. Because I am worried, you see.'

'Perhaps something came up with his family?'

'All he has is his old mum, and she died. And a brother, too, but he died ages ago in the war. His mum never got over it, Claude says. A box of his brother's things was sent back after he died, and she'd never been able to open it – just put it up on a shelf and left it. Isn't that sad?'

Mabel knew a woman in Peasmarsh who had never spoken her husband's name again after he'd been killed at Artois. 'The war was hard on people in so many ways.'

'I've been thinking and thinking, like you told me to do.' Florrie downed the last of her cocoa, and then scraped up the sugar that had settled at the bottom of the cup and licked the spoon. 'And I've remembered something Claude said about his poor dear mum. She was a cleaner at some enormous drinks factory.'

'At a distillery?' Mabel asked.

'Yeah, that sort of place. Could be a brewery. So, you see, if I can find out where he lives, then I can... I can ask why he's not come round to see me lately.'

'He owes you an answer to that,' Mabel said.

Florrie bobbed her head. 'The thing is, you would know better than me what to do, wouldn't you? And so, will you help me?'

'Help you find Claude?' Mabel asked. Find someone with only a Christian name who was living in his dead mum's house somewhere in Camden Town? The idea was preposterous. Although, how different was it from looking into Guy Despard's disappearance? Rosalind was happy to pay Useful Women for any work related to that private enquiry.

Mabel looked across the table at Florrie, who had grown still, her hands quiet in her lap. The young woman couldn't pay for a private investigation into Claude's whereabouts. When would Mabel have time? Where would she begin? Well, she supposed she could ask Cyril if he had seen Claude. And she could talk to this Martin. Perhaps Bert at the stage door had seen him.

Mabel looked back at Florrie and noticed her painted-on lashes had started to run.

'Of course I'll help.'

Florrie had left New River House the evening before relieved and happy at having handed her burden to Mabel, who now felt the weight of it. It was another puzzle to solve. Mabel liked a good puzzle, but she wasn't necessarily good at trying to solve two at the same time.

She was contemplating her approach on Saturday morning over a second cup of tea, when Mr Chigley came up to tell her there was someone on the telephone for her.

'Thomas has yet to bring the employee records to me,' Rosalind said after an initial greeting. 'He's being rather mulish about this, I must say. He'll be in his office – they work half a day on Saturdays – and so, I thought you could go and fetch them? I'll telephone and tell him you're on your way. And don't worry, I'll settle all this up with Miss Kerr.'

'Miss Kerr doesn't matter at the moment,' Mabel said. 'I don't want you to think you need to hire Useful Women to solve a murder.' And yet, as she said the words, she thought, *Why not?* 'I'm doing this because I want to.'

'How lucky I was that you were assigned to the wake,' Rosalind said.

'It was chance, you do know that?'

'Yes, I do,' Rosalind said with an annoyed tone. 'And I know what Park has said to you, but he sees danger where there is none.'

Mabel had toyed with the idea that the reason Winstone was so guarded about Mabel's interest in Guy and the dead man at the wake was because he had done something he didn't want his sister to know about. A protective nature could go too far, couldn't it? The idea had taken up residence in a dark corner of Mabel's mind and she'd as yet been able to turf it out.

Despard Shipping, Ltd., the official name of the company as stated on the brass plaque at the door, occupied the first floor of a Georgian house in Holborn, which, Mabel discovered, was not far from Lincoln's Inn Fields, that bastion of British law. Or, at least many of its barristers. Mabel walked into the office to be met with a stout young man at a desk in the centre of the room with doors arranged in a semicircle around him. One door stood open; the office beyond was dark, and the other doors were closed. The nameplate on one of the closed doors read Thomas Hardcastle, while another read Guy Despard.

Mabel explained her errand to the stout young man.

'He's taken a telephone call, but I'll let him know you're here. Please do sit down.' He gestured to a nearby chair and went into Hardcastle's office, leaving the door ajar and allowing the solicitor's telephone conversation to drift out.

'I will be clearing that up today,' he said. 'Yes... no. The other matter. Yes, but later. Four o'clock? Enniscorthy.'

An odd, stilted conversation. It seemed to Mabel that Hardcastle worked at revealing little. But he'd said enough for Mabel. Enniscorthy – the word drifted through her mind. Enniscorthy was a town in Ireland and there was little chance Thomas Hardcastle could get there by four o'clock that afternoon. Enniscorthy was also the name of one of Guy Despard's ships – Gabrielle Roche had mentioned it at the meeting while Mabel had been writing letters. As one of Guy's ships, it would be where Winstone said the 'working side' of Guy's business was – at St Katharine Docks.

Mabel filed these bits of information away when she heard

the telephone earpiece being hung back on its hook, and Hardcastle saying, 'Watkins, there's no need to hover.'

'Yes, sir,' the stout young man said in an injured tone. 'It's only you did say to tell you at once when Miss Canning arrived.'

Hardcastle mumbled a reply, and the young man came out and said to Mabel, 'You can go in now.'

The office had appeared comfortable but sparse, whereas the solicitor's office within felt a bit like walking into the British Museum. There were Chinese vases on the bookshelves and a Persian rug on the floor and a desk that dwarfed the man sitting behind it.

'How lovely,' Mabel said.

'William and Mary,' Hardcastle said, spreading his arms across its vast surface. 'Oyster veneer.'

Mabel remained standing. 'Well, Mr Hardcastle, I don't want to disturb your work for any longer than necessary.'

'Miss Canning, I don't understand why Mrs Despard is so impatient to take hold of the employee records,' he said, and then stopped as if waiting for Mabel to offer an explanation. When she didn't, he waved a hand at the several ledgers on a table in the corner. 'There they are. I expect to receive them in the same condition as sent the very moment she's finished. Later this afternoon, perhaps. This is, after all, a business.'

Mabel would make no promises. She picked up the ledgers.

'Thank you,' she said. 'Doesn't Miss Roche work in this office? I didn't see her and wanted to say hello.'

'Miss Roche,' Hardcastle said, 'does not come in on a Saturday.'

'Well now, what've you got for me?' Effie Grint asked. 'It's something about looking through old business accounts?'

The three of them – Effie, Rosalind and Mabel – stood in

the entry of the Despard house. Mabel admired the leather satchel Effie carried, worn at the corners and round the buckle from years of use. How handy it would be, Mabel thought, to have such a way to carry round a notebook as well as her purse and the odd sandwich for lunch.

Rosalind described the assignment to Effie in general terms because that was about all they knew. 'You'll be looking for irregularities.'

Effie nodded. 'Numbers need to add up properly,' she said. 'I have an eye for that sort of thing – I've always enjoyed running after those few pennies that try to get away.'

More than a few pennies, Mabel thought.

'Let's begin – I've got the table in the study ready for you.'

Mabel didn't last long in the study when Effie and Rosalind got down to business. Bookkeeping was not one of her skills – unlike seeing a person's handwriting as a musical expression, numbers were numbers to her and important only in adding or subtracting her own small accounts. Instead, she set herself grooming the flower arrangements she'd put together earlier in the week, going back to the scullery for a pail and meeting Gladys and Bridget coming up from the kitchen.

Leaning over to greet the dog, Mabel asked Bridget, 'Is Mr Winstone here?'

'Stopped for breakfast and left this one with us,' Bridget said. 'Don't know what to do with yourself, do you?'

Gladys *woofed*.

'You can come along with me,' Mabel said, and the dog did, following her up and down the stairs and in and out of rooms.

Mabel had come out from the scullery when a shadow fell on the privacy glass, and she reached the front door before the bell was pulled.

Cyril stood with hat in hand and brass-topped walking stick

in the other. His face lit up when he saw Mabel, followed quickly by a perplexed frown.

'Miss Canning,' he said, 'I hope you realise your talents extend further than being a housemaid. Not to say' – he looked past Mabel and into the entry – 'that a housemaid's skills are not legion. I'd never say that, no. Wouldn't want to get on Bridget's bad side.'

'Come in,' Mabel said, delighted to have an entertaining distraction. 'I don't mind answering the door when I'm handy. Rosalind is in the study with a bookkeeper working on the accounts.'

Cyril walked in and put his hat on the table and his stick in the stand.

'The house accounts?' he asked.

'No,' Mabel said, 'the business accounts.'

'She isn't?' he whispered with awe. 'Good for her. Time she took the reins in her own hands.'

'There's a discrepancy,' Mabel said. 'Although I don't know the details. Gladys and I would be glad for your company.' She looked round, but the dog was nowhere to be seen. 'There you are now, I must've worn her out. Why don't you go up to the drawing room and I'll bring coffee?'

Mabel found Bridget in the kitchen at the worktable.

'Lid for a pie,' she explained, wrestling with a lump of pastry.

'Beef? Pork?'

'It's a sort of pie I invented myself,' Bridget said with some pride. 'I fill it with colcannon.' At Mabel's bewildered look, she added, 'That's bacon and cabbage and potato. Reminds me of home.'

Having not had much of a cooked meal since she'd arrived in London, the dish sounded quite good to Mabel.

'Cyril is here, and Rosalind and Effie are still working so

I've sent him up to the drawing room. I thought we'd have coffee – I'm happy to sort it out myself.'

'You go on,' the maid said. 'I'll take it up.'

'Thanks, Bridget.'

Mabel and Cyril settled in chairs across from each other, but as soon as she sat down, Mabel noticed a wilted dahlia hanging over the edge of the vase on the mantel and so she rose, plucked it out and tossed it into the cold fireplace.

'There,' she said, sitting again.

'Well, Miss Canning, how is our Florrie?'

'Heartbroken,' Mabel said, 'and I don't blame her. It sounds as if this Claude led her on and then legged it – he should be ashamed of himself.'

'He should indeed,' Cyril said. 'Thank you for looking after the girl. I'm sure she'll come out the other end that much stronger.'

'She keeps hoping he'll come back, and she's asked me to help find him,' Mabel said. 'I told her I would, but I'm not sure what I can do. Did you meet him?'

'No, I never did. But if I saw him now, I would give him a piece of my mind, treating her the way he did.'

'I don't mind asking round for her. I'll look up this Martin, see what he knows.'

Cyril chuckled. 'You'll find that Martin knows very little about anything. Probably why being a Daft Boy suits him.'

A frenzied rapping from below startled Mabel, reminding her of the week before during the wake when the man fell dead on the doorstep. The rapping was followed by the doorbell. There was no sound of Bridget rushing to answer, and so Mabel said to Cyril, 'I'd better just—' and went downstairs, pulling the door to as she left.

It was Thomas Hardcastle, and he was a sorry sight. In the

short time since Mabel had seen him, he looked as if he'd been living rough for days. His eyes were bloodshot, with bits of leaves on his suit as if he'd spent the night in the shrubbery. He had pulled his hat down too far, and his hair stuck out from underneath like a fringe. His dark-blue suit looked as if he'd taken a dust bath in it, as birds do when trying to rid themselves of mites. His collar was askew, his tie loose round his neck and his boots scuffed and dull. He held his hat in his hands and Mabel could see a little spider crawling along the brim.

'Mr Hardcastle,' she said. 'Are you all right?'

'What? Yes. That is, I did have a small problem coming through the square and in my haste tripped over the corner of the path and...'

Mabel's eyes darted across to the square. Had he been attacked? She saw no one.

'I...' he began and then faltered. 'That is... good day, Miss Canning. I've come to see Mrs Despard to clear up a matter.' His voice was hoarse, and he swayed slightly.

'Mrs Despard is busy at the moment, Mr Hardcastle.'

'Well, then, perhaps I could take the accounts books back with me. They really should be in the office and not out and about. We must keep careful track of...'

'Of the money?' Mabel asked. He made it sound as if the ledgers had decided to go shopping on Oxford Street.

His eyes grew large, as if the question frightened him – as well it should.

'It's important that I explain,' Hardcastle said.

'Perhaps you could come back later.'

'No, I couldn't possibly.' The tic beside his right eye was twitching at top speed. 'I need to explain now. I need to say that if there's any problem...' Hardcastle began and then his voice seemed to catch. He cleared his throat. 'We all make mistakes, Miss Canning, but I want you to know that I have been a loyal employee of Mr Despard's and I always had an eye out for the best interests of the business. He valued my opinion, and I often advised him against bad investments that others may have attempted to badger him into, and although I am usually the soul of discretion, I will name names if I must, and I hope that for this information any other slight discrepancies may be... overlooked.'

He nearly ran out of air at the end of his speech and drew a long breath to recover. At that moment, Bridget came up from the kitchen carrying a tray and stopped where she was at the back of the house when she saw them.

'Is it coffee?' Hardcastle asked. 'Oh, thank you, Bridget.'

Mabel looked at Bridget and Bridget looked back, unmoving. If Hardcastle wouldn't leave, Mabel thought, they'd better put him somewhere he wouldn't find out what was going on in the study.

'Yes, Mr Hardcastle, coffee,' Bridget said. 'Go up to the drawing room, why don't you? Cyril is here.'

'Oh,' Hardcastle said flatly. 'All right.'

Mabel led the way and pushed open the drawing-room door to find Cyril at the front of the room looking out the window.

'Thomas,' he said, as if greeting a long-lost friend and paying no attention to the state of the solicitor's clothes. 'Good day. How are you?'

'Good day, Cyril,' Hardcastle said.

The three of them sat, and soon Bridget, who had gone back for another cup and saucer, brought up the tray and poured for them.

Mabel offered slices of fruit cake and as she and Cyril talked about the weather, she watched as Hardcastle nibbled at the cake without stopping until all that was left was a lone sultana in the palm of his hand.

They had finished with coffee and Cyril was telling a story about the time he met Harry Lauder and how if Harry wasn't finished with the music hall, then no one was, when all at once Hardcastle popped up from his chair and said, 'I must go.'

Mabel popped up too. 'Must you?' she asked, listening with one ear for any sounds downstairs, hoping Rosalind or Effie wouldn't choose this moment to emerge from the study.

'Yes, I'm going to sort it out,' Hardcastle said. 'Good day, Miss Canning.' He nodded. 'Cyril.'

'Yes, Thomas, good day to you.'

Mabel hurried in front to lead Hardcastle down to the front door and, she hoped, out without delay, but he paused when she'd opened the door.

'You think, Miss Canning, that one small thing will happen,' he said, 'and then, almost without you knowing it, this one small thing becomes quite large.' He put his hat on and left.

Mabel watched him go as she wondered – feared – what he meant by those words. Then she went over and tapped on the study door.

'It's only me,' she said.

Rosalind came out. 'Was that Thomas? Is everything all right?'

'Yes,' Mabel said.

It wasn't all right. Mabel saw the skin tighten round Rosalind's eyes and she felt the same in her chest. It was as if Hardcastle had sensed Effie's presence, which was meant to be on the strict q.t. He certainly knew something was up.

'He's nervous – more than nervous. At his wit's end, I'd say. He's meeting someone this afternoon,' Mabel said. 'This morning, I overheard him on the telephone in his office. It could be just his normal business, but he was speaking in an odd way. He said four o'clock and then he said Enniscorthy.'

Mabel watched Rosalind's face as the light dawned. 'The docks. That's one of Guy's ships – they're all named for places in Wexford, where he came from. Should we tell the police?'

'Tell them what?' Mabel asked. 'Where is your brother?'

'I haven't seen him today, but he usually stops in.'

Mabel looked at her wristwatch. 'It's gone one o'clock. We may not have time to wait for him. I'll see if he's in his flat. If we could get some information from this meeting, then it would be time to ring Inspector Tollerton. Don't you think?'

Agreeing, Rosalind returned to Effie and Mabel went back to the drawing room, where Cyril once again stood at the front window looking down at the pavement.

'There's a man troubled in his mind,' Cyril said.

THIRTEEN

At New River House, Mabel knocked on Winstone's door, but there was no answer.

'Gone out early,' Mr Chigley said, 'Gladys along with him. I told Mr Winstone he could leave the dog with me any time he wants, but he said she was no trouble and off they went. Shall I tell him you asked after him?'

'Yes, thanks, you may as well.'

There was nothing else for it. Mabel climbed the stairs once again, but this time all the way to the third floor, where she was happy to find Skeff and Cora at home.

'Am I disturbing you?' Mabel asked.

Skeff had answered the door with a newspaper in one hand and Cora sat at the table outside the kitchen sewing a needlefelt robin onto the side of a cloche.

'Not a bit of it,' Skeff said. 'Come in.'

'Tea, Mabel?' Cora asked. 'I'm gasping.'

'Thanks, yes.'

'Good, good,' Skeff said, as Cora went to the kitchen. 'Sit down, Mabel.'

Mabel sat on the sofa and quickly stood again and announced, 'I need to eavesdrop on a meeting at St Katharine Docks this afternoon at four, and I don't want anyone to recognise me. Can you help?'

Rather.

Cora went to work looking for a coat and hat – 'something drab that won't call attention to yourself' – while Mabel explained.

'It's the solicitor. He may be stealing money from the company and perhaps to keep it quiet, he killed the man in the greatcoat and possibly Guy Despard himself. I overheard him say he's meeting someone down at the docks. I only want to see who it is, and I'll go straight to the police.'

'What about Winstone?' Skeff asked.

'I would tell him, but I don't know where he is.'

'The thing is, Mabel, I wouldn't advise you go alone,' Skeff said.

Both fear and relief washed over Mabel. 'Will you come?'

'No, you don't want either of us – you want Flea. He's my man at the docks.'

'Is he called Flee because he's fast?' Mabel asked.

'No, he's called Flea because he jumps,' Skeff said.

'Oh yes, Flea is just the ticket,' Cora remarked. 'He's a nice young man.'

'I would trust him with my life,' Skeff said. 'He's my eyes and ears down there, if not my voice.'

'Flea doesn't speak,' Cora explained. 'Oh, wait now – a cape with a hood, that's what you need. Let me see what I have.'

Cora went off to the bedroom while Mabel gave Skeff as many details as she had. Skeff took it all in and then said she would go find this Flea, sort out a plan and return.

'Don't go far, Mabel.'

. . .

Cora located a long deep blue wool cape with a generous hood, and Mabel tried it on, examining herself in the half-length mirror on the wall.

'I look like a character in one of Mr Dickens's stories,' she said.

'You do have a bit of Little Dorrit about you,' Cora agreed. 'I've always thought she has such a sweet spirit.'

'As long as I'm not mistaken for Nancy,' Mabel said, as doubt nibbled away at her confidence.

They ate cheese and pickle sandwiches for lunch, and Cora went back to her latest hat project, while Mabel, as much as she told herself not to, found herself pacing in front of the fireplace.

At last, Skeff returned.

'We're set,' she announced. 'Mabel, you and I will meet Flea near the Tower. He knows the *Enniscorthy*, but he doesn't believe he's ever seen the man you described. Not too many toffs hang about the docks, so it should be easy to spot him. Flea will help you keep out of sight. I know you have more sense than to try to interfere with what you see,' Skeff said, sounding a bit like Mrs Chandekar telling eight-year-old Mabel to keep out of the deep end of the pond. 'All you need is to find out enough to tell Winstone or the Yard.'

'Just follow Flea's instructions,' Skeff said, as they stood in the chilly shade near Tower Bridge quay. 'You can trust him.'

Mabel smiled at the young man who appeared to be about fifteen or sixteen. He had an earnest, solemn face with a light cross-hatched scar on his right cheek. He was wiry, neither tall nor short and wore a floppy newsboy hat and trousers that came down just past his knees. They were either plus-fours or meant to be proper-length trousers on a young boy.

She had been unsure how she could follow instructions

from someone who didn't speak, but watching Flea and Skeff 'converse', Mabel saw that he was quite clear in his communication by employing other means – head nods, finger snaps, a whistle, a gesture. Who knew how much you could say with eyebrows.

'I'll be waiting up at the Waterman,' Skeff said. 'They have a lounge, and they know me there. Don't lose sight of each other in this fog.' She wished them luck and left.

The afternoon sky had been clear in Islington, but fog naturally gathers by a river and now the thin wisps Mabel had noticed when they'd arrived had thickened along the bankside.

'Right,' Mabel said, 'we'd best be off.'

As they turned to go, Flea trotted ahead and Mabel worried that she would lose him, but he came back in only a moment and stuck close to her. They walked into the fog, its cold fingers caressing Mabel's cheek. She shivered. Was she doing the right thing? She would get hold of useful information and give it to the police – that would be better than wasting their time. It wasn't as if she were trying to fulfil some sudden urge for adventure.

They reached St Katharine Docks – at least this is what Mabel surmised when Flea pointed to the wooden walkway. Now what?

She could see the ghostly form of a ship not much further. 'Is that the *Enniscorthy*?'

Flea nodded.

'Lead on.'

The docks covered more ground – and water – than Mabel had imagined. There were two basins, as well as the quay along the river. Warehouses lined the waterside, large and open and dark. They came upon a long, low building with lights blazing within. When they heard voices, Flea pulled them back behind a wooden shed until the voices faded. They watched and waited, and Mabel shivered at the groans and moans and clinking sounds made by the creaking of wood and the heavy chains that hung from cranes. Mabel squinted into the fog, but saw nothing, and she realised the futility of this surveillance. Thomas Hardcastle could have had his meeting and be gone by now.

Flea tugged on her sleeve and pointed at the ship.

'Yes, let's at least walk the length of it.'

The quiet was eerie, but Mabel reminded herself that mornings must be the busy time at the docks and almost everyone had finished work for the day.

But not everyone. Mabel heard steps and they were getting closer, but she couldn't sort out from which direction they came. She threw a look at Flea, who glanced over his shoulder and then nodded ahead. Mabel started off and then, further up the walkway, she saw someone – a man running away. He was swallowed up by the fog and Mabel hurried after him, although she couldn't have said why. To catch him?

Mabel caught her foot on a coiled chain at the edge of the quay and she fell onto her hands and knees, so close to the edge that her head hung over the walkway and she found herself staring at a narrow strip of water between dock and ship. There was something large and dark floating in the water, with the end of the chain wrapped round it.

She leant closer to take a better look. The water lapped at the edge of the dock, and it caused the object to bob and twirl and turn over and Mabel found herself staring at something pale and slimy, like the belly of a fish. But it was no fish – she was staring at Thomas Hardcastle.

Mabel cried out and leapt back, knocking into Flea. Someone grabbed hold of her arm and her first thought was that it was the man she'd seen running off and he'd come back for her. She screamed and fought, and Flea began pummelling whoever it was who had hold of her and he, in turn, shouted and cursed loud enough to be heard over the commotion.

Mabel gave up the fight and he loosened his grip enough for her to whirl round. The motion pulled off her the hood and Mabel knew that the look of shock on Park Winstone's face matched her own.

'What are you doing here?' they both shouted.

FOURTEEN

Flea continued to beat Winstone, whose attempts to hold the young man off with one hand were failing miserably.

'It's all right, Flea,' Mabel said. 'It's all right.'

Flea backed off but kept his fists up as if ready to go another round if need be.

'Who are you?' Winstone demanded of Flea, but didn't wait before he turned to Mabel. 'And what are you doing here?'

'That doesn't matter now,' Mabel said. 'Look down there.'

Winstone leant over, peered into the water and cursed again. 'Dead.'

'Yes, dead,' Mabel said. 'I saw someone running that way.' She pointed and added, 'Did you see him, Flea?'

Flea nodded once and put his hand up above his head.

'Tall,' Mabel said, 'and thin?'

Flea snapped his fingers and pointed at Mabel.

Winstone sighed. 'Well, we won't find him now, the three of us. Come on, we'll go up to the office and I'll ring the police.'

They started off, but Mabel heard two snaps and turned to see Flea backing away. He shook his head, a short, quick movement.

'You don't need Flea,' Mabel said to Winstone. 'He was only showing me the way.'

Winstone looked hard at the young man, who held his gaze. 'Yeah, all right, off with you.'

'Tell Skeff I'm fine,' Mabel said to Flea. 'Tell her I'm with Mr Winstone.'

Flea dashed off in the direction of the Waterman pub as it occurred to her that the young man wouldn't be able to tell Skeff that at all. Perhaps he could write.

Mabel swallowed hard and looked down once more at Thomas Hardcastle floating dead in the Thames. She saw a wound on his forehead – it was almost round and had bled, but much of the blood had been washed away. Who had attacked him? Then her eyes were drawn further up the dock, and she saw the fog shift and swirl as if someone had only just been standing there.

The dock offices for Guy Despard's business contained rough, utilitarian desks, tables and chairs and were a world away from Thomas Hardcastle's. Mabel sat by the paraffin heater and shivered, even with Cora's cape wrapped round her, while Winstone talked to the man running the office, who, when he heard the story, pulled a bottle of whisky from the bottom drawer of his desk, poured a drink for Winstone and offered one to Mabel. She took it. Winstone telephoned the police, then came over and knelt in front of Mabel.

'How are you?' he asked.

'I overheard him set this meeting up and then I followed him to see who he would meet.' She wiped her nose on the back of her hand. 'Is it my fault he's dead?'

'No,' Winstone said. 'But why didn't you tell me first?'

'I did try, but you weren't at home.'

'No, I've been loitering about the docks all day looking for Michael Shaughnessy.'

'Do you think he did it?' Mabel asked. 'Over money they'd been stealing from Guy?'

'And seven years after Guy disappears, they suddenly have a falling out?' Winstone asked.

'And seven years later, a letter from Guy surfaces and it mentions Shaughnessy.'

Winstone gave her a quick smile and a nod. 'Well done, Miss Canning.'

There were sirens in the distance and growing louder.

Winstone stood and put his hand out. 'Ready?' he asked.

'Yes,' Mabel said.

As they walked out, Winstone said, 'Tolly can get one of the constables to take you home, and then tomorrow, or the next day, you can go to the station to give your statement.'

'No,' Mabel said. 'I'm all right and I need to go to Rosalind. Who knows how long you'll be out here, and she should know what's happened.'

They left the fog behind them along the river and reached the police contingent – several cars and uniformed officers swarming round Detective Inspector Tollerton and Detective Sergeant Lett – and the former did a double take when he saw Mabel, telling her that Winstone hadn't mentioned her.

With a few words from Winstone, the inspector dispatched Lett and three constables to the quayside and then put his hands on his hips and said, 'What's all this?'

'I'm the one who found him,' Mabel said. 'I will give you every detail I know, but I want to go to Rosalind before some reporter gets wind of what happened.'

Tollerton's gaze darted from Mabel to Winstone to the quayside where Hardcastle's body was as if weighing the situation.

'All right.' Over his shoulder, he called, 'Drake' and one of the constables came forward. 'Drive Miss Canning to Mrs Despard's house. Park, you go with her.'

'Not a chance, Tolly. I'm staying here.'

When the police car pulled up to Rosalind's, Mabel's first thought was that the news had arrived ahead of them. The lights in the drawing room were on and the curtain twitched, and before Mabel had reached the front door, it flew open and there was Bridget like some Irish goddess of vengeance.

'What do you call this?' she demanded and, from behind a closed door somewhere, Mabel heard Gladys barking the same question.

Constable Drake had opened the car door for Mabel and now asked, 'Miss Canning?'

'It's all right,' Mabel told him. 'You can tell Inspector Tollerton we'll be waiting.'

It was not yet six o'clock, and Mabel marvelled at how much could go on in such a short time.

'Herself's in the drawing room,' Bridget said, closing the door and calming slightly. 'How bad is it?'

'Bad enough,' Mabel said, and went up.

The drawing-room door was closed and when Mabel opened it, Gladys flew out, gave Mabel's hand a lick and then proceeded to sniff out what news she could.

Rosalind stood near the fireplace, hands clenched in front of her and looking as if she might shatter at any moment.

'Is it Park?' she asked in a hoarse whisper.

'No!' Mabel exclaimed, and went to her. 'No, he's fine. Is that what you thought when you saw the police car? I'm so sorry, I should've said straightaway.'

Rosalind sank into a chair, the colour rushing back to her face. 'Park has been gone all day and I thought you'd come back and you didn't and so I rang your building and spoke with...'

'Mr Chigley?' Mabel asked, alarmed. 'Did you say I was missing?'

'No,' Rosalind said, and she seemed happy to be the one consoling and not in need of it. 'I didn't want to worry him even if I was. But I did leave a message for you.' Rosalind looked Mabel up and down, offered a wan smile and said, 'I like your cloak.'

Mabel had forgotten her disguise. She took off the cape and draped it over the sofa. Although she had shivered in the dock office, the evening wasn't cold, and she was glad to be free of its extra warmth. She took the chair next to Rosalind, reached over and laid a hand on hers.

'Thomas Hardcastle is dead.'

A shudder went through Rosalind and her hand flew to her mouth. Mabel thought she might be sick, but Rosalind took control of herself.

'He knew we knew, didn't he? Did he take his own life?'

Having been at the scene, that hadn't occurred to Mabel. She recalled the pale, slimy look to his skin and the wound on his forehead. 'I don't think so. Of course, the police will decide, but it looked as if he was killed. Murdered.'

'"Looked as if?"' Rosalind said. 'Were you there?'

Mabel gave her a brief account, knowing she'd have to do so again when Tollerton arrived.

'And you saw someone?' Rosalind asked.

'A glimpse, that's all,' Mabel said, trying to pull any detail she could from the image of the retreating figure, but she couldn't. She shook these thoughts away. 'How did you and Effie get on?'

'Ah! Effie found what looks to be phantom employees,' Rosalind said. 'A John B. Osgood appears on ten different payrolls – he's John Baker Osgood, then he's John Butler Osgood, John Beecham Osgood, John... you see.'

'Not a terribly inventive way to steal from the company,'

Mabel said. 'But I suppose criminals are not always imaginative.'

'Thomas a criminal,' Rosalind said, staring into the fire. 'It's so hard to take in – he's been a loyal employee. He was quite broken up when Guy went missing.' She gripped the arm of the chair. 'Had Guy become aware of Thomas's deceit? Does this have something to do with Michael Shaughnessy?'

'And what did the dead man know of it? Perhaps he'd tried to blackmail Hardcastle and was killed for that. This all seems to be down to the man who died on your doorstep.'

Perhaps, too, the blackmail concerned not only embezzlement, but also the murder of Guy Despard – at Hardcastle's hand. But Mabel kept that speculation to herself.

Their speculation ended with the sound of a car pulling up outside, followed by a knock. Gladys had settled on the floor between Mabel and Rosalind, but now rose, stretched and went to the closed drawing-room door. When Winstone walked in, she greeted him with glee and when Tollerton followed, the dog allowed him to give her a pat.

'Mrs Despard,' Tollerton said, 'I'm sure Miss Canning has told you what's happened. I hope you don't mind that we go over the details here.'

'You're very welcome,' Rosalind said. 'Would you like a drink?'

Winstone had already poured out two whiskies and handed Tollerton one. 'Miss Canning?'

'Sherry, Mabel? I'll have one,' Rosalind said, and Winstone served them.

'Now, Inspector, I have news that involves Thomas and may have something to do with his death. It's about a long-running embezzlement scheme at Guy's business run by Thomas and which may have involved Michael Shaughnessy.'

'How did you find this out?' Tollerton asked. 'And when?

You should've informed police of any suspicions you had, Mrs Despard, and we would've looked into it.'

Bridget appeared and set down a tray of coffee. 'I've sandwiches as well, and I'll take a plate to the one at the door.'

'I've left Constable Drake in the entry,' Tollerton said. He pulled out a pocket notebook and pencil. 'Let's see if we can take these things one at a time. First, a clarification. Miss Canning, remind me of your position in this house?'

'I have no position, Inspector,' Mabel said, trying not to take offence. 'That is, I work for the Useful Women agency, and in my capacity, I have carried out a few household and secretarial tasks for Mrs Despard.'

'And this working agreement has been going on for how long?'

'A week,' Mabel said. 'The wake was my first job.'

'But you were at the wake as a friend? That's according to Mrs Despard.'

'I may have been premature in that claim a week ago,' Rosalind said, 'but I can now say for certain that it's true. Mabel was a comfort to me at the wake, but now she is most certainly a friend.'

Tollerton wrote in his notebook. 'On the wake, Mrs Despard, did you notice any unusual behaviour from Mr Hardcastle?'

Looking for a connection between the dead man on the doorstep and Thomas Hardcastle, Mabel thought. *Good idea.*

'I was rather taken up with other things that day, Inspector,' Rosalind said. 'I'm afraid I won't be much help there.'

'Michael Shaughnessy's name was in the letter from your husband,' Tollerton said. 'Was he familiar to Mr Hardcastle?'

'Mabel heard me ask Thomas directly if he knew who Shaughnessy was,' Rosalind said. 'And he didn't answer but went off in another direction.'

'Do you believe Hardcastle killed the man in the greatcoat?'

Mabel asked. 'And that Michael Shaughnessy then murdered Hardcastle?'

'And you, Miss Canning,' Tollerton said, ignoring her question, 'did you notice Hardcastle in particular at the wake?'

'I saw him downstairs while everyone was in the drawing room,' Mabel said, this small detail shaking loose from her mind. 'It was when I'd taken Gladys down to the kitchen' – the dog raised her head at the sound of her name – 'and as I got back in the entry, Mr Hardcastle was coming back up the stairs here to the drawing room.'

'Where everyone else had remained?' Tollerton asked.

'Yes, I suppose – except for Miss Roche. I didn't know who she was at the time, but I saw her in the dining room talking with a few men.'

'This was not long before the dead man arrived,' Tollerton said, apparently unaware of the incongruity of his statement, 'when everyone was to have been upstairs. Did you mention this before, Miss Canning?'

'I was asked about my own movements,' Mabel said, 'as I suppose they were.'

Tollerton wrote in his notebook, but said nothing further about it, apparently accepting Mabel's defence. But Mabel fumed, annoyed with herself for forgetting until that moment what could be vital pieces of evidence. Where had Hardcastle been – out and around the corner beating a man to death? Who were the men Gabrielle Roche had held a quiet conversation with?

'Right, about this afternoon,' Tollerton continued. 'I want to hear your account, Miss Canning. Were you alone when you made your way to the docks? It seems a dangerous outing. How did you even know the way?'

Winstone cut in. 'I had told Miss Canning about the working end of Guy's business, Tolly. If you want to blame someone, blame me.'

'I'm always happy to blame you for whatever's to hand, Park, you know that.'

It was, Mabel could see, a jest between friends, but Winstone had saved her from mentioning or lying about Flea. Mabel believed Flea would want to be kept out of the story. She threw Winstone a grateful look.

'This morning,' Mabel said, 'I went to Thomas Hardcastle's office and overheard him making arrangements to meet someone at the docks. We had already suspected he may be involved in stealing from Mr Despard's business, and I, perhaps foolishly, took it upon myself to try to discover what was going on so that I could come to you, Inspector, with more than a wild idea.'

Mabel wished she were close enough to read Tollerton's notes upside down because his face gave nothing away. What was he writing about her? Was she down as a suspect in Hardcastle's death or just a meddling sort?

'Tell me about finding Hardcastle. Give it to me just as it happened.'

She did so, although she erased Flea from her narrative. When she finished, Tollerton questioned Winstone, who gave the story of being on the trail of Shaughnessy all day long, but never finding him.

'I asked in every pub up and down the docks. No one would tell me anything and that told me I'd just missed him.'

'So you spent your day drinking?' Tollerton asked.

'Wouldn't want to make anyone suspicious, now would I?'

Tollerton had gone and Rosalind had offered tea or coffee or a drink, but Mabel could only think about her own bed.

'Park's insisting on staying here tonight, although I don't know why. What good would it do for Michael Shaughnessy to try anything here? And if he did manage to break in, I doubt he could get past Bridget and that broom of hers.'

'It's a good idea to have your brother here,' Mabel said, glancing at Winstone. 'For peace of mind.'

'Why don't you stay too?' Rosalind suggested, sounding as if it were a house party in the making.

'That's kind of you, but it's best I return to my flat.' She stood and walked to the drawing room door.

'I'll see you home, Miss Canning,' Winstone said, rising and following. 'Rosy, I'll be back within the hour.'

Mabel stopped and turned. 'There's no need to see me home, Mr Winstone. I know the way.'

He narrowed his eyes at her joke. 'Regardless, I will.'

'You won't,' Mabel said with more force. 'I'm perfectly capable of walking to Piccadilly and getting the tram.'

Winstone's voice rose. 'Allow me to be concerned for your welfare, Miss Canning.' He put a finger up to stop her before she spoke. 'I will find a taxi to take you home. Wait here.'

He left.

Rosalind, who hadn't said a word during the exchange, came over, put her arm round Mabel's shoulders and gave her a squeeze. 'Infuriating, isn't he?'

Mabel laughed.

'The thing is,' Rosalind continued, 'Park has been alone for a while now.'

Mabel understood what she was to infer from this, and thought she'd better make herself quite clear.

'I've moved to London to be an independent woman.'

'You are independent,' Rosalind said, 'and I'm not saying you shouldn't be. But it can happen that a man and a woman are equal in a relationship. It was that way with Guy and me. He would never have told me I couldn't do one thing or should do another.'

'I'd say you two were a lovely but quite rare exception.'

'Perhaps,' Rosalind said. 'Come on.'

They went down to the entry, and when a taxi pulled up outside, Winstone got out. He pulled coins from his pocket, handed a few to the driver and said something to him that Mabel didn't hear. The cabbie's eyes grew large as they darted from Mabel and away. He pulled at his cap and nodded. Winstone held the door for Mabel, and, after the three exchanged goodbyes, she waved at brother and sister as the taxi pulled away.

Taxis were costly. Mabel knew that, although she didn't know quite how costly. Belgravia to Islington was not a short journey, and she was certain that the fare would have been too much for her budget. What had Winstone given the man? Sixpence? A shilling? A half-crown? Mabel sucked in her breath, shocked at the thought.

The taxi hurtled through the streets, and Mabel saw a different London from the one she observed on the tram or bus. It seemed more personal, somehow, and she felt protected inside the vehicle. No waiting at tram or bus stops, no being jostled as she held on to a strap when there were no seats. This was luxury. She mustn't get accustomed to it.

When the taxi pulled up to New River House, Mabel got out and turned to the cabbie. 'How much was the fare?'

'Taken care of, ma'am,' he said, and glanced at his watch.

'Yes, I know that, but I want to know how much it cost.'

He told her. It was nearly as bad as she had imagined.

'And what did he say to you before we left?'

Again, the cabbie checked the time. 'He explained the situation, ma'am. That he's a detective with Scotland Yard, and that I needed to get you home safe or he'd know why.' The man drummed his fingers on the steering wheel. 'He took my licence number and all, ma'am! Please, go inside. He said he would ring you at ten thirty to make certain you'd arrived.'

'Yes, all right, thank you.'

Mabel used her own key in the front door. No sooner had it closed behind her when the telephone in the foyer rang.

'I'll answer, Mr Chigley,' she called towards the open door to the porter's quarters. 'I believe it's for me.'

She waited a few more rings before picking up the earpiece.

'Present and accounted for, Mr Winstone. Good night.' She returned the earpiece to its hook.

The porter leant over the counter, stirring a cup of Bovril. 'Good evening, Miss Canning. All is well?'

'It is,' Mabel said. As well as could be expected. Under the circumstances.

'Good, good,' he said, tapping his spoon on the rim of the cup. It reminded her of the tapping she'd heard at the docks – the chain that dangled over the edge and Thomas Hardcastle's body floating in the river. 'Miss Portjoy and Miss Skeffington were asking after you earlier.'

'Of course,' Mabel said. 'They were expecting me and I'm later in than I planned. I'll just go up and say good night to them and return Cora's cape.'

Mabel hurried up the stairs before Mr Chigley thought of more pointed questions to ask her about her evening.

'Oh good, there you are,' Skeff said. 'Come in. Can you tell us about it?'

'I don't see why not. But first, here, Cora.' Mabel handed the cape over. 'Thanks – you're an ace at disguises, you know. Mr Winstone didn't know it was me until he saw my face.'

'Anything to help,' Cora said.

'Flea told me you were all right and with Mr Winstone,' Skeff said.

'Did he?' Mabel asked. 'How?'

'He draws quite well,' Cora said, and picked up a notebook and handed it to Mabel. Flea had done a pencil sketch and, in only a few lines the face was unmistakably Winstone's – round glasses, errant curl and all.

'That's amazing,' Mabel said.

'He's a talented fellow,' Skeff said.

'And he told you about the dead man in the water?' Mabel asked, as Cora guided her to the sofa and poured her a cup of tea.

Skeff gave a nod. 'Who was it? Are you able to say?'

'It was Thomas Hardcastle, solicitor. The very man I went to find. I had to explain that to the police, of course, and I'm not sure that Inspector Tollerton didn't want to arrest me for meddling – or whatever they would call it. What will they do now? What will Rosalind do? If Hardcastle had been involved with this Michael Shaughnessy—'

'The man mentioned in the note from Mr Despard to his wife?' Cora asked.

Mabel had forgotten how much she'd told them. 'Yes. So the two of them could've been involved in an embezzlement scheme. Did they have a confrontation, arguing about whether to continue or give up? Did one of them murder Guy seven years ago because he had cottoned on to their thievery?' She huffed. 'I don't know what I can do about it.'

'Had this Hardcastle gone down to do away with this Shaughnessy, or was it Shaughnessy's intent all along to get rid of the solicitor?' Skeff asked in a speculative way.

More questions with no answers.

'Thank you both for your help,' Mabel said. 'You may not be on Miss Kerr's rolls, but you are most definitely Useful Women. Now, I'm all in. Good night.'

Mabel went back down the stairs to her flat. Weary in both mind and body, she decided that tomorrow, Sunday, she could worry about the murder of Thomas Hardcastle, the murder of the man in the greatcoat, the elusive Michael Shaughnessy and what it all had to do with Guy Despard. Now, she wanted sleep.

She switched the lamp on in her bedroom and went over to the window and looked down on the road and across to the green. If there had been fog in Islington, it was gone, and Mabel could see a few couples returning home after a pleasant Saturday evening.

With a gasp, she pulled away from the window. There, across the road standing under a plane tree and looking up at her window was a man. A tall, thin man. He wore a brown suit and a hat pulled down, obscuring his face, but there was something familiar about him. She thought of the vanishing figure at the docks – a man running away from the murder of Thomas Hardcastle. Could this be the same man?

Mabel dropped to the floor and crawled over to switch off the lamp, then crawled back to the window and looked out. There was no one there. She felt a fool. A man pauses on his walk home and she thinks she's being followed? She really did need a good night's sleep. But when she did slip into bed, it was to remember her promise to Florrie to look for Claude. She must do something about that.

Mabel woke to the sun pouring in her window – here, at the end of September, summer had made a return visit. There was no cross breeze in her flat, and already it felt too warm, and so she splashed water on her face and thought about where Londoners might go on a Sunday morning to keep cool. Hyde Park?

She went to church. St Mary's was on Upper Street and a short walk away. It would be cool inside the stone church, and wouldn't Ronald and her papa be happy to hear that's where she'd spent her Sunday morning?

Even better, it was the harvest festival and Mabel returned from the service humming 'Come, Ye Thankful People, Come'.

But it was still morning, and would she keep cool lying out under a plane tree in the green?

Mabel met Cora and Skeff on the stairs. They were both wearing straw boaters and carrying a hamper between them.

'We're off to Hampstead Heath,' Cora said. 'We've got a picnic. Won't you come along?'

'Yes, do, Mabel,' Skeff said. 'It may not be the countryside of Sussex, but it'll do for today. Come cool off with us.'

It was as if they'd thrown her a lifeline. Mabel rushed back to her flat, changed into an older frock and rummaged through her larder for something to contribute. She settled at last on a jar of plums and a wedge of cheese. Both were gratefully received and added to Cora's hamper that already held a roast chicken, a few apples and three bottles of beer.

'Fortnum and Mason have nothing on us,' Skeff said.

They took the Underground from Angel Station just down the road and rumbled along a good while before reaching Hampstead. It was Mabel's first journey below ground and a bit disconcerting. Between stations, there was nothing to see out the windows except blackness and nothing inside but smoke and a great many people.

At last, they got off the train and moved with the crowd as one up and into the light, and when they emerged on the pavement at Hampstead, Mabel took such a deep breath of clean air, she thought her lungs might burst.

They walked up to Parliament Hill for the view. 'Would you look at that?' Mabel asked. 'The view at Box Hill of the North Downs is breathtaking, it truly is. But this lays all of London at our feet.'

'That's without the fog,' Skeff said.

They walked through wood and heath, sharing the weight of the hamper between two of them at a time.

'They've a ladies' bathing pond here,' Cora said. 'Next time, we'll bring our costumes along and take a proper swim.'

Mabel had no bathing costume. When she and Edith had taken themselves away to cool off on hot summer days, they would leave their clothes on bushes as a signal for others to stay away. *No chance of swimming in the altogether here*, Mabel thought.

They found the perfect picnic spot under a beech and within view of Whitestone Pond, already crowded with bathers of all sorts wading out into the shallow water. Settled, they ate and talked about nothing in particular and then fell asleep and awoke when the sun had moved their shade elsewhere. Too warm to resist, the women removed their shoes and stockings and joined the throng, holding their skirts above the water, which came up almost to their knees.

Keeping their clothes dry didn't last, though, because the children round them made it their job to splash everyone within reach, and so Mabel, Cora and Skeff made it their job to splash back. It was glorious, reminding Mabel of the family's occasional trips to the seaside when she was growing up. Those day-long events had engendered such excitement in her that Mabel often ran a fever the morning of, and Papa would threaten to keep them all home. As always, Mrs Chandekar found a way round him, and off they would go.

Skeff stepped up and out onto dry land and turned to help Cora, who extended her hand to Mabel. As Mabel emerged, shaking out her skirt, she looked across the grass into the sun and saw, under a large lime tree, a tall, thin man in a brown suit with his hat pulled down to obscure his face. She gasped, let go Cora's hand and almost fell back into the pond.

'Are you all right?' Cora asked, grabbing both Mabel's hands to steady her.

'Mabel?' Skeff asked.

Mabel whirled round and squinted. The spot under the lime tree was empty. She turned to her companions and said, 'I think I'm being followed!'

FIFTEEN

They huddled on one side of an ice-cream kiosk, each of them watching in a different direction like Cerberus. Mabel's outburst had taken her breath away. Was she truly being followed?

'But it couldn't be the same man I saw last night,' she told them and herself. 'I'm just too jumpy after yesterday.'

'You weren't jumpy until you saw him,' Skeff said. 'Don't second-guess yourself. You feel as if this is the same fellow and he's following you, then that's enough. A woman knows when there's trouble. Do you recognise him from somewhere?'

Mabel shook her head, but not with conviction.

'So, he is familiar to you?' Cora asked.

'Is he? I don't know. It's just, there may be something about him I recognise.' That thought chilled her. What if he were Michael Shaughnessy? Had she met the man and hadn't realised it? How did he know she was involved in the enquiry?

Skeff glanced at the sea of people on the heath. 'He's probably still out there. If he wants to keep an eye on you, he wouldn't've gone. Let's see if we can trap him. Are you game, Mabel?'

Without a pause, she said, 'I am.'

. . .

Mabel made a show of separating from Cora and Skeff, who waved at her and went off in an entirely different direction – to circle back at a distance and then watch Mabel from within nearby shrubbery. They were away from the heaving crowd but near enough to Mabel, who leant against a nook at the base of a beech tree near the wood. Tilting her hat forward just short of covering her face, she sighed dramatically and closed her eyes, but not completely. In a moment, she let one hand fall from her lap as if she had nodded off to sleep.

The minutes ticked by, and no one passed. Mabel found it difficult to keep her eyelids mostly closed and wanted to either open or shut them completely and so she chose the latter. She would hear the man if he approached, and if not, she would hear the signal from Cora and Skeff if they saw him.

One second or ten minutes later, Mabel heard Skeff whistling 'Knees Up Mother Brown'. She bolted upright at the signal, blinking herself awake in time to see a man in a brown suit rushing towards her.

She tried to scramble to her feet, but lost her balance. Her legs went out from under her, and she cried out as he caught his foot on hers and fell forward. In that split second, Mabel saw that he was heavy rather than thin and also that he had an ice cream in his hand. The man's boater flew off his head and he landed on her with an *oof*, the ice cream squished between their bodies.

At once, Cora and Skeff ran up and pulled him off. Mabel, gasping for the breath that had been knocked out of her, shook her head at them.

'Oh dear, sir,' Cora said, as they attended to him, 'are you all right? What a bad fall.'

Mabel took a finger and wiped the ice cream off her front. 'Yes, bad luck, sir,' she said.

'It's the ground,' Skeff remarked. 'It's uneven. Could happen to anyone.'

'*Humph,*' was his reply. He walked off, but not before throwing Mabel a suspicious look.

As the three of them came up from Angel Station, Skeff said, 'Just to be on the safe side, you make certain Mr Chigley knows not to let anyone of his description in the door.' When Mabel hesitated, she asked, 'Won't you?'

'My description is so vague, Mr Chigley might stop half the young men of London. And I must be careful, or he'll write to Papa and say I'm in danger – which I'm not – and Papa will come riding up on his white charger to save me.'

Cora smiled. 'What a lovely image.'

'Would you feel safe telling Winstone?' Skeff asked. 'Because the more people who know to look out, the better.'

'Perhaps so,' Mabel said.

Light was fading and the gas street lamps had come on, but that didn't stop Skeff and Cora from scrutinising the people passing on the pavement and those milling about in the green, and even craning their necks to see further up Essex Road just in case. But there was nary a man in a brown suit.

Inside New River House, they all three greeted Mr Chigley.

'Got a bit of sun, did you?' he said. 'Lovely day for it and we must enjoy it while we can.'

'Indeed,' Mabel said.

'Good night,' they all called and continued up to the first-floor landing, where Mabel knocked on Winstone's door. There was no answer.

She shrugged at Cora and Skeff. 'I'll tell him tomorrow. Whoever it was I saw, he isn't out there now, is he?' Mabel said. 'So, I've nothing to worry about this evening.'

. . .

Mabel had made certain to survey her surroundings when she walked out of New River House the next morning, but no one loitered on the streets of Islington. Instead, the landscape was a sea of people going to work. Mabel joined them, taking the tram to Piccadilly and then walking to 48 Dover Street.

'Good morning, Miss Kerr,' she said.

Miss Kerr looked over her glasses. 'Good morning, Miss Canning. I've had a good word from Mrs Despard about Mrs Grint's work.'

'Did she say anything else?'

'You mean did she ask to engage you for a job today? No.'

That wasn't what Mabel had meant, but then again, why would Rosalind tell Miss Kerr about Thomas Hardcastle's murder?

'About today,' Mabel said. 'I'm afraid I won't be available for a job this morning.'

One of Miss Kerr's eyebrows twitched ever so slightly. 'Oh? Your initial eagerness to be one of the Useful Women wearing off a bit, is it?'

'No,' Mabel said with some force. 'That isn't it at all – it's a personal matter. But now that I think about it, it can wait a bit. Do you have something for me?'

'Mrs Marsden would like a book collected from Hatchard's and delivered to her,' Miss Kerr said without looking up.

'Hatchard's, right,' Mabel said. She'd seen the bookshop on Piccadilly. And then off to Rosalind's.

Miss Kerr opened the Jobs ledger and held her fountain pen poised over a page. 'Wait now. Miss Canning, do you play the piano?'

'Yes, I do.'

'Mrs Orping has had her piano tuned in anticipation of her grandson visiting, but as she doesn't play herself, she would like a demonstration. Would you rather this job or the bookshop?'

A chance to play the piano? 'I'll take both,' Mabel replied. 'And I will return after lunch.'

Now, this was the sort of morning Mabel could enjoy. It had cooled off considerably and the blue autumnal sky, the leaves in Green Park turning buttery, golden yellow, and two Useful Women assignments that suited her perfectly made for what looked like a perfect day. Too bad she had so much on her mind.

Had the newspapers reported Hardcastle's death and connected him to the Despard business? Did Miss Kerr suspect her involvement and had wanted to remind her who it was that Mabel worked for? How would it look if Useful Women had its name entwined with not one, but two murders – plus an unsolved disappearance?

Mabel went directly to Hatchard's and collected the book for Mrs Marsden. But then, her thoughts lingering on the weekend murder, she noticed a display of detective novels and she had picked up several, including a new one about a Belgian detective. Then she remembered that she was on the job, and so returned the books to their table. If her budget could take it, she'd come back for them.

Mrs Orping took Mabel into the study and gestured to the grand piano at one end of the room.

'He wants to be a concert pianist,' she said of her grandson, 'and his parents want him to be a doctor. I want him to do what he likes. So, here you are. Play whatever you like.'

Mabel found the selection of sheet music well-rounded, and for variety chose a lively piece by Debussy and followed that with 'Moonlight Sonata'.

'Well now,' Mabel said, 'how does it sound to you?'

Mrs Orping thought the piano sounded fine. And that was that.

Mabel would've played longer if asked. She missed it. Too bad Mrs Orping didn't need someone to come and play for her once or twice a week when her grandon wasn't visiting. She could ask Rosalind about playing the piano in the drawing room, but would that be taking liberties?

Once finished with her Useful Women duties, Mabel went directly to Rosalind's.

'Thank God you're here,' Rosalind said, taking Mabel's arm and gently pulling her in. She glanced over her shoulder and continued in a quiet voice, 'Gabrielle is in the study. Inspector Tollerton met her at the office first thing this morning and told her about Thomas and put a few questions to her. I'll go and see about coffee. You wouldn't go in and sit with her, would you?'

Rosalind went downstairs and Mabel to the study, where Miss Roche sat like a wilted rose, shoulders sagging, head down and holding her bag in her lap. She looked up at Mabel with red-rimmed eyes but attempted to recover her usual poise. She did a poor job of it.

'Miss Canning,' she said.

'Hello,' Mabel replied, forgoing the usual 'good morning,' because it wasn't really. 'I'm very sorry about Mr Hardcastle.'

'The inspector came to tell me this morning. He asked if Mr Hardcastle had any family to notify, but there is none as far as I know. He also asked me about Michael Shaughnessy and Mr Despard's former dealings with his Irish concerns. I would never be a party to such acts, but it's always easy to blame the Irish,' she added in a bitter tone.

'The police explore all possibilities,' Mabel said. 'They look for connections and must see one concerning Mr Despard and the man who died at the wake and this Michael Shaughnessy. And Mr Hardcastle.'

'Yes, of course they do. And I understand that people will kill for money or something they desperately desire, but we would never do that.'

'We?' Mabel asked.

Miss Roche took a leaflet from her bag and handed it over.

LECTURE TONIGHT

'IS IRELAND FREE?'
7 p.m.
Archway Methodist Church Hall
Sponsored by the Committee for Irish Families

'Mr Despard was a great supporter of the cause,' Miss Roche said. 'We care for families torn apart when the government split Ulster, keeping part of it in Great Britain and letting the other part go free. This isn't politics, it's about people. We had hoped Mr Despard would make a permanent commitment, but then...'

But then he disappeared? He discovered that the cause had been siphoning off money regardless of his support and he was killed hoping that his widow would step up?

'It isn't what you think!' Miss Roche cried, as if she'd heard Mabel's thoughts. 'We would never use violence of any kind and we certainly do not take money that does not belong to us.'

Red blotches broke out on Miss Roche's face and her eyes filled with tears. In their few brief encounters, the woman had been confident and assured, and this flood of emotions put Mabel on the back foot.

'I didn't mean I thought you'd done any of this,' she said. 'You or the people you help. It's because I wasn't here when Mr

Despard went missing, and I'm unfamiliar with everyone's situation.'

Miss Roche swiped the back of her hand across her cheek and then drew out a handkerchief. 'If you'd like to know more about what we do, then you should attend tonight's lecture. Archway is easy to find. Where is it that you live?' Miss Roche asked.

'Islington,' Mabel replied.

'I'm quite familiar with Islington,' Miss Roche said. 'The lecture is just down the road. I hope to see you there.'

Rosalind came into the study as the secretary readied to leave.

'Aren't you staying for coffee? I'm sure Bridget will be bringing it up soon.'

'I won't, Mrs Despard, thank you. I'd best go back to the office. Watkins is in bits, poor fellow. And I need to continue my search for any correspondence between Mr Despard and Michael Shaughnessy before I'm suspected of something dire.'

Rosalind followed her out, saying, 'Don't play the martyr, Gabrielle. It doesn't suit you.'

When she returned to the study, Mabel said, 'I should go too.'

'Please don't,' Rosalind said. 'No, I shouldn't ask – you must have your own work to do.'

'Not until this afternoon,' Mabel replied.

'We'll go up to the drawing room. I'll just run down and tell Bridget.'

Mabel had got as far as the entry when the bell was pulled, and she answered the door to Inspector Tollerton on the doorstep.

'Ah, Miss Canning,' he said, sounding not at all surprised.

'Do you have news?' Mabel asked.

'About Mr Despard's disappearance? About the dead man from the wake? About who chucked Thomas Hardcastle in the

Thames?' Tollerton shook his head. 'Sorry, Miss Canning. I have nothing to tell you.'

'Forgive me, Inspector. Good morning. Come in.'

Directly behind him, Winstone appeared, along with Gladys, who slipped past them all and headed for the kitchen.

'Tolly,' Winstone said. 'Miss Canning.'

'Yes, good morning,' she said. 'There'll be coffee in the drawing room.'

Rosalind walked in and saw Tollerton on the sofa and Winstone at the piano, and Mabel noticed a fleeting look of apprehension cross her face.

Tollerton rose. 'Mrs Despard, I hope you don't mind I've come. I have nothing else to tell you, but—'

'It's all right, Inspector,' Rosalind said. 'You're in time for coffee. Bridget will be up soon. What can I help you with?'

'I'd like to go over the day your husband went missing – I know it's a while ago and memories fade but—'

'Some memories never fade,' Rosalind said, and a faraway look came into her eyes. 'I was out all that day and didn't return until evening, and so Bridget had taken the day off too. Neither of us knew he'd gone, but he would often dash off for two or three days. Guy was never one to sit behind a desk in a big office, something Miss Roche often complained about. It was because he liked to spend his time with the men who worked for him. "We came from the same streets," he would say. He relied on Thomas to run things in the office, and that's how the business carried on these seven years.' She frowned. 'All the while, Thomas stealing from him.'

'And that day, Mr Hardcastle was in the office?'

'They all said so,' Rosalind replied. 'Gabrielle and his secretary at the time, a young man named Griffin. He signed up after that autumn and was killed – where was it, Park?'

'Gallipoli,' Winstone replied.

'No one was out of place that day, Inspector,' Rosalind added. 'When I arrived home that evening and Guy wasn't here, I thought, well, he's delayed or gone for a drink with someone. That's what you do, you see, tell yourself "just a little longer" and you make excuses until there are no more excuses to make.'

Bridget came in and set down a tray of coffee and sandwiches. 'I heard voices,' she said. 'Thought you might need more than cake.'

'Didn't Guy take a case or valise when he travelled?' Mabel asked.

'He kept rooms in boarding houses where he travelled the most,' Winstone said. 'Dublin, Glasgow, Portsmouth.'

'The people at those boarding houses,' Mabel said, 'no one had seen him?'

'No one,' Rosalind confirmed. 'I understand how it looked suspicious, Inspector, but for a while there, I thought that Inspector Burge was going to dig up the yard here and look for where I'd buried him.'

Winstone muttered a curse under his breath.

'I'm sorry for how you were treated then,' Tollerton said. 'If it had been up to us' – he gave a nod in Winstone's direction – 'we would've done things differently.'

'Thank you, Inspector.'

'As for the two of you,' Tollerton said, looking pointedly at Winstone and then Mabel, 'I will remind you that meddling is not welcome in a police enquiry.'

'Good afternoon, Miss Canning,' Miss Kerr said. 'I trust your morning went well.'

'Yes, Miss Kerr, and here I am, just as I said.'

'Good.' She reached for a paper at the corner of her desk.

'Mrs Neame needs assistance in hanging a picture – if your afternoon is free?'

'Just the one picture?' Mabel asked, taking the assignment. 'That shouldn't take all afternoon.'

Mrs Neame welcomed Mabel profusely. She was in late middle age and over her day dress wore a loose silk coat with a peacock-tail design running up the deep sleeves. When she gestured to welcome Mabel in, the sleeves of the coat floated through the air.

'I can't tell you how grateful I am for your assistance, Miss...'

'Canning.'

'Canning. I'm in such a muddle about my Millais.'

She led Mabel to the library and gestured towards a painting propped against the bookcase. The picture showed a ghostly woman's figure standing at the foot of a four-poster bed wherein lay a surprised-looking soldier. The painting – not small – was dwarfed by its heavily carved and gilded frame.

'Arthritis in my hands, you see,' Mrs Neame said, holding them out and rubbing a knuckle. 'And I'm afraid Cribbes is well past carrying much more than a tea tray these days.'

'What a lovely picture – I'm delighted to hang it for you.'

'Well, now, bring it along, and you can help me decide where.'

Mabel picked up the painting, staggered under its weight – forty pounds if it was an ounce – and followed the client down a long corridor.

'I knew Ruskin,' Mrs Neame said over her shoulder. 'Rather, my father knew him and was a great admirer, although that didn't stop Father from supporting Millais. This is one of his minor works, of course.'

There was nothing minor about it.

When Mrs Neame stopped at the end of the corridor and

gestured to a small table against the wall, Mabel set the painting on it with care and then shook out her arms.

'Hmmm,' the client said, standing back a few feet and studying the painting in situ. 'No, I think not – the space is a bit too close to get the full effect. Let's try it out on the landing.'

And so it went. Mabel carried her burden, lumbering behind Mrs Neame along corridors, in and out of rooms, and up and down the stairs, all the while trying to keep up with the client's stories of many encounters with a host of Pre-Raphaelites, dropping names such as Edward Burne-Jones and Dante Rossetti and the like as Mabel tried not to drop the painting.

Two hours later, Mabel had to take a stand or collapse.

'Wouldn't it look lovely on that wall,' she said, setting the painting against the back of a sofa in a second-floor drawing room with a grunt. They'd been in the room once before already.

'Well, perhaps not. But I do so appreciate your kind attitude,' Mrs Neame said. 'You're much more patient than the lady Miss Kerr sent on Friday.'

Mabel didn't breathe as she let that statement sink in. 'Someone else from Useful Women came to help you with this same painting?'

The client nodded. 'Yes, and another one earlier in the week. I do have a difficult time deciding. Would you care for tea?'

Late afternoon, Mabel made her way home, her arms feeling like jelly. She'd had to hold onto her teacup with both hands and had come to the conclusion that Miss Kerr had known the job for Mrs Neame would take the entire afternoon and had used it as a way of reminding her who was in charge at Useful Women. Perhaps Miss Kerr believed Mabel had been spending

too much time with the Despard affair – unpaid and not repre-
senting the agency. Mabel believed Miss Kerr was being short-
sighted. All of the help she had given Rosalind could be under
the guise of Useful Women. It should be some sort of job of its
own, really – not flower arranging or writing letters of condolence, but a job of... what? Finding dead bodies? Perhaps not the
description Miss Kerr would like in the Useful Women booklet
number eight.

SIXTEEN

The Methodist church hall in Archway looked benign enough, and Mabel chastised herself at the thought that the hall might be the place for fomenting a rebellion. There was a mixed crowd of men, women and a few young lads who were playing war among the seats until a chair crashed to the floor, after which the boys' ears were pulled and they sat down quietly.

Across the room and at the foot of a low stage, Gabrielle Roche looked busy talking with several men and women and gesturing as if she were director of the event. She saw Mabel and lifted her chin in greeting but didn't approach.

Mabel chose a seat at the side and about halfway back in the room so as not to look either too eager or too reluctant.

The lecture was about families, just as the flyer had said. Several people spoke about how close relatives had been torn asunder when the nine counties of Ulster had been broken during partition, leaving six in the North still attached to Britain and three in Southern Ireland.

'My brother and his family are in County Cavan,' said one woman who spoke. 'We live just a few miles away in

Fermanagh, but practically overnight it was as if a wall had been thrown up between us. Did we deserve that?'

There was a plea to support the effort by giving a few shillings a month, but the connection between the separated families and the money given through subscription to the committee was lost on Mabel and so, when the general movement was towards the table where one of the women poured tea and a man took names, Mabel headed for the door, only to be intercepted by Miss Roche.

'I hope you enjoyed the evening,' she said, her clear blue eyes burning brightly.

'I did,' Mabel said. 'Thank you for inviting me.'

'You can help, you know. You can tell Mrs Despard about our efforts, that we're an organisation that works with families, and that she's nothing to worry about.'

At that moment, Gabrielle was called away and Mabel left, wondering if 'nothing to worry about' was meant as a vague threat – that Rosalind would need to pay up, that is, donate to the cause, or what happened to her husband and her solicitor would happen again.

Mabel stepped out of the church hall, where the blaze of the gas lamps along the road created pools of light on the pavement with inky darkness between. She could walk back to her flat, but she had the pennies in her purse, and here came a bus going her way. She boarded and took a seat along the side, then noticed someone jump on – a tall, thin young man wearing a brown suit with his hat pulled low. Mabel felt sick. Here he was again. The man she'd seen running away on the docks? The man who had watched her window from the green and had followed her to Hampstead Heath? And now had he followed her from the lecture. Had he been one of those talking with Gabrielle Roche in the hall?

She looked straight across the bus at her own reflection in the window as her mind and her heart raced.

Had he first been at the wake? The thought occurred to her in a flash as she remembered Miss Roche talking with several of the men downstairs while everyone else – apart from Thomas Hardcastle – was in the drawing room. And then, only a short time later, the man in the greatcoat arrived on the doorstep.

The man at the back of the bus grabbed a pole as the bus lurched forward. Mabel longed to get a good look at his face, but he stayed in the shadow. What was it that was so familiar about him?

At St Paul's Road, the bus turned away from Islington, and so Mabel decided to walk the rest of the way. Several others got off behind her, but she didn't turn to see if the man was one of them. She walked along briskly, glad to reach Upper Street. Not far now.

As she turned the corner, she paused and looked over her shoulder and saw a figure, about twenty steps behind her, pause and dip into the shadows. She quickened her step, dodging around a few slow walkers. When she plunged into the dark between gas lamps and heard him close behind her, she broke into a run – New River House was in sight. When she reached the door, she touched it as if it were a talisman, then pushed it open and looked behind her. There was no one there.

She shut the door and leant against it, panting. The foyer was quiet. A low lamp burnt on Mr Chigley's desk, and another light shone through from his living quarters. Mabel slowed her breathing, and told herself not to be a silly goose. Then someone pushed open the street door behind her, and she stumbled forward, crying out.

'Dear God, Miss Canning!'

Mr Jenks caught her a second before she hit the floor and pulled her up with his free hand, keeping hold of his samples case in the other.

Mabel straightened herself and adjusted her hat, but couldn't speak with her heart pounding so. *It's Mr Jenks*, she told herself – *only Mr Jenks*.

He had continued talking: '... so terribly sorry... I had no idea... are you injured? Shall we ring for an ambulance?'

Mr Jenks – neither tall nor wearing a brown suit – appeared flustered, almost to the point of tears.

'What's this then?' Mr Chigley said, bursting out of his room.

'Nothing!' Mabel said with a little laugh. 'Nothing at all, Mr Chigley. I had come in just a moment ago, and when Mr Jenks opened the door, it startled me, that's all. I'm fine.' She turned to the young man and smiled. 'Thank you for your concern, Mr Jenks, you're very kind.'

Mr Chigley looked unconvinced as his gaze went from Mabel to Mr Jenks, where it hardened.

'We're lucky for your attention, Mr Chigley, aren't we, Mr Jenks?' Mabel asked. 'Always an eye out to who comes and goes.'

Jenks mumbled something and hurried up the stairs.

'It's my job, Miss Canning,' Mr Chigley said. 'Until the door is locked at ten and only those who live here have a key to get in.'

Mabel felt both constrained by Mr Chigley's watchful eye over his domain and, at the same time, grateful he would always be there.

The next morning, fretting about her day, Mabel burnt the toast and stewed her tea. She drank the tea and, after scraping the worst bits off, ate her toast, although with plenty of marmalade. She wanted to go to Rosalind's to keep abreast of the investigation – had Michael Shaughnessy been found? – but didn't know how would she manage that and not be struck off the Useful Women rolls?

And so, Mabel arrived at the Useful Women office just after nine o'clock and was promptly sent out on a job to repair Miss Newton's lace-edged camisole. This required delicate work and Mabel smoothed the garment out on her lap to keep the stitches from puckering, continuing to dwell on the police enquiry. Did they believe Shaughnessy involved in both murder and embezzlement? Guy's letter connected the man to something. If Hardcastle had killed Guy and Shaughnessy had killed Hardcastle, then who else might Shaughnessy want to get out of his way of a steady, but stolen, income? Thoughts of murder and deception distracted her so much that she realised too late she'd sewn the lacy camisole to her own skirt.

'Damn!' she muttered.

'Finished yet?' the client asked, looking in on her.

Mabel's head shot up, her face hot as she covered the stitching with her hand. She smiled. 'Nearly.'

'Would you like to come back to the library for a cup of tea?'

'No, thank you,' Mabel said. 'I've good light here by the window. I'll just crack on, shall I?'

Mabel allowed herself a grumble as she set about unstitching her work in order to stitch it all over again.

She made it back to the Dover Street office in time for Mrs Fritt's tea-and-bun trolley and had already finished her bun when the telephone rang.

'Miss Kerr, the Useful Women agency. How may I help you?'

Mabel counted as one of her skills the ability to listen to one side of a telephone conversation and fill in what the other person was saying, but in this instance, she picked up no clues, neither from her employer's face nor from the faintly heard female voice on the other end of the line. That is, until her employer locked eyes on her, and Mabel felt a frisson of excitement – Rosalind had thought of a job for her.

'Yes, of course,' Miss Kerr said into the telephone. 'She's in the office at this moment. I will send her at once.'

Mabel climbed out of the taxi at Victoria Station and paid the driver, grateful that this fare would not go on her personal account. She marched through the entrance and straight to the stationmaster's office. Just inside the door, a man sat at a desk.

'Hello, I'm Mabel Canning from the Useful Women agency. I've been told you have an escapee, and I've come to claim him.'

From behind her came a cheery voice. 'Hello, Miss Canning!'

Mabel looked over her shoulder at the eight-year-old boy sitting in a chair three times his size.

'Hello, Augustus.'

It hadn't been Rosalind, Winstone or the inspector on the telephone. Instead, it had been Mrs Malling-Frobisher, frantic that her dear, sweet Augustus had disappeared from his school before breakfast that morning and had been seen getting on a train to London. He'd been apprehended upon arrival and now needed to be escorted safely home.

The stationmaster seemed all too eager to release his prisoner into her custody, and so it was only moments later that Mabel and Augustus stood in the middle of the station while people rushed past in all directions.

'Ready to face up to it?' she asked.

Augustus looked at the station clock and said, 'I missed my breakfast this morning.'

'Whose fault was that?'

'I might faint from hunger before you can get me home.'

Mabel laughed. 'We can't have that, can we? Your mother will have to pay Useful Women an exorbitant fee if I need to revive you.'

They went to the station café, where they both had sausages, fried potatoes and tea.

'How did you do it?' Mabel asked.

Augustus, his mouth full of potatoes, tapped a finger on the side of his nose.

This boy is older than his years, Mabel thought. 'In that case, why did you do it? I thought you liked school.'

'I do, but my dad is coming home from Australia today.'

'Did your mother tell you?'

'No, Miss Canning. My dad wrote to me at school. Mum won't even talk about him except to say Australia is the ends of the earth and that's the best place for him.'

Mabel must have been turning soft because she had a stab of pity for Augustus. 'Do you see him often?'

'I saw him last Christmas, but after he gave me my present, Mum made him leave.'

'What did he give you?' Mabel asked.

'A sword!' Augustus waved his fork in excitement, and a piece of sausage went flying through the air. 'A real pirate's sword.' His high spirits evaporated. 'Mum took it away.'

In the taxi on the way to his house, Augustus said, 'I thought it would be you come to meet me, Miss Canning. I made sure to write to Mum about when you took me to the station that you weren't any fun and you never let me out of your sight.'

'That's not strictly true, is it?' Mabel asked.

'Maybe not,' Augustus said, 'but it worked. And don't you and I get along well?'

He may be a scamp, but Mabel had to admire Augustus's organisational skills and his ability to elude capture until he'd

arrived at his destination. He and Flea were of the same ilk –
intelligent, resourceful – the only difference being their circumstances. Still, she imagined they'd get along well.

Once Augustus had been safely delivered, Mabel thought it
possible to return to work by way of Belgravia and so rang the
bell and was greeted with joy by Rosalind.

'I need a distraction,' she said. 'We won't have to talk about
anything, will we?'

'I've only stopped to see how you are,' Mabel said, worrying
slightly at Rosalind's feverish cheer.

'Have you eaten lunch – yes, long past lunch, isn't it?
Would you like tea? Come up to the drawing room.'

The grey skies outdoors seemed to have infiltrated the
drawing room, creating a dim atmosphere, but Rosalind set
about turning on the myriad of lamps and sconces until the
place was ablaze.

Mabel walked over to the piano and nodded at the open
music. 'Have you been playing?' she asked. 'Oh, it's four hands.'

'Park and I used to play on the old cottage piano at home,'
Rosalind said, 'and we still do now and then.'

'Edith and I played four hands,' Mabel remarked. 'That
seems a long time ago.'

'Let's you and I play now,' Rosalind said, 'shall we? Do you
see one you know?'

Mabel shuffled through the pieces. 'What about "*Jeux d'en-
fants*"? Shall I do left? Edith and I always traded back and
forth.'

'I'm afraid I'm strictly right, so you're stuck with the left.'
Rosalind set the piece on the music rack and gave it a pat to
flatten it. They sat on the bench with hands poised over the
keyboard. Mabel prayed she wouldn't make a dog's breakfast of
her part.

Rosalind nodded the time, and they began, but not far in, Mabel felt something wet touch her arm. She looked down to see Gladys.

'I'm in time for the concert, am I?' Winstone asked from the door. 'Carry on then.' He walked over to the drinks cabinet and poured himself a whisky.

Mabel waited for a word from Rosalind, but she was watching Winstone, her head cocked. Then she rose and, giving Mabel a backward glance, said to her brother, 'I must go and ask Bridget for tea. Park, come over here and play four hands with Mabel.'

Winstone took a swig of his whisky. 'My sister has always been skilled in telling people what to do without asking if they want to do it.'

'Stuff and nonsense,' Rosalind said. 'It's Bizet.'

'Is it?' he asked, as if that made a difference. He took another drink. 'Well, Miss Canning, shall we give it a go?'

'Yes, all right, let's,' Mabel said.

Rosalind left them to it. Mabel scooted to the right side of the bench, and Winstone went round to her left and sat beside her. The piano bench seemed suddenly very small and Winstone very close – her left side was snug up against him and their arms touched. Mabel swallowed, nodded the time and they were off.

Although she had continued to play in the two years since Edith's death, there had been no one to play four hands, yet, after a nervous few measures, her fingers, for the most part, remembered the way. They made it through the languid beginning and the frenetic 'Spinning Top'.

Now, Mabel was quite enjoying herself. Winstone played well. He didn't try to outplay her, rush the tempo or take over her own notes. But when she cut her eyes at him, she saw a mischievous gleam, and the next time she had to reach deep into his left-hand territory, he tried to trap her hand under his elbow.

She gave a shout of mock outrage and kept playing and, at the first opportunity, stole a run from his right hand and played it herself. After that, it became a war of keys, and soon chaos reigned, ending in Winstone snorting and Mabel in a fit of giggles.

'I call a truce,' Mabel said. 'I'll need to practise before we go again.'

'You held your own,' he said, cleaning his glasses with his handkerchief. 'And you have a certain flair.'

'You're too kind, Mr Winstone,' Mabel said. They remained seated. 'She seems a bit tightly wound today, don't you think?'

'Hmm,' Winstone replied.

'No word on the enquiry?'

'We've been told to mind our own business, Miss Canning. Remember?'

Mabel left brother and sister to their tea and returned to the Useful Women office, where Miss Kerr asked after Augustus.

'He left school because his father is visiting from Australia,' Mabel said. 'He only wanted to see him.'

'Well, Miss Canning, I must say you have a certain knack with the boy.'

As Miss Kerr said that, she made a note in the Useful Women register, and even without reading the words upside down, Mabel knew she would be on-call for any future Augustus Malling-Frobisher antics. Oh well, it could be worse.

'Now then,' Miss Kerr continued, 'I can provide a calming task for you this afternoon. A Mrs Sturham who lives in Marylebone requests someone who can read her to sleep.'

'What, now? During the day?'

'Yes, during the day. Will that suit?'

'Thank you, Miss Kerr, I'll take it.'

. . .

Mrs Sturham's maid answered the door and, in a whisper, said that 'milady is in her bedroom ready and waiting,' and led the way upstairs.

Mabel found the client, an elderly woman, tucked up in bed wearing a satin bed jacket and a white muslin nightcap. She had a long plait of grey hair, the end of which rested on top of the counterpane.

'I don't sleep well at night, you see,' she explained, 'and so I'm going to try sleeping during the day as if it were night. It is, as they say, an experiment.'

The curtains were pulled to darken the room, and apart from the blazing fire, which made the room warm and a bit stuffy, the only light came from a small lamp on a table by the bed. Mabel settled in the wing chair next to it and accepted the book Mrs Sturham handed to her – a collection of poems about sleep.

The maid arrived with glasses of warm milk. Mabel took a sip of hers, opened the book to 'Cradle Song' by William Blake and began.

When Mabel awoke, it was dark. Where was she? Not in her own bed. Not in any bed. She was sitting up with her head resting against the upholstered wing of a chair. A sound like an explosion went off and shook her fully awake. It was followed by another, quieter explosion, and after that, the sound of heavy breathing. It all came back to her. That had been no explosion, but Mrs Sturham snoring. Mabel had been reading poetry to put the client to sleep, and it had worked for both of them. That and the warm milk.

Who had switched off the lamp? What time was it?

Mrs Sturham shifted into a light snore as Mabel crept out of the room and went looking for the maid. She found her drinking tea in the kitchen. 'Sleeping peacefully,' she reported. 'I'll be on my way, but first, may I use your lavatory?'

Having freshened up, she stood out on the pavement blinking into the sunlight. It was only three o'clock, but, with her head still full of cotton wool, Mabel had thought it well past six. She never slept heavily during the day. Perhaps events were catching up with her.

After a moment to get her bearings, she made her way to Marylebone Street, and found a bus.

At the Angel, Mabel alighted and walked slowly to New River House as she thought how she should be spending every waking minute helping to solve the mystery of the dead man on the doorstep and therefore the disappearance of Guy Despard. What was she doing instead? Taking afternoon naps.

She walked too slow for some, apparently, because just as she reached New River House, a young woman knocked into her from behind, causing Mabel to stagger forward.

The young woman continued on her way, throwing a quick 'sorry' over her shoulder.

'*Hmph*,' Mabel said, and glanced round to see if anyone had noticed the collision. No one paid a whit of attention.

Wait – someone across the road in the green had noticed – a tall, thin man wearing a brown suit standing under a plane tree.

SEVENTEEN

A cold wave of fear washed over Mabel. She hurried the last few steps up to New River House, opened the door and threw herself into the foyer and straight into Cora and Skeff.

'Whoa now,' Skeff said, catching Mabel.

'He's out there,' Mabel whispered furiously. 'The man who's following me. I saw him last night and here he is again. He's there on the green.'

She pointed at the closed door, and Cora and Skeff followed her gesture and narrowed their eyes as if they could see through wood and concrete.

'Should we call out to Mr Chigley?' Cora asked quietly. 'He's gone back to make himself a cup of tea.'

Mabel frowned. The porter's office was empty, but the door to Mr Chigley's living quarters was ajar, and she could hear him humming. 'No,' she said. 'What could he do or say now? I want to know who this fellow is. I'm going out after him.'

'Wait,' Skeff said in a low voice. 'You shouldn't let on that you realise he's following you. Keep him off guard, and you have the chance to get the measure of him.'

'Good point,' Mabel said. 'I'll just stroll by and take a look. Closer up, I may recognise him.'

'But when he sees you approaching, he might get skittish and bolt,' Cora said. 'Here, let's exchange coats. He's just seen you come in wearing a green one and if you go out in my red, he won't realise it's you.'

'Cora, you're brilliant.'

'It's nothing,' Cora said, her face flushed as she took off her coat. 'It's only, I've seen husbands walk straight by their wives if the wife is wearing a new hat, so I know it doesn't take much. Ooh, here, take my hat too.'

Mabel tore off her brimmed hat and put on Cora's picture hat that was so wide one side dipped nearly to Mabel's shoulder and was weighted with an enormous silk rose. She plunged her hands in the pockets of Cora's coat, felt something and drew out a pair of round-framed spectacles.

'My glasses!' Cora cried. 'Put them on.'

Mabel did so, and the world became fuzzy. 'I'll need to look over the tops to see clearly,' she said. She struck a pose. 'What do you think?'

'I think if I didn't know it was you, I wouldn't know you,' Skeff said.

'Right then. Here I go.'

Mabel threw open the door, stepped out and paused. Lowering her chin slightly so that she could see, she surveyed the world round her. People passed on the pavement without giving her a second glance. Well, they would, wouldn't they, because they didn't know who Mabel Canning was. But what about him?

He was still there, loitering at the edge of the green, leaning on the trunk of a plane tree and facing New River House. When the door opened and Mabel walked out, he had cast a glance at her, but only for the briefest of moments. Uninterested in her, was he?

Mabel went to the kerb, waited for a clearing in the traffic, and then boldly walked across the road towards him, her head bobbing up and down in order to catch glimpses of the world in focus. She kept her eyes on him as she drew close, and he continued to pay her no heed. When she passed him quite close – only inches away – his eyes darted to her and then away. He didn't recognise her, the fool!

But neither did she recognise him. She could go no further than to confirm her first impression that he was a young man. Yet, there still was something familiar about him, something that reminded her of Mr Jenks. Because he was young?

Mabel continued walking straight across the green, thinking that this would niggle at her until she remembered where it was she'd seen him and found out why he was stalking her. Had he followed her after the lecture on Ireland? There was something in her that would not commit to that.

At once, she was impatient with the ruse, and it came to her that she should walk straight up to him and ask who he was and why he was doing this. With her heart in her throat, she spun round and marched back to the spot.

He was gone.

Mr Chigley looked up from sorting the afternoon post when Mabel swept open the door of New River House and walked into the foyer.

'Hello, Mr Chigley.'

'Miss Canning, is that you?'

Cora and Skeff, sitting on the bottom step of the stairs just out of sight of Mr Chigley, leapt up.

Mr Chigley peered closer at Mabel. 'I didn't realise you wore spectacles.'

Mabel whipped them off and stuck them back in the pocket of Cora's coat. 'They're Cora's – just trying out a new fashion,' she said. 'I've borrowed Cora's hat too. You know she designs hats, don't you?'

'Yes, I see that isn't your hat. I see it now you call attention to it,' Mr Chigley said, scratching the scarred side of his face as he studied her. 'Quite fetching, it is.' He leant out over the counter and looked back at Cora and Skeff. 'Post for you, Miss Portjoy. And for you, Miss Skeffington.'

Mr Chigley may not be a connoisseur of the latest fashion in hats, but he knew how to keep an eye on his building.

Cora and Skeff hopped up to collect their letters.

'And one for you, Miss Canning.'

Mabel's was from Ronald. Had she posted her latest letter to him? The days seemed to be getting away from her lately.

'Well?' Skeff asked, after the porter retreated to his private quarters.

While Mabel and Cora reclaimed their own coats and hats, Mabel said, 'He never blinked once, not even when I was as close to him as I am to you. I'd no idea how easy it was to disguise yourself.'

'Did you know him?' Cora asked.

Mabel shook her head. 'Now, I'm not even sure he's familiar. Perhaps I've talked myself into that. Thanks again, Cora, for your help.'

'It was rather fun,' Cora said, 'although, at the same time, worrying that someone is doing this.'

'What does Winstone say about it?' Skeff asked.

Mabel had not mentioned it yet – so much else had gone on. She admitted as much, promised to do so forthwith and marched up the stairs, with Skeff and Cora watching from the foyer. But when Mabel dutifully knocked at Winstone's door, there was neither an answer nor a *woof* from Gladys. Mabel looked down at the two women and shrugged her shoulders.

. . .

A quiet evening alone brought the return of unsettling thoughts. Was she suited to be one of the Useful Women? Miss Kerr ran a tight ship, there was no getting round that. In barely more than a fortnight, Mabel had danced close to the edge of what Miss Kerr deemed the proper sort of employee. True, Mabel had been witness to murder and got herself involved in the enquiry, but she had also carried out a myriad of other jobs assigned to her without complaint and she believed, on the whole, they balanced out – the exciting and the mundane. Mabel wouldn't mind the occasional dog washing if she could solve a mystery once in a while. But, aside from Florrie's request to find Claude – which Mabel had done little about – she couldn't offer to work for free.

She carried a chair into her bedroom and sat beside the window in the dark looking down at the pavement and across the road to the green and late in the evening she saw him again – the man following her. He stood out of the light with his hat pulled down, hands in his pocket idly watching New River House as if he had nothing better to do.

But he hadn't been there long when he turned round and looked into the green as if someone had called to him. He disappeared under the canopy of the trees and didn't return.

The man's presence confused, annoyed and frightened Mabel – in equal parts – but at that moment, in her low spirits, fright had the upper hand.

She left her flat and walked down to the first-floor landing, where she heard music coming from Winstone's flat. It was that sweet Chopin nocturne. Tears came to Mabel's eyes, and without a thought, she tapped lightly at his door.

The music stopped, and she heard a scratching on the floor and a whine. Gladys!

She tapped again. 'Mr Winstone, it's Mabel.'

The door flew open. Winstone had no coat or waistcoat on,

and he had dropped his braces, which he was pulling back up in
a hurry. Mabel looked away, concentrating on greeting Gladys.

'Miss Canning?'

'I know it's terribly late,' she said, 'but it's only that when I
heard you playing, I thought perhaps you wouldn't mind if
I... You see, I've had a very odd...' She stopped for a moment and
sniffed. 'It's just that – I'm being followed.'

Winstone abruptly stuck his head out the door and looked
downstairs.

'Where is he?' he asked. 'Tell me what he looks like.'

'He was in the green, but he's gone now.'

'Come in.' He put his hand on her arm but took it away
quickly. 'That is, will you come in?'

Mabel nodded.

Winstone guided her to the sofa. 'Would you like a brandy?'
he asked.

'Yes, thank you.'

Winstone poured himself one, too, and pulled a chair over
so that he could sit across from her, their knees almost touching.
Gladys hopped up on the sofa and put her head in Mabel's lap.

All at once, she didn't know where to begin and wasn't
entirely sure she could speak without losing composure, so
instead she asked, 'What news of Mr Hardcastle's death?'

'Sadly, I've been told nothing,' Winstone said.

They each took a drink. He watched her, his eyes dark and,
Mabel thought, full of concern. She wished they could stay this
way – quiet, close – but knew it couldn't last.

'Miss Canning – you're being followed?'

'Yes, all right. Here it is. After finding Mr Hardcastle in the
river on Saturday, I thought I saw someone running away – you
know that, and you know I didn't get a good look at the man, but
only an impression. But it matched Flea's description of him.'

'Flea,' Winstone said. 'He's a remarkable young man. How
was it you met him?'

'He's a friend of Skeff's,' she said. 'So then, when I arrived home that evening, I noticed a man on the green and he seemed to be looking up to my window, keeping watch or something. He's tall and thin and he was wearing a brown suit. I couldn't see his features because of his hat.'

'You've seen him again this evening?' Winstone asked.

'Before this evening,' Mabel said. 'Sunday, I went to Hampstead Heath with Cora and Skeff and he was there. I'm sure – I'm *nearly* sure it was him, but he's elusive. Last evening, Miss Roche invited me to a lecture about families in Ireland at the Methodist Hall in Archway and I went, and on my way back, a man followed me onto the bus and then back here. At least he might've been following me.' At once, her story seemed weak and full of holes. 'I can't be sure it's the same man and I can't be sure he's watching me. I could be imagining the entire thing.'

Her voice ended on a tentative note, and Winstone must've heard it.

'But you aren't. What else has happened?'

'This afternoon, I saw him on the green and I walked across the road and straight past him and got a good look.'

'You didn't recognise him?' Winstone asked.

'There is something familiar about him, but I can't say from where.'

'Could he have been at the wake?'

The question chilled Mabel. She thought of Gabrielle Roche in the dining room talking with three men while everyone else was upstairs in the drawing room. One of them wore a brown suit, but that was all she could remember.

'It's possible. Do you believe Michael Shaughnessy could've been at the wake and no one knew him – or someone is keeping quiet?' Mabel asked. 'And now he's watching me because he thinks I'm somehow involved in what all has happened? No. This man is young – he would've been a boy when Guy was alive, so I don't know how that would fit.'

'You should've told me this before.'

'I haven't had the opportunity.'

'You put yourself in danger by going out after him,' Winstone said.

'Cora gave me her coat and hat to wear as a disguise. And her glasses. The fellow never gave me a second look.'

'Miss Portjoy? Is she a costumier?'

'No, she works at a milliner's and designs hats, but she knows how easy it is to alter your appearance, and she has a good eye for it. It was her cape I wore on Saturday.'

'Whoever this fellow is, he doesn't sound terribly bright.'

'You didn't realise it was me in the cape at first.'

Winstone narrowed his eyes at her.

Mabel finished off her brandy. 'If we find Michael Shaughnessy, will we find out what happened to Guy?'

'I'm still not convinced Shaughnessy killed Guy – there are too many questions to be answered.'

'It must've been frustrating for you, the way the investigation went.'

'It was maddening to see what it did to Rosy. She should've stayed down on the Isle of Wight longer, but she insisted on coming back up to London after a few months. I looked in on her as often as I could.'

'You looked in on her from where?' Mabel asked.

'Ah,' he said, sounding at once evasive. 'I joined up at the end of '14.'

'Yes. You saw action?'

Winstone finished off his drink, took his glasses off and polished them while he spoke. 'I wasn't in the trenches. I worked in the diplomatic corps, in Paris for the most part. I sat at a desk and read letters that were not addressed to me and wrote a few pretending to be someone else,' he said in an offhand way. 'I would like to have had you there with me, Miss Canning. You and your handwriting skill.'

For the briefest moment, Mabel imagined them together in Paris in one of those glittering hotels, drinking champagne and dancing every evening, then working late into the night in deserted offices lit by a single lamp, intercepting secret war documents in order to foil the Germans' latest plot until, at last, in the early hours of the morning, unable to resist any longer, falling into each other's—

'Another brandy?'

Mabel took a sharp breath. 'No, thank you. I believe I've had enough. I'd best go.'

'About the man following you,' Winstone began.

'Is he following me or am I imagining it?' Mabel said, rising. 'I'd like to get my hands on him and ask.'

Winstone stood. 'May I see you home?'

'Up the stairs and down the corridor?' Mabel giggled. 'Yes, you may.'

They walked to her flat and paused.

Winstone said, 'You will take care.'

'I will,' Mabel replied. 'My only activities will be good and proper jobs for Useful Women. Oh, and trying to find Florrie Hart's beau.'

'Who is this?'

'She's in the show at Collins,' Mabel said. 'I met her when I'd gone to the stage door to tell Cyril how much I enjoyed my first ever visit to a music hall. Florrie is worried because the fellow she was seeing has stopped coming round and asked me if I could find him for her. I'm not certain what I can do, but I did say I'd try. Quite innocuous work, I promise. But thank you for your concern,' she added.

'You mean "Thank you for your concern and good night, Mr Winstone"?'

'Yes,' she said. 'And good night to you, too, Gladys.'

. . .

Mabel had spent a restless night, disturbed by dreams of being in Paris and searching for Gladys, who had become a dancer at the Folies Bergère, where Serious Cyril was Master of Ceremonies. Mabel awoke disoriented and sat hunkered over a cup of tea until it went cold and then dressed and left for the agency, stopping first at the porter's window.

'Good morning, Mr Chigley,' she said brightly, hoping he wouldn't notice her puffy eyes. 'Do you know a drinks firm in Camden Town?'

He folded up his newspaper. 'Gin? Wine? Don't I just? That's Gilbey's. Your father and I ordered Gilbey's Gin for the army's stores in India.'

'Did you now?' Mabel thought of her Bacon's walking map. 'Camden Town isn't too far, is it?'

'Just down the road.'

'It must be a big place, this Gilbey's.'

'Massive.'

Gilbey's would employ a great number of people, including cleaners – such as Claude's mum.

'Do you need to go there?' Mr Chigley asked, and Mabel heard the unspoken *And if so, why?* in his voice.

'Do you remember Florrie from Collins?' Mabel asked. 'She mentioned that her beau's mum worked there as a cleaner, that's all.'

Appeased, Mr Chigley picked up his newspaper again.

There now, Mabel thought, pleased with herself. She had something to report to Florrie, and Mabel could begin the search for Claude where his mother had worked. Perhaps Mabel could make it back for the matinee that afternoon.

But upon her arrival at 48 Dover Street, Miss Kerr handed Mabel three jobs that took up nearly her entire morning. She delivered a dress from one client to the drapers and collected a pair of boots from the cobblers for another client who had tried them on, said they still didn't fit and had Mabel return them to the cobblers. After that, she repaired a stuck drawer in a writing desk by rubbing candle wax on the runners and, in the process, found a lost letter from the client's son in Australia.

At the end of her morning, Mabel thought she would report in to satisfy Miss Kerr and go to lunch, but Miss Kerr had other ideas. She had taken a telephone call from a distraught client. Mrs Littledale, due to sail from Southampton to Italy the very next day, had lost her passport. Could Miss Kerr send round one of her Useful Women to find it?

Mrs Littledale was in an agitated state when Mabel arrived, and flew into an emotional rage when asked to retrace her steps from the previous afternoon – the last time the document had been seen. It was only with a great deal of persuading that the client reluctantly led Mabel from bedroom to corridor to bathroom back to bedroom and finally down the stairs, where she gestured to a tea tray on a table.

'My maid left on her own holiday yesterday,' the client said, as if to explain why the tray hadn't made it all the way to the kitchen. 'I had to bring it downstairs myself.'

Mabel picked up the tray and there, underneath, was the passport.

'How ever did that get there?' Mrs Littledale asked in an accusatory tone.

Mabel smiled, but inwardly wondered why people said they'd looked everywhere for a lost object when they hadn't?

At last, lunch, but Mrs Littledale lived in Fitzroy Square, and that was too far from Belgravia for Mabel to make a quick stop at Rosalind's and so straight back to Dover Street she went.

During the morning, Mabel had kept telling herself that this was not work for work's sake, but the essence of being one of the

Useful Women, and that Miss Kerr had not assigned her this string of menial tasks just to put her in her place. She wasn't sure she believed herself on that point.

She ate an apple for lunch walking back to Piccadilly, and when she arrived at the agency, Miss Kerr gestured to Mabel's chair across the desk.

'Miss Canning, is our work here at Useful Women not enough for you?'

Mabel felt her face go hot. 'No, Miss Kerr. That is, I find the work good. Satisfying.'

Miss Kerr's eyebrows twitched in disbelief. 'You must make a decision,' she said. 'Either you work for me or you don't. At first, I had thought you were dedicated to the principles of Useful Women, eager to carry out any job, knowing that even the most insignificant assignment is worthwhile to our clients and they come first. But, Miss Canning, you have allowed yourself to become distracted by events which do not actually concern you, to the point I am not sure I can rely on you.' Miss Kerr moved her fountain pen from one side of the Jobs ledger to the other and continued. 'Perhaps Mrs Despard is paying you separately for other work, and if that is the case, then, as much as it grieves me to say, you will be removed from the Useful Women rolls. I will not have my workers poached and must set an example.'

Miss Kerr rested her forearms on the desk and waited.

'I don't want to leave Useful Women, Miss Kerr,' Mabel said in earnest. 'I suppose you could say that my attention to the Despard case has gone beyond what you thought was required, but I am not being paid by Mrs Despard for anything other than the jobs she has arranged with you. She is not trying to poach me.'

Miss Kerr nodded, looking appeased by Mabel's explanation, although Mabel herself felt she was leaving something out of the argument that needed to be brought up. She would think of it later.

'I do have a job for this afternoon, if you're available,' Miss Kerr said.

Drat. Mabel had already made plans for herself that afternoon. She hoped to look in on Rosalind, she intended to talk with Florrie about Claude's mum being a cleaner at Gilbey's, and she'd thought that perhaps she could make a visit to Camden Town herself. Didn't every enquiry need on-the-ground research? But, Useful Women first.

'Yes, Miss Kerr, of course I'll take it.'

'Good,' Miss Kerr said, and handed over the details.

Mabel went to a fashionable house in Kensington, out of which a Madame Franc ran a dressmaking business. She had so many women working for her, in every stage of the process from office to design to sewing, that she had her own exchange right there on the premises. The telephonist was out ill, and Mabel was to fill in for the rest of the day.

Madame Franc gave her a brief, vague lesson on how to run the board and left her to it. Immediately, Mabel began to handle all manner of calls coming in and going out about every dressmaking detail, from importing French satin ribbon to the supply of pins. Some callers would ask for a person – 'Miss Rimington, please.' Others would request a step in the dressmaking – 'Sleeves.' Occasionally, callers didn't know what they wanted – 'Can you tell me who it is that buys thread?'

It began well. Mabel moved the keys to their proper position, plugged and unplugged cables to transfer calls. She answered in a calm voice and, after running her finger down the list of who was who at the business, connected the person ringing to the proper telephone. But the work was exacting, and her nerves taut. By late afternoon, the number of calls increased, and it seemed everyone wanted to speak to someone else 'at once'.

Mabel became lost in a confusion of flashing lights and cables that criss-crossed the board in front of her. Quite by accident, she connected a caller to the wrong telephone. In her haste to correct the mistake, she unplugged two other calls in progress and then reconnected them to the wrong person until, with an exasperated cry, she pulled every single cable from the board, tore the earphones from her head and sat staring at the lifeless thing in front of her. A trickle of sweat ran down her temple.

'Cuppa tea?'

It was a girl sweeping up in the corridor, and she must've seen what Mabel had done.

'Never ends, does it?' the girl added.

'No, it doesn't seem to,' Mabel said weakly. 'Thank you, I'd love a cup of tea.'

The incoming line began to ring.

Mabel made certain to ring Miss Kerr at the end of the day – using her new skills at the switchboard – to report she'd carried out the job to Madame Franc's satisfaction. 'Satisfaction' might've been too strong a word, given that mid-afternoon, the dressmaker had shouted down the stairs, 'Is anyone on the bloody telephone?' But, then again, no one came to replace her. Mabel left with a new respect for telephonists.

'Hello, Bert,' Mabel said, approaching the stage door. 'Am I too early to catch Florrie?'

Bert looked at the time. 'You are. The girl usually slides on in about half an hour before the show.'

'I'll come back then,' she said. 'I only want a quick word with her. Will you tell her?'

'I will.'

Mabel trooped back across the green and into New River House as Mr Chigley emerged from his quarters with a cup of tea in hand.

'Miss Canning,' he said, laying the cup on his desk and going over to the wall of letter boxes. 'You are much sought-after today.'

'Thank you, Mr Chigley,' she said, and stuffed them in her pocket.

She went up to her flat and ate a boiled egg, along with the dried end of a loaf and the last of the butter. She checked out the window, where she saw no tall, thin man in a brown suit watching her window.

About half an hour before the first evening show at Collins, she walked back across the green and to the stage door, where Florrie stood waiting.

'Bert said you were looking for me. Have you found him?' Florrie said, bouncing slightly on the balls of her feet.

'I have a bit of news,' Mabel said, at once aware how small that bit was. 'Do you have a few minutes?'

At that moment, there was a commotion from the backstage corridor behind Bert and a group of young men came tumbling out, laughing and knocking into each other. They sobered up as they passed Bert, who gave them the eye, and went off into the night.

Florrie clicked her tongue. 'Daft Boys,' she said to Mabel.

'Are they?' Mabel asked. 'Let's stop Martin – I want to ask him a few questions about Claude.'

'Oi!' Florrie called after the men. 'Where's Martin?'

The four looked at each other as if counting their number and then turned round, walking backwards.

'Forgot his hat?' one of them suggested. And off they went.

'Never mind,' Mabel said. 'Let's go and sit on the green, shall we?'

They sat on a bench at the edge of the green. Dusk had started to settle and even though the sky was not completely dark, the gas lamps had come on and one blazed nearby. People rushed past on the pavement. In London, Mabel had learnt, everyone was in a hurry.

Florrie looked at Mabel and said, 'So?'

'I realise I haven't come up with any news for you,' Mabel said, 'but I believe I've found the place where Claude's mum worked. Gilbey's in Camden Town – they distil and brew and import wine. Now that I know that, you see, I can go to their offices and ask about her and that will lead us to Claude. But anything else you can tell me about him, Florrie, even the smallest detail, would help. For example, I don't know what he looks like.'

'Oh!' Florrie laid her hand on her heart. 'He's terribly handsome.'

When the young woman offered nothing else but a lovesick sigh, Mabel said, 'I'm sure he is. But what are his features? Try to describe him to me, so that if I saw him, I would know it was Claude.'

'Yes, all right.' Florrie screwed up her mouth in concentration. 'His hair is sort of reddish. He's not a ginger, though – it's darker than that. And he has a sort of round face and a really lovely smile.' She looked off into the middle distance with a smile of her own. 'I can just see him now walking through the green towards me wearing that old greatcoat.'

EIGHTEEN

Greatcoat?

The word slapped her across the face. Claude wore a greatcoat? They were not a rarity, Mabel reminded herself, but
neither were they that common. When soldiers returned from
the war, they exchanged their uniforms for clothing vouchers,
and so, many greatcoats were handed back to His Majesty's
Government. But not all. Mabel knew an old fellow in Peasmarsh who wore his son's greatcoat as a sort of memorial. His
son had returned from war but had died at home not long after
Armistice Day.

'You all right there?' Florrie asked, looking closely at Mabel.

'Yes, yes,' was all she could reply as her mind built connections with what she knew, rather like working the telephone
exchange. The man in the greatcoat who fell dead on Rosalind's
doorstep had no name, and no one of his description had been
reported missing. Claude had a name – if only one, at the
moment – and he'd gone missing. Had no one reported him?

Mabel glanced at Florrie, who appeared lost in her
daydream, and saw the benefit of talking over and over again
with a witness. If you just kept them talking, there was no

telling what detail may shake loose from the rafters of their minds and come tumbling out. The greatcoat meant nothing to Florrie, but for Mabel, it was the key.

'That'll show Martin, when you find Claude,' Florrie said with glee. 'The more I think on it, the more I don't know that Martin himself hasn't said something to Claude to scare him off.'

Martin, again. What's he got to do with all this? Mabel wondered.

'I'd best get back for the second show,' Florrie said, and Mabel accompanied her to Collins with one more question.

'When was the last time you saw Claude?'

Florrie paused at the start of the passageway that led to the stage door and screwed up her face. 'Friday week,' she said. 'He came round between shows. He was ever so sweet – promised to take me out for a proper meal in a restaurant soon.'

Friday week? The day before Guy Despard's wake.

As she returned to New River House, Mabel thought on what she'd just learnt. Here he was, the man in the greatcoat, presented to her on a platter by Florrie. But was it Claude who fell dead on Rosalind's doorstep, or were these two different men wearing greatcoats? What would Florrie's beau have to do with Guy Despard?

Mabel couldn't untangle this without help, but she couldn't go to Scotland Yard with such a flimsy notion. No, first she would go to Camden Town and find Claude's mother's house and perhaps something concrete that would connect them.

She hurried up the stairs and knocked on Winstone's door and as soon as he opened it, she said, 'We need to go to Camden Town. The man in the greatcoat – I may have found out who he is.'

Winstone took his hat from a peg by the door. 'I'll find a taxi.'

Later, Mabel would remember how he had believed her without question, and acted on the spot. It was the first true vote of confidence in her skills, apart from his admiring her ability to copy handwriting.

'Wait,' Mabel said, putting a hand on his arm, because her mind had raced ahead and seen a problem. 'Now that I think about it, perhaps you should ring Inspector Tollerton. There'll be a search involved, and we can't do it all on our own. I can explain more on the way. Will he take your word for it?'

'I'll do my best.'

But the only telephone in the building was on the wall in the foyer, mere inches from the porter's window. How could Mr Chigley not hear a call to the police?

'I'd rather you didn't telephone from here,' Mabel whispered, even though the door was closed. 'Mr Chigley is in regular contact with my papa, and I haven't had the opportunity yet to explain my—'

'Your new career in crime?' Winstone asked. 'I'll go to the Underground station and use theirs.'

'Yes,' Mabel said, 'you can tell them you're with Scotland Yard, as you did my cabbie.'

'It worked, didn't it?' Winstone crouched in front of Gladys. 'You stay here, girl, and I'll take you out for a long walk when I return.' To Mabel, he said, 'Where shall I tell Tolly to meet us? "Somewhere in Camden Town" is a bit vague.'

'At the offices for Gilbey's – it's possible Claude's mum worked there.'

'Who is Claude?'

'I suspect he is the dead man in the greatcoat.'

Winstone nodded. 'I'll see you outside in fifteen minutes.'

He left, and Mabel took the opportunity to dash to her flat

to freshen up. On her way back to the landing, she heard Cora and Skeff coming down the stairs and so waited for them.

'May I walk out with you?' Mabel asked quietly.

'You may walk out with us and all the way to Notting Hill, if you like,' Skeff said. 'There's a coffee house there that's a favourite of ours.'

'Is it about the man who was following you?' Cora whispered. 'Do you need another disguise?'

'No, it's...' Mabel lost her train of thought for a moment as images of the music hall popped into her head. 'It isn't that. I want to explain all this to you as soon as I can, but for the moment, I'd rather Mr Chigley didn't enquire about where I'm going.'

'Righto,' Skeff said. 'Leave it to us.'

They proceeded down the stairs, where Mr Chigley greeted them warmly, and out of the blue, Cora and Skeff began a lively description of an organisational meeting of the National Union of Societies for Equal Citizenship they'd recently attended.

'Previously known as the National Union of Women's Suffrage Societies, as you may recall,' Skeff said, and began a potted history of the movement as the three women moved out the door, each of them giving a wave before it closed.

They stopped on the doorstep, and Skeff nodded to Winstone, who waited with a taxi.

'I see you have another engagement,' Skeff said.

'Yes, I'm off,' Mabel said.

'Toodle-oo!' Cora called.

'Inspector Tollerton agreed?' Mabel asked. The taxi swerved round a stopped bus, and Mabel was thrown against Winstone. 'Sorry,' she said.

'"Agreed" may be too strong a word. I told Tolly you had a

lead, and I told him where we would be. He'll see us there, but he'll want to know more. And so do I.'

Mabel had gathered her thoughts as best she could.

'Remember I told you I was helping Florrie from the music hall find her beau, Claude?' Winstone nodded. 'It seemed as if he'd gone off her and she was taking it hard, and so I thought I could at least look for him for her – make him tell her to her face that he was ending it. Thing is, she doesn't know his surname and all I had to go on was that he'd lived with his mum who worked at a drinks firm in Camden Town before she died in the summer.'

'Gilbey's?'

'Yes, Gilbey's. I thought I might go and ask about her myself, but first I needed a description of him and just now when I talked with Florrie, she told me that he always wore a greatcoat.'

Winstone's brow furrowed. 'You believe he's the dead man?'

'She described him as I remembered him – dark red hair, round face. And the last time she saw him was the day before the wake.' Mabel frowned. 'It isn't much, is it?'

The taxi took a sharp left turn as Winstone exhaled.

'No, it's good,' he said. 'It's more than the police have at the moment.'

Mabel looked out the window of the taxi.

'Where are we?' she asked. 'What's that round building?'

'Piano factory, ma'am,' the cabbie said.

'Are these all warehouses?'

'They've everything here – bottle stores and their own railyards.'

But it was the end of the day and no one was about. They came to an office building, and the taxi stopped behind two police cars already parked. Tollerton got out of one and three uniformed police constables out of the other.

Winstone paid the cabbie, who drove off.

The inspector stuck his hands in the pockets of his coat and said, 'Miss Canning, what are you doing here?'

'It's Miss Canning who has got you this close, Tolly,' Winstone said. 'Let her explain.'

She did. She put it to the inspector as she had to Winstone, explaining the tenuous connection of a greatcoat between Florrie's Claude and the dead man on the doorstep. And his description.

While she talked, Tollerton wrote in his notebook, frowning all the while. He was still frowning when she'd finished.

'Why did Miss Hart ask you to look into the disappearance of this Claude?' Tollerton asked.

'He'd been attentive and then stopped coming round. The last time she saw him was the day before the wake. She was afraid he'd thrown her over and asked me for help because she could tell I sympathised with her and was willing to listen. It isn't the sort of thing you go to Scotland Yard with, is it? You see, I wasn't intentionally looking for the man who died on Rosalind's doorstep – if that's who he is.'

'All right, thank you, Miss Canning for this information.' Tollerton nodded to the dark building. 'All gone home in there, but there are a few streets of houses that have been split into flats. We'll go door-to-door this evening and come back to the business tomorrow. Now, I'll have one of the constables drive you home.'

'What?' Mabel said. 'No, I'm here to help find out what happened to Claude.'

'This is a police investigation,' Tollerton said, 'and we may uncover vital details in a murder case.'

'Which you wouldn't be able to if it hadn't been for me.' Mabel put her hands on her hips. 'You can't stop me from knocking on doors.'

Winstone wiped his face in what may have been an attempt to cover a smile, but the snort that escaped betrayed him.

'Miss Canning and I will work a street together, Tolly,' he said. 'Will that satisfy you?'

The inspector chewed on the inside of his cheek for a moment and then muttered, 'You might as well because you're two of a kind.'

'Thank you, Inspector,' Mabel replied.

She and Winstone crowded together in the back of one of the police cars and rode the short distance back beyond Gilbey's buildings to the bottom of a street with terraces on either side that appeared to go into infinity. Mabel saw a finger of fog creep round the corner at the top. The gas lamps were few and far between. A few heads popped out of the houses nearest them, but the rest of the street was quiet.

People were indoors sitting down to their tea, Mabel thought. *Too bad we'll interrupt.*

'Hello, I'm Mabel Canning, and this is Mr Winstone. We are looking for a man named Claude whose mother was a cleaner at Gilbey's. She died in the summer, but she might've lived round here, and we believe Claude stayed in her house. He often wore a greatcoat. Do you know him?'

By the tenth door, Mabel had her piece off pat, but it was to no avail. Most thought that Mabel and Winstone were from the Salvation Army. The women who came to the door spoke to Mabel readily, but the men addressed their answer to Winstone. Neither Claude nor his greatcoat struck a chord with anyone.

The going was terribly slow because almost every house had been divided into flats, and that multiplied the number of doors they knocked on fivefold. They made a note of the flats where no one answered. Mabel tried not to despair but knew at this rate, it would be days before everyone had been tracked down. What if it all came to naught?

The fog rolled towards them as they made their way up the

street, so that when at last they reached the top, the houses at the bottom had vanished. Children had come back out for one last bit of play before bedtime, but they couldn't be seen, and their voices echoed in strange ways that made them seem near one second, then far in the distance the next.

'We'll move one street over and work our way down,' Mabel said to Winstone, her determination fighting with a sense of hopelessness.

'No, you won't,' Tollerton said, emerging from the fog.

'I'm sorry if I've led you on a wild-goose chase, Inspector,' she said.

'Not at all, Miss Canning,' he replied. 'This is the nature of police work. We'll go as long as we can this evening and finish tomorrow.' One of the police cars pulled up. 'Drake here will take you home.'

'Tolly—' Winstone started.

'Both of you.' Tollerton turned, spoke to the other constables and they walked off.

Winstone glared after Tollerton's disappearing figure.

Police Constable Drake climbed out of the car and opened the door, and Mabel got in, followed, after a moment, by Winstone. He huffed and grumbled as they started off, but then he leant forward and spoke to the constable in a conversational tone.

'Long day, Drake?' he asked. 'At least it can seem like it sometimes, can't it?'

'Yes, sir,' Drake said.

'But Inspector Tollerton's a good man, I know that. We worked together before the war.'

'Did you, sir?'

'Have you been in the force long?'

'Joined up as soon as I got back in '18.'

'Where were you?' Winstone asked.

By the time Drake had turned the car and driven down to

the bottom of the terrace, the two men had fallen into an easy exchange about French champagne.

'Can't drink it,' Drake said. 'Gives me wind something terrible.' He glanced in the mirror at Mabel. 'Begging your pardon, ma'am.'

'Would you drive us back through Gilbey's, Drake?' Winstone said.

'Yes, sir,' Drake replied.

It was well and truly dark, and the thick fog made the world seem impenetrable, the warehouses, bottle shops and railyard appearing only at the last minute as the constable drove along the deserted lanes. Then Mabel saw a smudge of light up ahead, and as they neared, she recognised the offices where they'd met the police.

'I'll get out just here, Drake,' Winstone said. 'You take Miss Canning back to Islington. No need to wait for me.'

Mabel's head whipped round as the car came to a stop.

'But, sir—' Drake said.

'And I'll explain to Inspector Tollerton that I insisted.' He laid a hand on Mabel's. 'Go home, and I'll see you there.'

Winstone hopped out the door and closed it.

'Park!' Mabel shouted after him, with half a mind to follow.

He gave her a quick smile through the window and hurried off.

'Miss Canning,' Drake said, looking back at her, 'where in Islington am I taking you?'

It took Mabel only a moment to decide. 'To Collins Music Hall, please.'

'Do you live close, ma'am?' PC Drake asked, when he'd pulled up in front of Collins.

The journey to Islington had been torturously slow as the

police car crept along the roads, but finally they'd arrived. The delay had not lessened Mabel's decision.

'Only a few steps,' she said. 'I can see my way from here.'

From Camden Town to Islington, they'd driven in and out of the fog. Here at the green, it was quite thick, but the street lamps would guide her. But she wasn't finished with the day and needed someone to talk with.

'Thank you, Constable. Good evening,' Mabel said, giving Drake a wave before turning and making her way down the passage to the stage door.

'Hello, Bert,' Mabel said. 'Has everyone left? I was hoping to catch Cyril.'

Although not far, the journey from Camden Town had seemed interminable because of the fog. She had assured Constable Drake that letting her off in front of Collins was best because she wanted to 'check on a friend.' She'd hurried out of the police car and had given him a wave before he could ask any questions.

'The second show's not long finished,' Bert said, 'and Cyril's still round. You'll find him inside – down the corridor, first door on the left. He's the only one with his own dressing room. Want me to show you the way?'

'No, it's fine. Thanks.'

Mabel had never been backstage at any sort of theatre. The church hall in Peasmarsh had been the best venue for plays and shows and pantomimes. It had a stage a couple of feet high, but there were no backstage passages and certainly no dressing rooms. In the church hall, when a performer went off stage to change costume or make the next entrance from the opposite side, there was a mad dash down the three steps into the audience, along the side aisle, out the door and round to the other door, and then up the opposite aisle. All this added up to missed cues, out-of-breath performers and, often, costumes hastily pulled on backwards. It also meant that often the best part of the show was not actually on the stage.

But Collins Music Hall was a true theatre. It carried the scent of paint and glue and the lingering smell of paraffin that had been used for lighting in the days before electrification. Passages led off the main corridor to who knows where – the place was dark and labyrinthine and lit with only the occasional dim sconce. The building creaked and sighed as if glad the day was over.

Mabel found Cyril's dressing room marked with a gold-painted star. She knocked, but there was no answer. She waited a moment and knocked again, then, because the door wasn't closed all the way, she put her nose in.

'Cyril?' she asked the emptiness, just to be polite, and then stepped in.

A small lamp burnt on the dressing table, doubling its light in the reflection of the mirror, which itself was strung with bulbs like a necklace, although these were switched off. Half-squeezed tubes of make-up and pots of colour were lined up in an open wooden box that showed its age. There were brushes and combs and wigs. A cloth stained with a rainbow of colour hung off a peg, and there was a hat rack and a long rod that held costumes.

There were photographs stuck in the frame of the mirror, on the back of the dressing screen in the corner and lining what little wall was available – and they were all of Cyril on stage. It was a veritable cavalcade of his music-hall career. In some photos, Cyril was alone. In others, he stood in front of a chorus of young women. In one, he posed with a partner and when Mabel looked close, she saw that it was Rosalind wearing the shimmering dress that Florrie now wore on stage.

'Miss Canning!' Cyril exclaimed.

She whirled round. 'Hello. I hope you don't mind I came in – I did knock first. I haven't touched anything.'

Cyril laughed. 'You're very welcome any time.'

'I was admiring your photographs,' she said.

'Mmm,' he said with a smile of chagrin. 'It's beginning to look a bit like a museum in here, I'm afraid. But never mind, we'll soon fix that.' He reached over to his make-up table and picked up a half-empty bottle of whisky. 'Gert and I were just sitting down for a wee dram at the end of the day. Won't you join us?'

NINETEEN

Mabel followed Cyril out, further down the corridor and into a large room. Along one wall were mirrors and counters piled with make-up. A row of counters and mirrors ran down the middle, too, and the other wall held a rack of costumes. At the far end of the room were a few chairs, one of them occupied by Mrs Farraday.

'Look who I've brought back, Gert,' Cyril said. 'Miss Canning stopped in for a visit.'

'Hello, Mrs Farraday,' Mabel said. 'We met at the wake for Guy.'

'Hello, love, wouldn't have forgotten that now, would I? Lovely to see you again.'

'Has your daughter already left?' Mabel asked.

'Yes, she and her friends have gone off to the cinema.'

'The cinema,' Cyril said with a growl, as he poured the drinks and handed them out. 'They're getting too familiar with the enemy there, Gert. You should tell her as much. If we let it, cinema will be the death of us. We need to prepare for battle.'

'Oh, go on, Cyril,' Mrs Farraday said, and gave a short laugh. 'It's just a picture show.'

'The enemy is at the gate,' Cyril remarked, 'and we must do all we can to repel him.'

'I've a good few years on you, Cyril,' Mrs Farraday said, 'and I don't hold out much hope of a music hall revival.'

'But you must,' Cyril insisted. 'It'll come round. I know that for certain. Yes, it may seem like a never-ending stretch of closures, but we are going to put a full stop to that.'

Mabel reckoned Cyril could be one of those street-corner preachers if he set his mind to it – his intensity and enthusiasm would catch on.

'We'll see,' Gert said amiably. 'Now, Miss Canning, how is Mrs Despard doing? I know Cyril gets terribly worried about her.'

'Holding up,' Mabel replied, unwilling to go into further detail.

Cyril gave Mabel the slightest of nods and a fleeting smile.

'Miss Canning and I are keeping an eye on her,' he said.

'And her brother is too,' Mabel added.

'Indeed,' Cyril said, lifting his glass. 'We mustn't forget Park.'

Mrs Farraday had finished her whisky, and when Cyril offered another, she declined.

'I've mending to do tomorrow before the matinee or Anne will fairly burst out of her dress for the chorus, so I'd best be home now.'

'Good night, Gert,' Cyril called.

'Good to see you again,' Mabel said.

When Mrs Farraday had gone, Cyril rested his elbows on his thighs and said, 'Now, Miss Canning, what did you want to see me about?'

'It's been quite a day, and I'm not sure where to begin. Here's one thing – I may be closer to finding Florrie's Claude.'

'You never are?' Cyril asked, sitting up at once. 'How did you manage that?'

'I'm getting ahead of myself,' Mabel said. 'Really, it's only an idea. Do you remember what Claude looked like?'

'I never saw the fellow,' Cyril said, 'and I confess that I was suspicious of Florrie making the whole thing up. She does have quite an imagination.'

'I believe he's real, but it's only today that I got a fair description of him from Florrie. He wore a greatcoat.'

It was a significant statement as far as Mabel was concerned but appeared lost on Cyril because he looked as if he expected more.

'The man who died at the wake,' Mabel prompted. 'He wore a greatcoat too.'

'I didn't see the man at the wake,' Cyril said. 'I'd left for the matinee by the time that all broke loose, and by the time I returned, he'd been tidied away.'

Yes, Mabel remembered now that Mrs Farraday said as much. Cyril hadn't missed a show in twenty years, and he hadn't let Guy's wake stand in the way of his record. She chastised herself for that thought – look at how much of a comfort to Rosalind he'd been over the years.

'Well, I believe they are the same man. Could be at least. Florrie says that Claude's mum, who died, worked as a cleaner at Gilbey's in Camden Town, and so now Mr Winstone and the police are there trying to find out more. It may all have to do with a Michael Shaughnessy, the man mentioned in the letter Guy wrote to Rosalind.'

'Now,' Cyril said with a nod, 'there's a name I recognise. She's talked of nothing else these last few days since Hardcastle was found – wait now, that was you, wasn't it?'

'Yes,' Mabel said.

'Not part of your remit from that agency of yours, is it?' he asked.

'No.'

'And so, police believe this Shaughnessy murdered the solicitor,' Cyril said, as if going through it all in his mind. 'And Guy as well?'

'Possibly,' Mabel said. 'And if that's true, won't he go after Miss Roche, thinking she knows too much?'

'I suppose he would. But what are we to do, Miss Canning – you and I?' Cyril said, putting his glass down hard on the counter. 'What are our roles in all this except to commiserate?'

'I don't know,' Mabel admitted, 'I really don't. Police didn't seem all that happy for me to put my nose in their enquiry. And Mr Winstone wasn't too sure about me to begin with.'

'But you've proved yourself to him, surely.'

Mabel didn't answer.

'Look now,' Cyril said, 'we'll have to see what tomorrow brings, don't you think?' He rose and Mabel did likewise.

They walked back down the corridor and stopped at his dressing room, where Cyril collected his hat and walking stick. He tapped it twice on the floor.

'I say, Miss Canning. I went to the doctor and waited for hours. "Doctor, doctor," I said, "you're ignoring me." The doctor said, "Next!" *Boom-boom!*'

Mabel laughed.

Bert had gone when Mabel came out the backstage door and down the passageway and into the fog. The green, shrouded in grey with the trees half-materialised beings, looked as if it were playing a part in a Victorian ghost story. She'd left Cyril in his dressing room, assuring him that it would be no trouble getting back to her flat.

Now, she took a moment to orient herself. The fog compressed the light from the gas lamps to glowing orbs, but Mabel thought she could make out the one outside New River House – the one she could see from her flat. She wouldn't walk across the green, but instead, kept to the pavement, moving from lamp to lamp with care. There were few people about and even fewer cars, and she felt quite alone in the world.

When she reached the doorstep of New River House, her hair damp and even a bit greasy, she heard noises coming from the green. She turned, although could see nothing, and listened. Some shouting and then laughter. Perhaps the Daft Boys were having a night out.

The porter's office was empty as Mabel stepped into New River House, but the door to Mr Chigley's living quarters stood open. He'd be locking the front door soon, and alert to any key in the door, so Mabel had slipped in just before he might've made a comment on the hour. She made her way quietly up the stairs, pausing at Winstone's door. Had he returned? Shouldn't he come to her and tell her what he'd found? No, she thought, annoyed with being sent home by the police and Winstone. They were back in Camden Town in the thick of things and here she was, waiting.

In her flat, Mabel made herself a cup of tea and dunked a jumble in it. She looked out the window to a wall of grey, then sat on the sofa with her book. She wouldn't go to bed until she'd had word from Winstone, even if the word was that Mabel's wild hair about Claude had been a waste of police time.

She put her head back on the sofa and closed her eyes, but jerked awake at the sound of a car horn, panic gripping her chest. What was she doing? She shouldn't go to sleep now. Instead, she leapt up, and paced in front of the gas heater. To keep the panic at bay, she threw her energy full force into being annoyed at Winstone. Where was he? She would knock on his door, that's what she would do. Because how could he not come and tell her something. Anything.

He'd got out of the taxi when he saw lights in the offices at Gilbey's, and in her pique, Mabel had thought he was going

back to Tollerton, but now it came to her. The offices were
closed, but the lights were on because the cleaners were there.
He'd gone to ask about Claude's mum.

She pulled her hat and coat on and dropped her key in her
pocket. There was something else in there – Mabel patted the
pocket and remembered the post Mr Chigley had handed over
earlier.

At Winstone's door, she raised her hand to knock, but
paused when she heard Gladys whining.

'Gladys?' Mabel said.

The dog whined again, this time combined with a half-bark,
making it sound as if she were giving Mabel what for.

Winstone may not come back to New River House for
Mabel, but he would come back for Gladys because he'd
promised her a walk. So, where was he?

'Gladys, I'll be right back.'

Mabel hurried down to the foyer.

'Mr Chigley!' she called, knocking on the counter.

A light went on inside the porter's quarters, and he
appeared almost immediately.

'Miss Canning? What is it?'

'It's... you see...' It was no good telling the truth, it would
take too long. 'I told Mr Winstone I would take Gladys for a
walk while he was out, and I'm afraid I'm long overdue.'

'But it's late and the fog,' Mr Chigley said. 'It isn't a pea-
souper, but it's bad enough.'

'It's all right, I'll only go over the road to the green, and I'll
stay right along the edge. Could you let me into his flat to get
her?'

'Will do.'

The moment the door opened a fraction of an inch,
Gladys's nose was there to push her way out. She was a bundle
of wiggles, and all the while talking to them in half-barks and
throaty sounds.

'There now, girl,' Mr Chigley said, giving her a scratch.

Gladys licked his hand, but then gave Mabel her attention.

'I'll just go in and get her lead,' Mabel said, but instead of reaching for it on the wall by the door, she walked into the flat and all the way to the bedroom. No one was there. Nothing looked disturbed. She put away the fear that someone had somehow broken in. Ridiculous – Mr Chigley wouldn't allow it and even if the fellow had slipped by the porter, Gladys would've taken care of him. She turned and crossed back to the door. 'Silly me, here it is.' She took it off the peg and hooked it to Gladys's collar. 'Thank you, Mr Chigley. Here we go, Gladys.'

Mabel stepped to the kerb and looked back. The fog had instantly created a grey wall between her and the door of New River House. She listened. Although she couldn't see far, she could hear voices. She looked behind her to see a man and a woman, huddled together, walking by. She heard an engine, and when the car appeared on the road, Mabel judged that she could see about ten feet. The car crept by her, and Mabel caught a glimpse of the driver gripping the wheel, leaning forward and squinting. No one was speeding on this night. She listened for the sound of another car or the clop of a horse but heard nothing.

'Now, Gladys.' They hurried across, and Mabel stopped when they were safely on the other kerb and near a lamp, for all the good it did. 'Look, here's some grass and a few shrubs and a tree for you. We won't have to go far.'

Footsteps rushed towards her from the direction of Angel Station, and Mabel had time only to turn before the man knocked into her. She cried out and he grabbed her with one hand and his hat with the other.

'Sorry,' he said. 'Didn't see you—'

Mabel looked up at him, this tall, thin, young man wearing a brown suit.

'You!' she shouted and pulled away. Gladys barked and pulled on the lead and the man's eyes widened.

'Bloody hell!' he cried, turned tail and ran off in the direction he'd come.

Gladys went wild, barking, and nearly yanked the lead from Mabel's hands, but the dog wasn't after the tall, thin man. Instead, Gladys took off like a shot, barking furiously and pulling with such single-minded strength that Mabel had to clutch the lead with both hands to keep hold. She looked over her shoulder at where the man had been, but the fog had reclaimed his place. The dog dashed down paths, zigzagging into the depths of the green, Mabel dodging obstacles in her path as she saw them. What had seized Gladys's attention – a squirrel? A rat? Another dog?

They passed no one as they raced through the fog. Mabel attempted to cajole the dog into holding up, but Gladys was having none of it, straining against the lead if Mabel showed even the smallest inclination to slow. They reached the far corner of the green that resembled a thick hedgerow more than a city park, where the shrubs were as tall as Mabel. Here, the dog stopped, then began to burrow into the tangle of stems.

'Gladys, come out of there,' Mabel said, as she followed, the briers scratching and catching at her coat.

The dog responded with a *woof*, and then a groan.

A groan? That hadn't been the dog – there was someone in the thicket. Mabel thought the best course of action was to leave the person be.

'Gladys, come out!' she whispered furiously, and tugged on the lead. Gladys tugged back. All Mabel could see was the dog's backside, which wriggled with excitement.

There was another groan, and when Mabel pushed

through, she saw the head and shoulders of a man lying on the ground, his hat partially covering his face, but not so much that she didn't recognise him.

'Park!' she cried, and sank to the ground at Winstone's side.

TWENTY

Winstone groaned again and struggled to sit up, made more difficult either by his injuries or Gladys sitting on his chest in joyous reunion. He had a swollen eye, and a stream of blood from his forehead.

'Can you speak?' Mabel asked. She reached into his coat pocket, pulled out his handkerchief and dabbed at his face. The bleeding had stopped, but it was fresh. 'Are you badly hurt?'

'Yes, I can speak, Miss Canning,' he said in a rasping voice. 'No, I'm not badly hurt.'

Gladys sat down near the edge of the path as if acting as lookout.

'Who did this?'

Winstone put his hand to his head. 'I didn't see. He came from behind, whoever it was. I heard something and turned and had just time to—' He put his arm up as if to ward off a blow.

Mabel took his hand. A red wound ran across the back of it. 'Looks like you took the brunt of the blow here,' she said. 'Can you move your fingers?'

He wiggled them and winced.

She looked closer at the bloody mark on his forehead. 'It's

round,' she said. 'Like the one on Mr Hardcastle's head.' Hardcastle was dead and here was Winstone, alive, but he so easily could've ended the same. She shuddered. 'When did it happen? How long have you been here?'

'Not long, I don't think. When Tolly found me still at Gilbey's, he made certain I left. Drake brought me back and told me where he'd left you and so I was going to Collins to look for you. Whoever it was might've finished me off but for a group of yahoos coming through the green. He legged it.'

'I heard them,' Mabel said, remembering the shouting as she went back to her flat. 'Well, you can't stay here all night. Can you stand?'

'Yes, Miss Canning, I can stand,' Winstone said.

Exasperated, Mabel said, 'Oh, I do wish you would stop calling me "Miss Canning"!'

Winstone laughed, then coughed. 'You're giving me permission?' he asked.

'Yes,' she said, softer now. 'I give you permission.'

Winstone reached over, cupped her face in his hand and stroked her cheek with his thumb.

'Oh God,' he said, pulling his hand away, 'I've smeared blood on your face.'

Mabel laughed. 'Give me your handkerchief.' She found the cleanest spot and wiped her cheek. 'Better?' she asked.

He nodded. 'We can't both look as if we've been through the wars.'

They stood for a moment so that Winstone could get his balance.

'Do you think it was Shaughnessy,' Mabel said, 'and he's after anyone who might recognise him?'

'It could be,' Winstone said, 'but he's got the wrong end of the stick if he thinks I can identify him.'

'So, he's going after anyone he believes may be able to identify him. That would be you, Miss Roche and—'

'And Rosy.'

Mabel grabbed his arm. 'We need to tell the police,' she said.

'We need to get there. Let's go. No, wait,' Winstone said. 'My glasses.'

Mabel scanned the ground, but when Winstone raised his arm again, she said, 'Here – they caught on the sleeve of your coat.' She took them and polished the lenses with the hem of her skirt. 'At least they aren't broken.'

He put them on, and they emerged from the shrubbery. Gladys shook herself thoroughly, Mabel straightened her hat and Winstone brushed himself off. They crossed the road with care and went into New River House.

'He'll hear, so we might as well wake him up,' Mabel said. 'You go on, I'll try to explain.'

In the foyer, Winstone went straight to the telephone on the wall and, once the exchange answered, asked for Rosalind's number.

Mabel stopped at the porter's window and knocked lightly on the counter. 'Mr Chigley?'

The porter came out, pulling his jacket on over his pyjamas. 'Miss Canning, is something wrong? Oh, hello, Gladys.'

Gladys had stretched far enough to put her front paws on the counter.

Mabel glanced at Winstone, who gave her a dark look as he listened and waited. No one had answered and so he depressed the hook and spoke to the exchange again. 'Scotland Yard,' he said. 'Detective Inspector Tollerton. Yes, it is an emergency.'

Mr Chigley leant out over the counter. 'What's this about?'

'Mr Winstone was attacked in the green.'

'Dreadful,' Mr Chigley remarked. 'Well, he shouldn't have

to ring the police himself. Have him come and sit in the office here and I'll put the kettle on.'

'No,' Winstone was saying into the telephone. 'No, I won't wait. Find him and give him the message. Tell him to get to Rosy's. Tell him it's important, that—'

That it's a matter of life or death.

'That he's needed.' Winstone hung up and turned to Mabel. 'Let's go.'

'But the police,' Mr Chigley said. 'And you're hurt, I see.'

'We're going to meet the police at Mr Winstone's sister's house,' Mabel said, as they left. 'Everything's fine. I'll explain later.'

Out on the pavement, Winstone glared at the fog. 'We'd best go on the Underground. It would take too long in a taxi, even if we could find one.'

Mabel blocked her mind from defining 'too long' as they hurried down to Angel Station, Gladys trotting along beside. They bought tickets, rode down to the platform in the electric lift and soon a train came. Once settled in the car, there was nothing to do but think. She turned to Winstone.

'Good thing Bridget is there,' she said, hoping to hear encouraging words back from him.

Winstone didn't answer but took Mabel's hand and tucked it in the crook of his arm.

There was something Mabel didn't like about all this. Was it Shaughnessy protecting himself because he'd been stealing money from Guy's business? Hadn't Hardcastle been part of the scheme? Had the solicitor decided to give himself up and his partner in crime didn't like the idea? Where did Claude – that is, the man in the greatcoat – come into all of it? He had learnt of what they'd done, but kept it quiet for seven years? The only reason Mabel could think of for Claude to keep quiet was because he had been in on the plan, too, and the three of them needed to continue siphoning off money even with Rosalind running the company.

Too many holes.

The train rattled along. Gladys, at their feet, gave them the occasional anxious look. Mabel didn't enjoy her third journey on the Underground any more than she had enjoyed the first two. Cigar, pipe and cigarette smoke created a miasma that caught in her throat. She didn't like the darkness outside the window.

Winstone had them change from the Northern to the Piccadilly line at King's Cross, and when at last they got off for good at Hyde Park Corner Station, Mabel could breathe again. As they hurried off, she imagined that the fog was thinning, or perhaps she was becoming accustomed to making her way in it.

In Belgravia, Winstone stopped at the end of Rosalind's terrace where a path ran along the back of two terraces. The brick walls on either side stood six feet high.

'Shouldn't we go to the front door?' Mabel wondered aloud.

'And announce ourselves by pulling the bell?' Winstone said. 'If there's nothing going on, all we will face is Bridget's broom. If there is, we can at least be quiet about our entrance. I'll go this way. You wait out on the pavement. I'll go through the house and let you in.'

'Not likely,' Mabel said. 'I'm going with you.'

'There's no gate in the back,' Winstone replied.

'I've climbed a brick wall before,' Mabel said. She didn't mention there had been a handy buttress to give her a leg-up and that she had been ten at the time. 'Let's go.'

Mabel attempted to count the houses as they passed, but it was Winstone who knew when they reached Rosalind's. He stood tall enough to just see over the wall. Mabel stretched an arm up and could put her hand on the top easily but couldn't pull herself up that far.

'Right,' Winstone said. He locked his fingers together, bent down and put his hands in place. 'Over you go.'

She hitched up her skirt, put her foot on his makeshift step and, as she jumped, he lifted. She landed on her tummy atop the wall and clung there for a moment so she wouldn't go head-first down the other side. Her hat fell off and drifted to the ground. Trying not to think of the state of her stockings or what sort of picture she presented from behind, she wriggled her body until she'd turned herself round and then dropped into the yard and onto her hat.

'Mabel?' Winstone called.

'Yes, I'm all right.'

'Here comes Gladys, look out.'

Winstone set Gladys on top of the wall, and the dog nimbly jumped down. Winstone heaved himself over as Mabel looked at the house.

'There's a light on in Rosalind's bedroom.'

No other light showed, but their eyes had grown accustomed to the dark. They crept through the yard to the scullery door. It looked as if it had been kicked open, the lock hanging loose. Mabel's heart went to her throat.

Winstone put a hand up as caution, but Gladys had put her nose in the air and immediately trotted over to the door of the broom cupboard and scratched at it. There was a thump from within and then another. Gladys gave a low *woof*.

They tiptoed over. Winstone motioned for Mabel to stand back, then he lifted the thumb latch. The door flew open, and out tumbled Bridget.

She lay on the floor, her hands and feet tied together with what looked like garden twine. Her white apron looked stained with what Mabel prayed wasn't blood. Bridget's shock of red hair still exploded from the top of her white cap, but the cap sat askew. With all four limbs tied as one, she couldn't walk or scoot or roll, only wiggle. Her mouth was stuffed with rags and tied over with a strip of linen, but that didn't stop her from talking in a fierce tone. The words were unintelligible, but the meaning clear.

'I need a knife to cut this,' Winstone said.

'Here.' Mabel leant over to the dresser, pulled open a drawer and retrieved the garden shears she used for flower arranging.

Bridget held still while Winstone cut the string at her hands and feet. Once freed, she stretched and rubbed her hands and continued her tirade until he'd got her gag untied. She pulled the rags out of her mouth, spat and struggled to stand.

'Where is he?' she shouted. 'Wait'll I get my hands on him!' The words choked out of her with a cough. 'He's not long for this world, I can tell you that. Help me up here, I'll strangle him with my own two hands.'

'Where is he? Does he have Rosy?' Winstone asked.

'Don't you know?' Bridget asked, holding on to the back of a chair. 'Don't you have her? Mother of God.'

That news had taken the steam out of Bridget's advance, and she sank into a chair, breathing heavily.

'Listen now,' she said, 'and I'll tell you what I know, although it isn't much.' She put her hand on her forehead and closed her eyes. 'I heard a noise back here and I came to see and heard something else, like a *tap-tap*. There was the door open. But, before I could think, he was on me.'

'Who was it?' Winstone asked. 'Can you describe him?'

'Never laid eyes on him – he came at me from behind. When he grabbed me, I put up a fight, but he had the advantage of surprise, I suppose. And then... well, the next thing I knew, I woke up in the broom cupboard.'

Winstone leant close to Bridget and sniffed. 'Chloroform,' he said.

Mabel came close, too, and caught a whiff of a sweetish odour.

'He wouldn't take her anywhere,' Mabel said. 'They must still be here.'

'You know who it is?' Bridget asked. 'Tell me who and I'll see to him.'

'We think it might be Michael Shaughnessy,' Winstone said. 'Come on.'

They crept out of the scullery to the entry, Bridget with broom in hand, and stopped at the bottom of the stairs. From somewhere above came the faint sound of singing – a woman's voice, the notes echoing in the stillness.

'That's "Let's Go Down to the Strand",' Bridget whispered.

'Stay here,' Winstone said, and put his hand on the newel. 'I'll go up.'

Mabel put her hand on his. 'I'm going too.'

He nodded. 'Bridget, we've sent Tolly a message, but I don't know when he'll get here. You go down to the corner. You know what to do. Take Gladys with you.'

Bridget nodded. 'C'mon, girl,' she said to Gladys, and the two headed for the front door.

Winstone led the way upstairs and Mabel followed, putting her feet just where he had, hoping he knew the stairs well enough to avoid any loose boards that would creak. They turned on the first-floor landing and climbed to the second floor, and it was there on the landing that a board squeaked. Winstone and Mabel froze. The singing stopped, and there was a small cry. They rushed into the room but pulled back at once.

They stood across the room. He had Rosalind's arms pinned to her side and he held a straight razor to her throat.

It was Cyril.

TWENTY-ONE

Rosalind was the picture of calm. She wore silk pyjamas and over them her silk dressing gown in a Chinese print with a king-fisher-blue background. Her face was pale as cream with two bright pink spots on her cheeks as if she'd put on make-up. Her eyes were large and dark.

'It's all right,' Rosalind said in a trembling voice. 'I'm all right.'

They were next to Guy's dressing table, and Mabel glanced down to the neatly laid-out shave set that was missing one item – the straight razor held to Rosalind's throat.

'Cyril,' Winstone said in a calm, even voice. 'Let Rosy go.'

'I should've known it would be the two of you,' Cyril said. It was almost a snarl as if his face, always on the verge of a smile, had dropped its mask. 'The nosy parkers, interfering where they're not wanted.'

'Let her go,' Winstone repeated. 'Please.'

'Are you giving me orders?' Cyril said. 'You think I don't know what I'm doing? That I would ever hurt my girl? You could never understand it, could you – all the plans we've made for her return? You'll soon see our names in lights. Electric lights and all.'

'Then you don't want to hurt Rosalind by accident, do you?' Mabel asked, as her mind filled with questions. How had she not seen this? Had no one suspected him? Did Cyril have such a winning façade he could pull the wool over all their eyes?

'You,' Cyril said, pointing his chin at Mabel. 'Where did you come from? There's one thing Park and I can agree on, Miss Canning – we were both highly suspicious of your convenient appearance in this house. You're not even family.'

'Neither are you,' Winstone said. He had stepped sideways so slowly Mabel hadn't noticed.

'I'm better than family,' Cyril said, and Mabel saw the hand that held the straight razor shake. 'I didn't steal her away from what she loved.'

A long, high-pitched whistle sounded from outside – away, perhaps at the corner of the square, and as if to cover it, Rosalind said, 'Let's sing another song, Cyril. You join me this time. Let's sing "Where Did You Get That Hat". Remember when you did that one? Why don't we go down to the drawing room, and Park can play for us?'

'Oh no, none of that,' Cyril said. 'The boy doesn't believe in us, and I won't let him steal your limelight. We'll show them, we'll show them all.'

'Like you showed Claude?' Mabel asked. She, too, moved away, and now Cyril had to take his eyes off one to see the other. 'You remember Claude, the man who wore the greatcoat? Just this evening, I told you we'd found out who he was.'

'That poor man who died here?' Rosalind asked. 'Cyril?'

Mabel saw Cyril loosen and then tighten his grip on the razor.

'There was no point in him,' Cyril said with derision. 'He was telling second-hand stories and thinking it would get him somewhere. Saying I was at the station talking with Guy.'

'Guy?' Rosalind echoed.

'That was a lie,' Cyril said. 'Everyone knows I haven't missed a show in—'

'Twenty years?' Mabel asked. 'That's the lie, isn't it?'

The razor jerked as if Cyril would like to be holding it to Mabel's neck instead. 'Twenty years – everyone knows it's true.'

The whistle sounded again, and Mabel rushed to cover it.

'Or you think there's no one left who will remember it isn't?' Mabel asked. 'I daresay Bert will remember. You shouldn't've boasted about that, Cyril. Now, all Bert has to do is look it up in his ledger, and it'll show if you played the matinee that day or not.'

Cyril's eyes widened, and Mabel knew she'd hit her mark, but she saw the razor tremble. They were tantalisingly close to finding out what had happened to Guy, but had she gone too far? How could they get Rosalind free?

'What's that?' Cyril asked.

A long, low growl had replaced the whistle coming closer. It grew louder, and here came Gladys slithering in the door like a snake. She worked her way around furniture and people in the room, heading for Cyril and Rosalind.

'Get that thing away from me!' Cyril shouted, as he kicked out at the dog. 'Go on!'

With a loud bark, Gladys leapt at him, and Cyril threw out the arm holding the straight razor to defend himself. In midair, the dog twisted her body, avoiding the blade and clamping down on the wrist holding it.

Cyril screamed, let go of the razor and Rosalind and fell to the floor. Mabel ran to her, while Gladys held fast to her prey until Winstone put his foot down none too gently on Cyril's arm.

'Good girl,' Winstone said. 'That'll do.'

Gladys released Cyril's wrist, but he kicked out at her again, and so she snapped at his ankle. 'Not my legs!' he cried.

Winstone pulled him off the floor roughly and pushed him down on the chair. 'Shut your gob, or you'll find it stuffed with the same rags you used on Bridget.'

Mabel took Rosalind by the shoulders. She could feel Rosalind shaking – or was that Mabel herself? 'Come on, let's get you over to the sofa.'

Winstone pulled Cyril's arms behind the chair and tied him down with the cord from the curtain. 'We'll need something for his feet. Rosy?'

For a moment, Rosalind looked lost, and then she seemed to regain her strength. 'Here,' she said, taking the long silk belt from her dressing gown and holding it out. 'Use this.'

'You don't listen to them, my girl,' Cyril said to Rosalind. His tone was intimate and sugary. 'Don't listen to what they say.'

'She isn't a girl, Cyril,' Mabel said. 'Time doesn't stand still – not even for you.'

Winstone cinched Cyril's feet to the chair legs with a jerk.

'Why did you kill Claude?' Mabel asked. 'He did have proof, didn't he? Proof that you were with Guy the day he disappeared. And you wanted that proof, you wanted to get your hands on it before anyone else did.'

'What did you do to Guy?' Winstone asked. He leant over from behind and spoke in Cyril's ear.

Cyril cringed. 'That husband of yours could've restored you to your rightful place on the stage,' Cyril said, speaking only to Rosalind. 'But he refused.'

Rosalind had regained her colour and more. She rose, stalked across the room and stood over him. 'Tell me, Cyril. Tell me what you did to Guy.'

'He didn't believe in you.' Cyril shook his head. 'What sort of a marriage is that? He had the solution to our trouble in his pocket – all he had to do was buy us a music hall. The Albion was under the gavel – I begged him. But he refused.'

'I will never go back to the music hall,' Rosalind shouted at him. 'Haven't I said that enough?'

'But you...' Cyril struggled as he spoke, and Winstone jerked so hard on the man's collar that it popped open. When he loosened his hold, Cyril gasped and said, 'I only wanted to talk with him! That's why I followed him to Euston Station, to try to talk some sense into him. He wouldn't listen, but I had to give it another go, so I got on his same train – just to watch and wait for another opportunity. We'd got almost to Holyhead before he saw me and got off. Colwyn Bay. What did he think he was going to do there?' Cyril's story had taken him away from his present situation as if he could see the scene playing out on the stage. 'You needed to know the sort of man you had married,' Cyril said to Rosalind. 'It was his own fault. That he would take you away from all you loved.'

'What happened?' Rosalind's words were deliberate and void of emotion.

Cyril began to fidget, but Winstone, close behind, kept a grip on his arms. There was nowhere for him to go, and Cyril must've realised it because his bravado began to fade, leaving behind a weary man showing his age.

'We had a few more words. I tried to make him see the light, but he struck out at me. You remember that, my girl – he struck out at me. What else could I do but defend myself? It was only one kick.'

'The same way you murdered Claude,' Mabel said.

Cyril muttered something unintelligible.

'Did Guy get up?' Rosalind asked.

'Rosy,' Winstone said.

'I want to know,' Rosalind pressed. 'Did Guy get up again?'

'He didn't quite...' Cyril said, and his gaze dropped to the floor. 'We had walked down the platform, you see, to where the tracks curve, and when he hit me and I kicked out, he lost his balance and tumbled down the embankment into the wood. I couldn't stop him.'

The silence in the room grew heavy.

'And you walked away.' Rosalind's voice was thick. 'And said nothing.'

'I only wanted him to buy you a music hall,' Cyril repeated. 'What would that have been to him – nothing but pocket change. But now, my girl, it's all your money, isn't it?'

Rosalind balled up her fists, but Mabel reached her before she could attack.

Gladys barked an alarm, keeping it up as heavy and hurried footfalls were heard on the stairs. Winstone called the dog over, and a few seconds later, Inspector Tollerton burst into the room, followed by six or seven uniformed constables and, behind them, Bridget with her broom.

Tollerton took in the scene as Rosalind moved back to the sofa with Mabel. Gladys gave a final *woof*. At last, he looked at Winstone and said, 'Could you not have waited for me?'

Winstone reached for the straight razor where it had landed on the floor and held it up between thumb and forefinger. 'He had this to her throat when we arrived. No, I couldn't've waited.'

Tollerton took a sharp breath and turned to Rosalind. 'Are you all right, Mrs Despard?'

She nodded. 'Yes, Inspector. I'm quite glad to see you.' She nodded at Cyril. 'He's confessed to killing Guy.'

'Just as well he has,' Tollerton said, 'as we now have a witness statement that puts you at Euston Station and talking with Mr Despard.'

'Was it Claude in the greatcoat? Was it Claude who saw Cyril with Guy?' Mabel asked.

'Claude was the man in the greatcoat who died on the doorstep. It was Claude's brother who was the witness, as it turns out,' Tollerton said. 'We have written testimony as to that.

But, in addition to Mr Despard's murder and the murder of Claude Elliott, there's a third death Mr Godfrey here will need to answer for. Thomas Hardcastle.'

Cyril's eyes flickered to the inspector and away. 'Poor old Thomas,' he muttered. 'Such a loss.'

Three of the constables took Cyril downstairs, where Detective Sergeant Lett waited. The local constables, who had been called to the scene by a policeman's whistle, went back to their beats.

'A policeman's whistle,' Tollerton said, 'but not, as I understand it, blown by a policeman.'

'No, sir, that was me blowing the whistle,' Bridget said, broom at her side, standing at ease.

'Do you have your own Metropolitan Police whistle?' the inspector asked.

'It's mine,' Winstone said. 'My old one. I gave it to her.'

Tollerton sighed.

'Inspector,' Rosalind said, 'you won't be leaving yet, will you? I'll get dressed and come down to the drawing room, and Bridget can bring us coffee. Can you stay? I want to know what's happened.'

It was as if Tollerton suddenly became aware that Rosalind was in silk pyjamas and a loose silk dressing gown. He averted his eyes and spoke to the floor. 'Yes, thank you, Mrs Despard. I'll just have a word with Sergeant Lett before they take Mr Godfrey in.'

Mabel and Rosalind remained behind, as did Winstone. He came over and sat on the arm of the sofa next to his sister.

'How could I be deceived all these years?' Rosalind asked.

'You were grieving, and Cyril took advantage of that,' Mabel said. 'But he saw your fond memories as hope for what he wanted. It was all about him.'

'But why couldn't I see it?' Rosalind persisted.

'Sometimes, Rosy,' Winstone said, 'even when you are faced with incontrovertible evidence, if you don't want to believe something, you won't.'

Rosalind looked up at her brother with a half-frown, half-smile. 'That's a very wise thing to say.'

'It is, isn't it?' Winstone asked with good cheer. 'But it isn't my wisdom – it's Mabel's.'

'Is it now?' Rosalind said. She touched her brother's face. 'Did Cyril do that?'

'He did.' Winstone held out his hand with the mark across it. 'I realise now it's the brass knob on that damned walking stick of his. Knocked me out, and it was Gladys and Mabel who found me.'

Rosalind put her hand on Mabel's and gave it a squeeze. 'Well done. At this moment, it finally feels over, but I have to remind myself it isn't. Because tomorrow, the newspapers will start up, won't they? But for now, Park, go and wash your face and let me get dressed. Mabel and I will see you in the drawing room.'

As Winstone left, Bridget came in and took Mabel's coat for a good brushing. 'Found your hat in the scullery,' the maid said. 'Looks like you danced a jig on it. I'm not sure what I can do.'

'Never mind, I'll give it to Cora,' Mabel said. 'Hats are one of her specialties.'

Bridget left, and as Mabel washed her face and hands in the bathroom, she told Rosalind about Skeff and Cora.

'Are they part of Useful Women?' Rosalind asked.

'Not strictly, no,' Mabel said. 'They have their own work, but they've been ever so helpful. Skeff has a friend who guided me down to the docks. Cora's got quite the talent for disguises. She's the one who dressed me up so that I could walk right by that fellow following me and—' A blinding revelation hit her, and she stood stock-still with water dripping down her neck.

'Martin!' She saw his face clearly now, even though he'd tried to hide it under a hat. 'Martin is who has been following me. All along, I had thought it was something to do with Miss Roche's Irish lecture or Michael Shaughnessy, but instead, it was one of the Daft Boys.'

'I didn't know someone was following you,' Rosalind said with a voice of complaint.

'There was enough going on here,' Mabel said, 'it never occurred to me to tell you.'

'And, the Daft Boys. Is that the act at Collins?' Rosalind asked. 'You mean Cyril has had a hand in that too?'

'He must've. I saw Martin once the first time I went to the stage door. He'd been cheeky enough to wink at me and so the only impression I had of the man in the brown suit, even when I saw his face again, was that he reminded me of young Mr Jenks, who lives in our building. Cheeky sort too. He sells bobbins.'

Rosalind laughed. 'I need to be caught up on all this,' she said. 'But now, if Cora designs hats, what does Skeff do?'

'Skeff is a newspaperwoman.'

Rosalind's face dropped.

'No,' Mabel said, 'don't worry. She works for her uncle's paper, the *London Intelligencer*. Her uncle wouldn't give an inch to innuendo and rumour – he has integrity, as all newspapers should. Let the rags print what they like, Skeff would write an even-handed report of this entire affair. Your story, Guy's story. You could give her an exclusive and beat the others to the punch. You can trust Skeff.'

'I trust you,' Rosalind said, 'and if you trust Skeff, then so will I. Bring her round tomorrow.'

Rosalind donned a yellow day dress that reminded Mabel of autumn chrysanths. Mabel combed her hair and dusted off her dress. There was little hope for her stockings – the holes were too large.

The women met the men in the drawing room, where Gladys was stretched out in front of the fire.

'I believe it's brandies all round, don't you think, Mabel?' Rosalind said.

Winstone poured, and they sat down as if it were not – Mabel looked at her watch – one o'clock in the morning. Bridget brought a tray of coffee and sandwiches and then gave Tollerton her account of events, up until she was put out with chloroform. Then she said good night.

The four of them began talking through what had happened then.

'All right, Inspector,' Rosalind said, 'tell us everything.'

'I'm hoping to learn something myself,' Tollerton said, eyeing Mabel and Winstone. 'But first I'll say that Michael Shaughnessy gave himself up this afternoon, apparently at the urging of Miss Gabrielle Roche.'

'So she did know him,' Mabel said.

'She knew him under another name,' Tollerton said.

'It wouldn't be Osgood, would it?' Rosalind asked.

'Yes, it would, Mrs Despard.' Tollerton waited for more.

'I found a discrepancy in the business accounts, and with the help of a bookkeeper Mabel knows, we could see that Thomas had been stealing from Guy for years using fake employees. They were all named Osgood, but with different Christian names. I'll give you the details.'

Tollerton smiled at Rosalind. It was a small smile, but the first one Mabel had seen from the man, and it occurred to her he could be quite pleasant if he set his mind to it. 'Thank you, Mrs Despard. I have to say, Hardcastle wasn't one of those fellows to put his ill-gotten gains away for a rainy day. Have you ever been to his house?'

'Never,' Rosalind said.

'It's like walking into one of the rooms at the British Museum – chock-full of vases, urns, figurines – all breakable and all apparently quite expensive. I was afraid to turn round in the place. In addition to his charwoman, he employed a valet, a butler, a housemaid and a cook.'

'How many servants does one man need?' Mabel asked.

'He had a chauffeur, but no car,' Tollerton added. 'He liked his rich life, and he found a way to pay for it.'

'Cyril thought he could make Mr Hardcastle's murder look as if it were part of the theft?' Rosalind asked.

'Cyril must've heard us talking about it,' Mabel said. 'He was here in the drawing room and you and Effie were in the study, but you and I spoke in the entry. Mr Hardcastle came and was so nervous and told you he knew someone who had wanted money from Guy. I wonder if he was only talking out of his hat or did he know something about Cyril? And then I told you about the meeting Mr Hardcastle had down at the docks.'

'And so it was Cyril at the docks,' Winstone said.

'Mr Hardcastle had the same sort of round wound you do,' Mabel said. *But he's dead*, she added to herself.

'His walking stick.'

'I want to hear about Guy,' Rosalind said. 'I want to know about the man who died here and what he had to do with it all.'

Winstone poured another round.

'During the investigation of your husband's disappearance in 1914,' Tollerton said, 'Park wanted to ask at Euston Station if anyone remembered seeing Mr Despard, knowing he had so much business in Ireland, and thinking he might've taken the Irish Mail to Holyhead and then over to Dublin on the ferry. The inspector at the time ignored the idea, but Park asked regardless.'

'Inspector Burge,' Mabel said, and Tollerton's gaze went from her to Winstone.

'We could've found someone if we'd kept asking,' Winstone said, 'but we were called off.'

'But that's just what Guy intended, wasn't it?' Rosalind

asked. 'He must've been on his way to see Michael Shaughnessy about the discrepancy in the accounts. I wonder if he didn't already suspect Thomas, but wanted to work his way up. Guy always preferred face-to-face talks with the men who worked for him.'

'Cyril said it was Colwyn Bay where they got off,' Winstone said. 'Where there's a curve in the track, and some woods at the bottom.'

Tollerton nodded. 'We'll contact police there tomorrow.'

'You found Claude's mother's house?' Mabel asked.

'We did, Miss Canning,' Tollerton said. 'We've got the connection now, and it's thanks to you and your interest in helping that young woman. Claude Elliott had been living in Southampton since before the war. He wasn't fit for service, but did work in the boatyards. Claude came back to London this summer when his mother wrote to say she was ill. Mrs Elliott had worked as a cleaner all her life, the last ten years or so for Gilbey's. The elder son was killed early on in the war, and a box of his effects was sent back. A neighbour who knew her well told us Mrs Elliott could never get up the strength to open it. "She was that broken up about the boy," the woman said.'

'We all deal with grief in our own way,' Rosalind said.

'After his mother passed, Claude opened the box,' Tollerton explained. 'At least we found it open and assume it was him. Inside, there was a letter written by your husband, saying that the brother, James Elliott, would have a job with him when he returned from the war. There was another letter, this one from James to his mother, but never sent. It might've been written in the trenches nearly upon his arrival. He told her how he had met Mr Guy Despard at Euston Station and had been offered work after the war. Apparently, his mother loved the music hall because James made special mention of spotting Serious Cyril from the Grand. He wrote that he'd seen Cyril talking with this Mr Despard in the station. It was the day James left for the war – the twenty-third of September.'

'Claude was using the letter his brother had written to their mother and was blackmailing Cyril?' Mabel asked.

'Or attempting to,' Winstone said. 'It was his mistake if he thought that because Cyril was on the stage, he had money. So Cyril had to stop Claude before the truth got out that he'd seen Guy on the day Guy disappeared.'

'Cyril killed him without a second thought,' Rosalind said. 'Cyril killed Guy because Guy wouldn't give him money and he killed Claude to cover that up. Cyril wanted money. He wanted it to buy a music hall, no matter how many people he had to murder to get it.'

TWENTY-TWO

It was after two o'clock when the gathering broke up. Bridget had not gone to bed, after all, but brought up Mabel's coat and hat and stood waiting for Rosalind. Tollerton sent Winstone, Mabel and Gladys home in the remaining police car and telephoned for another to collect him.

The insides of Mabel's eyelids felt as if they were coated in grit, and her entire body cried out for bed. On the journey back to Islington, Gladys yawned on the seat between them, Winstone put his head back and dozed and Mabel might've fallen asleep, but for the fact that when she put on her freshly brushed coat, she felt paper crackle in the pocket, and remembered the post Mr Chigley had given her. As they motored through the deserted streets – clear of both people and fog – she pulled the letters out. Here was one from Ronald. His handwriting carried something of the ecclesiastical about it with its little serifs and extra dots and when she saw it, she heard organ music.

Mabel,

I'm having dinner with the bishop this evening. After dinner, I will come back to your building, before I catch the last train, because your father told me in no uncertain terms that I am not to return to Peasmarsh without seeing with my own eyes that you are well. You know how he is.

In good faith,

Ronald

'Ronald!'

'*Umph?*' Winstone said, jerking awake. 'What?'

'Oh, no.'

Winstone's key was no more in the lock of the front door at New River House than Mr Chigley was out of his bed and in his porter's office – unless he'd been there all night.

He didn't speak as he took in their appearance and Mabel knew that a brushed coat could not cover for her dishevelled appearance or Winstone's injuries.

'Good... morning, Mr Chigley,' Mabel whispered, as if she might wake up the entire building if she spoke too loudly.

'Miss Canning. Mr Winstone.' His tone was cautious. 'Reverend Herringay was here for you earlier, Miss Canning.'

'Mr Chigley, there was a police incident this evening,' Mabel said. 'That is, yesterday evening, I suppose.'

'Police?'

'Miss Canning and I were helping Inspector Tollerton of Scotland Yard with a matter,' Winstone said. 'You're very welcome to ring him for the details, but I'd wait until later in the day if I were you.'

'Police,' Mr Chigley repeated, his gaze darting back and

forth between the two of them. 'I see. Well, I'm happy you are both safely home. Yes, you too.' Gladys had put her front paws on the counter.

'Was Ronald – Reverend Herringay – concerned I wasn't here?'

'No, Miss Canning,' the porter said, 'it's all right. I told him you often went out in the evening, to a lecture or whatnot, and so there was nothing for him – or your father – to worry about.'

'Oh, Mr Chigley,' Mabel said, 'you covered for me. That's so kind of you.'

The porter blushed. If Mabel had dared to lean over the counter and give the man a kiss on the cheek, she would've.

Mabel slept only a few hours before rising imbued with what felt like superhuman strength, but she realised this could not last the day, and so got busy. She dressed wearing her second-best day dress and her only other pair of stockings, and drank tea while writing an account of her part in all that had happened. She folded the paper and put it in her bag and then wrote letters to Ronald, to her papa and to Mrs Chandekar with a sketchy account of events, a clear affirmation of her health and well-being and a promise to visit soon.

She went upstairs to Cora and Skeff's, but only Cora was at home. Mabel held out her brimmed hat, which looked as if it had been through the wars.

'Can you do anything with it? I landed on it last night when I came over the back wall at Rosalind's,' she said, and then laughed. 'I had no idea how that would sound.'

'My,' Cora said, giving the hat a quick inspection. 'I'll see what I can do. In the meantime, try this one out.' From a coat peg, she picked a bicorn hat that had a strawberry motif across the turned-up front brim and handed it over, then ushered Mabel out the door and followed her. 'I'm so sorry, but I must run, or I'll be late for work. When you weren't back last evening, we thought there might be something going on with regards to your enquiry. This morning, Mr Chigley said you were fine, but we didn't want to disturb you too early. Is it finished?'

'It is and I'll tell you all later. I'm going to see Skeff at the newspaper – Rosalind's agreed to talk with her.'

'Well done!' Cora said. 'Cheerio now!' she called, and dashed off.

Mabel stopped in her own flat to take a look at the bicorn hat in the mirror. Quite stylish.

On her way down the stairs, she paused for a moment near Winstone's flat. He and Gladys had walked her to her door in the early hours of the morning and, for a moment, they had stood in silence, all three of them nearly asleep. 'Good night' seemed an inadequate end to the day and yet Mabel – and, she suspected, Park as well – had not one drop of energy to speak additional words. Not that she had any idea what those words would be.

When she reached the ground floor, Mr Chigley commented on her spritely step, and she thanked him once again for his discretion and told him no doubt he would read details of yesterday's affair in the newspapers. But not just any paper.

Mabel made her way to the offices of the *London Intelligencer* on Shoe Lane, just off Fleet Street.

The smell of ink and paper and hot metal hit Mabel when she walked in. A man sat behind the front counter. He had the sleeves of his shirt turned up and held fast with bands. His fingers were stained with ink, and he had a piece of paper as large as a table spread out in front of him. He looked up only after Mabel cleared her throat.

'Hello, I'm Mabel Canning. I'm looking for Miss Skeffing-ton.' It was at that moment she realised she didn't know Skeff's Christian name. 'Is she here?'

'Skeff!' he bellowed over his shoulder.

'Coming!' Her voice came through a doorway from a room filled with desks, people shouting and boys running past with stacks of papers.

'Thanks, Davey,' Skeff said to the man at the counter as she emerged. 'Mabel, there you are! Mr Chigley advised not to knock you up first thing this morning, and Cora and I were on pins and needles. What's happened?'

'Do you have a few minutes?' Mabel said. 'I'll explain. Also, I have a proposal.'

Skeff led her to a room empty apart from a plain deal table and two chairs. She closed the door, which dropped the noise to a mere din, but Mabel still felt as if the building were throbbing. The presses, she thought, and a thrill went through her that she sat so close to the heart of a newspaper. Through the glass in the top half of the door, she could see the boys dashing about and hear the occasional shout of 'Copy!'

Skeff pulled her cigarettes out of her pocket, lit one and said, 'What do you have for me?'

'Good morning, Miss Kerr,' Mabel said.

It wasn't Friday, when pay packets were handed out, but another one of those occasional days when, for no particular reason, the Useful Women office was unusually busy. Several women sat in chairs along the wall, and one had been brazen enough to sit in the chair across the desk from Miss Kerr. Mabel's chair.

'Good morning, Miss Canning.' Miss Kerr glanced at the time as if to point out Mabel had been skiving off work coming in at this time of the day.

Mabel stood next to the woman who was sitting in her chair. 'I've come to say that I have several things to attend to today and may not be available for assignments.'

The woman sitting in Mabel's chair raised a suspicious eyebrow at her and then pointedly turned back to Miss Kerr. 'As I was saying, Miss Kerr,' she said, 'you can call on me any time of the night or day for a job, that's how dedicated I will be. You can come and drag me out of my bed if necessary. The reasons I want to be one of Useful Women are so many in number that I would not be able to enumerate them on one hand only. But let me just say this—'

'Yes, yes, Miss Applegate,' Miss Kerr said. 'Take a seat if you please.'

'But I am sitting.'

'A different seat.'

'Well, I—'

Mabel swallowed a snigger, saved by Mrs Fritt rattling in with her tea-and-bun trolley.

'Would you look at all these Useful Women,' she said, hands in the pockets of her apron. 'Now, who's for tea?'

Every one of them. The queue formed quickly, and Mabel waited her turn, paid her five pence and took a bite of her bun.

Miss Kerr nodded her into her proper chair. 'Sit down, Miss Canning. Now, are you saying you are not available for any job today?'

'Oh no, I wouldn't say that.' At least not within Miss Apple-gate's earshot. Mabel licked a bit of sugar off her thumb, reached into her bag and drew out the account she'd written of recent events. 'First, I believe this will explain things and after you've read it...' *Don't lose your nerve, Mabel.* 'After you've read it, I'd like to have a word. Now, I do have rather a full day, but I'm perfectly willing to take on whatever you deem appropriate for me.'

'Good,' Miss Kerr said, 'because as it happens, Augustus

needs escorting to Victoria Station for his return to school.'

Mabel and Augustus Malling-Frobisher indulged in sausages and fried potatoes at the café at Victoria Station before he boarded his train.

'It's become a sort of tradition, hasn't it?' the boy asked, hanging out the window of his compartment as the train lurched forward.

'Two times doesn't make for tradition,' Mabel said from the platform. 'But I suppose it could be considered our usual.'

Augustus grinned. 'See you at Christmas, Miss Canning!'

Mabel arrived at Rosalind's after lunch.

'How was it with Skeff?' she asked.

'Brilliant,' Rosalind said. 'Not to say I'm not a bit nervous. She said it'll be in the late-afternoon edition. That's awfully fast, isn't it?'

'It's the way things are these days – news at your fingertips. Now, people will know the true story.'

'I told her about this idea I have,' Rosalind said. 'It's been brewing for a while now. I've thought about what would've happened to Bridget if she hadn't come with me, and what will happen to Gert Farraday when she can't work any longer and all those singers and dancers who keep at it for years and have so little to show for it. So, I'm going to open a home for them – a place they can be comfortable and live out their days.'

Mabel hugged her. 'Perfect.'

Before Mabel left, Rosalind said, 'Inspector Tollerton said there are still forensic matters to verify.'

It was a kind way to refer to the search that would be carried out to find what remained of Guy's body that had been flung over the embankment and into the wood seven years ago.

'Also,' she said, brightening, 'will you come to dinner tomorrow night?' Rosalind asked. 'Please. Park will be here, of course, but' – her face flushed a deep pink – 'I've asked Inspector Tollerton too. Should I have done that? It's just that he's been square with me the entire time and—'

'What a grand idea,' Mabel said, taking Rosalind's hand. 'We can find out about the man behind his police façade. Perhaps he grows parsnips in his spare time.'

They were standing at the front door, and Mabel's heart skipped a beat when a shadow fell across the privacy window at the side and someone rang the bell – for a fleeting moment, she wondered if it could be Cyril.

But it was Miss Roche. She wore her usual business suit and smiled when Rosalind opened the door, but Mabel saw a softness round her mouth – an uncertainty or sadness.

'Good afternoon, Mrs Despard,' she said. 'And Miss Canning.'

'Gabrielle, come in.'

'I won't, no, but thank you.'

'I planned to go into the office this afternoon and talk with you.'

'I'm glad to save you that journey,' Miss Roche said. 'Here you are.' She handed Rosalind an envelope.

'What's this?'

'I am tendering my letter of resignation,' Miss Roche said, but her voice failed her on the last word and it came out in a whisper.

'Gabrielle, come in here,' Rosalind said.

Miss Roche obeyed, stepping over the threshold and as far as the entry table.

'I should go,' Mabel said.

'There's no need,' Miss Roche said.

'And there's no need for you to resign,' Rosalind said.

'There is every reason,' Miss Roche said, her voice thick

with emotion. 'I have failed you and Mr Despard by harbouring a thief. I brought that man Shaughnessy here to this very house for Mr Despard's wake. He has been involved in my committee for Irish families.'

'But you didn't know it was Michael Shaughnessy, did you?' Mabel asked.

Miss Roche shook her head violently as her chin quivered. 'I knew him as John Boyle Osgood – he said his father was English. I'm mortified at how I was duped.'

Rosalind stuffed the letter into Miss Roche's hands. 'I do not accept your resignation. How in the world would we run things without you, now that Thomas is... gone. You must stay.'

'You're so kind, but—'

'I insist,' Rosalind said, 'and I'll hear nothing else about it. Now, off you go, and I'll stop in later. All right?'

'Thank you,' Miss Roche said. 'Thank you.'

When she'd gone, Mabel turned to Rosalind and said, 'That's a good start to running the business – wouldn't Guy be proud?'

Mabel went back to Islington and when she alighted from the tram, she glanced at the newsstand near the station and saw the afternoon edition of the *London Intelligencer*.

'SERIOUS CYRIL' CHARGED WITH MURDER OF BUSINESSMAN GUY DESPARD SEVEN YEARS AGO

WIDOW CLEARED OF SUSPICION HOLDS NO GRUDGE AGAINST POLICE

'I KNEW HE HADN'T LEFT ME'

*BELOVED ENTERTAINER SAID TO HAVE ALSO
MURDERED SOLICITOR AND MESSENGER*

At the bottom of the page was a related article.

ROSALIND DESPARD WILL OPEN HOME FOR FORMER MUSIC HALL ENTERTAINERS

'Just not Cyril,' Mabel muttered.

She bought two copies and walked over to Collins and to the stage door.

'Hello, Bert.'

'Miss Canning.' Bert, perched on his stool, looked over his glasses at her. 'I've heard the strangest news.'

Mabel handed over the newspaper. 'I imagine you have. Here's the whole story. Is Florrie free, do you think?'

Bert sent for her, and Florrie came out still wearing her street clothes but with her make-up on, along with a bewildered expression.

'Mabel, have you heard?' she said. 'Cyril's missed the show. The manager is putting me on with Martin for the duet.'

'Martin?' Mabel exclaimed. 'Bert, I need to talk with Martin when Florrie and I finish. Don't let him out of your sight.'

'Is Martin mixed up with this?' Bert held up the paper.

'No,' Mabel said. 'It's... I'll explain in a bit.' She turned to Florrie. 'Do you have time for a quick chat?'

Florrie let herself be led to the green, where they sat on a nearby bench. 'Is Cyril in trouble? It doesn't have to do with my Claude, does it?'

Mabel drew the simplest picture she could to explain what her Claude had to do with a seven-year-old murder case, and Florrie drummed her fingertips on her knee as she listened. Before Mabel reached the bad news, she said, 'Cyril said he'd never even seen Claude.'

Florrie gasped. 'Would you credit it? Of course he's seen him – I saw them talking out here on the green. Twice, maybe three times.'

Metropolitan Police would want to hear this eyewitness account, but that could wait.

'The thing is, Florrie, I'm very sorry to tell you that Claude is dead.'

For the first moment, Florrie had no reaction, then she flushed red with anger and tears.

'Stop it,' she shouted. 'You can't say that. It isn't funny.'

Gently, Mabel told her what had happened and gradually Florrie's anger turned to tears.

'Cyril did that to my Claude?' She took a shuddering breath. 'I suppose he wasn't my Claude, not really. I asked him once about what he and Cyril were talking about, and Claude put his arm round me and gave me a squeeze. He says, "I have something that Cyril wants" and I said to him, "Oh, Claude, Cyril can never take me away from you."' A fresh flow of tears coursed down her cheeks. 'But he wasn't talking about me, was he? He was talking about that letter.'

Mabel put her arm around Florrie's shoulders. 'It wasn't right what Claude did,' she said. 'But he didn't deserve to die for it, did he?'

Florrie sobbed. 'So it's all right if I still miss him?'

'Of course it is.'

Florrie had wiped most of her makeup away mopping up tears, and so had to hurry back into the dressing room to sort herself out for the final number.

'I'll go drag Martin out here for you,' Bert told Mabel, 'but I'll warn you now the boy is thick as two planks. Why don't you come and wait in my office?'

He opened a door behind him, switched on a bare bulb that

hung from a low ceiling and gestured with a flourish for her to enter.

'I won't be a tick.'

Mabel stood in the centre of Bert's office, which was about as big as their airing cupboard at home in Peasmarsh. It held a chair and a half-sized writing table and a bookcase made from old boards and old bricks filled with ledgers marked on the spine with 'Grand' or 'Collins' or 'Seabright'. Bert's accumulated history of music halls. The room had no window and smelt of old paper and paint and whisky. Playbills covered the walls, from the Empire in Hackney, the Three Crowns in Woolwich, the Bull and Bush in Hampstead and so many others.

'Right, here he is,' Bert said. He had hold of Martin and gave him a light shove into the office.

When Martin saw Mabel, he was like a pigeon startled by the blast of a shotgun that flaps about wildly trying to escape, flying here and there in everyone's face until at last he thinks he sees blue sky and makes for it, only to run smack into a brick wall. The brick wall being Bert, who stood in the doorway.

'I didn't do anything,' Martin said, his arms still flapping. 'I didn't touch her. It isn't my fault. I was minding my own business and I can't help it if I happen to be where she is. It wasn't my idea. I was just doing what I was told. He told me he thought you were in danger, and I was like a guard or something, but not to show myself and then to tell him what you were doing, so he could... Has he really murdered someone, Bert? Am I in trouble?'

'Martin,' Mabel said sharply, and the young man quieted and stood still.

'Yes, ma'am.'

'Are you saying Cyril put you up to following me?'

'Yes, ma'am.'

'You didn't think there was anything wrong with that?' Mabel asked.

'Well, now that you mention it, it did seem a bit odd,' Martin said. He'd broken out in a sweat and reached up and ran the sleeve of his jacket across his forehead.

'I'll have you know, Martin,' Mabel said, 'that I am acquainted with a detective inspector at Scotland Yard, and I have half a mind to ring him this minute and tell him what you've been doing.'

'Oh no, ma'am, please,' Martin said in a whinging voice. 'I'll lose my place here.'

Mabel knew her threat was empty – what could the police do? – but empty or not, it was enough for her to put the fear of God in him.

'Well, Bert,' she said, 'I know you'll keep an eye on Martin, so I'll let it go this time. You mind your Ps and Qs, young man.'

'Thank you, ma'am. I will.'

The Useful Women office was blessedly empty when Mabel returned, apart from Miss Kerr, who took Mabel's report from the corner of her desk and gave her a look that was difficult to read.

'Hello, Miss Kerr, good afternoon. I've brought you a copy of the afternoon *London Intelligencer*.'

Miss Kerr scanned the headlines and said, 'Oh, I see, Miss Canning. And your name is mentioned in the article, describing how you helped catch a murderer?'

'No, my name isn't mentioned – but the Useful Women agency is.'

Miss Kerr picked up the paper and read. Mabel remained standing and waited.

'Serious Cyril,' Miss Kerr said, and tsked. 'Dear God, what is the world coming to? This article was written by someone named "Skeff". Is that, as they say, a nom de plume?'

'That is Miss Skeffington,' Mabel replied.

'Does she not have a Christian name?'

'She prefers to be known as Skeff.'

And no wonder – her Christian name was Hippolyta, as Mabel had learnt only that morning.

'It's because you sent me to help at the wake that he was caught,' Mabel said. 'And so you see, Miss Kerr, I – that is, the Useful Women agency – was instrumental in assisting police on many fronts. This will bring in more business, don't you think?'

Miss Kerr seemed to mull this over. 'I'm not certain I want to put my Useful Women in danger.'

'I was never in any danger,' Mabel said, just as she had told herself several times since she realised Cyril could just as easily have given her a swift and deadly kick on a dark corner in Islington and that would've put her off the scent for good. 'Nor would I place any other of the Useful Women in danger if we were to take on assignments that involved any sort of enquiry into... murder.'

'What are you suggesting, Miss Canning?'

Mabel backtracked to less dangerous territory. 'If we can find lost things,' she said, 'why not lost – or missing – people? Why can't we be employed to put a client's mind at ease by looking into the background of a new acquaintance or maid or butler and thereby rooting out a cat among the pigeons before he does any harm? What if an agency offered investigations of this sort and advertised it? I mean, after all, who better to undertake such a delicate job?'

Miss Kerr narrowed her eyes and raised a brow. 'Are you proposing to break off and form your own agency?'

'Not at all,' Mabel said fervently. 'I would never be able for that. You know the specific talents of your Useful Women, and I would never attempt to copy you. I would only organise particular jobs of enquiry within the agency. Through those successful jobs, I would encourage more of the kind to come in. I may want to offer parts of an overall enquiry to select Useful Women, but only under your watchful eye because it's you who has cultivated their skills, whether that is bookkeeping or speaking fluent Italian or—'

'Yes, yes, Miss Canning, you've stated your case. No need to over-egg the situation.'

Trying to be optimistic, Mabel said, 'Does that mean you'll think about my proposal?'

'That means, Miss Canning' – Miss Kerr rested her fore-arms on the desk and folded her hands – 'that I am willing to give it a go. I will add another speciality to the list of tasks Useful Women are capable of taking on. It will be number one hundred – Private Investigation.'

Mabel sat down.

'That isn't to say we can expect to receive such exciting assignments as a murder enquiry every day of the week.'

'No, Miss Kerr, certainly not.'

'There will remain, for the bulk of your work here at the agency, mundane, shall I say, tedious jobs? Jobs that it will be necessary to take on.'

'Of course, Miss Kerr.'

'Well, then, Miss Canning, with that understanding, I would like you to coordinate this venture. Under my aegis, you understand.'

'I understand, Miss Kerr.'

Mabel Canning, private investigator.

At the first-floor landing, Winstone's door opened, and Gladys wiggled out.

He looked better than he had the night before – that is, earlier that morning – although the purple under his eye had deepened and the round red wound was still prominent.

'That's a fine hat,' he said.

Mabel touched the edge of the bicorn. 'Thank you. It's one of Cora's.'

'Do you have time for a turn round the green?' he asked. 'I was just taking Gladys out.'

Mabel turned round and went back downstairs. They stepped out the door into the afternoon autumn sunshine. She'd been rushing round all day, but now that she paused, Mabel detected a change in the sun's angle from its summer height and felt a certain feeling in the air. This day, even London air smelt good.

Gladys chose their route, and for the next half-hour Mabel and Park criss-crossed the green talking of nothing more serious than which of Chopin's études was the most difficult. But eventually the conversation turned to what weighed heaviest on their minds.

'I can't believe I fell for Cyril's song and dance,' Mabel said.

'His song and dance?' Winstone asked.

'When Ronald was here, he reminded me Edith used to say I was smart enough not to fall for anyone's song and dance – although we couldn't remember the right words. I remember now. It was an expression she picked up from a magazine – "song and dance" is someone's pretence. But I did fall for Cyril's song and dance. More fool me.'

'You knew him only a few days,' Winstone pointed out. 'We've known him for years and we were taken in. Even Bridget.'

Gladys gave a tug at the lead, and they turned towards home, waiting at the kerb across the road from New River House.

'I spoke to Tolly this morning,' Winstone said. 'He's been round to Rosy's and she's invited him to dinner tomorrow. I'm not altogether sure that's a good idea.'

'Do you have a say in the matter?' Mabel asked.

'No, I don't,' Winstone said. 'But she's also asked me, and I know she's invited you. May I escort you?'

Behind his glasses, she saw the gleam of mischief.

'You and Gladys?'

'Of course.'

'Yes, you may.'

She slipped her hand into the crook of his arm, and he gave it a squeeze. The traffic cleared and off they went.

Mabel stopped for a word with the porter as Winstone and Gladys continued upstairs.

'Now, Miss Canning.'

'Mr Chigley,' she said, thinking it best to be on the offence, 'you're probably wondering how my work with the Useful Women is going.' *You and Papa.* 'And so I will tell you. My duties with the agency are broadening, and I will now be in charge of the private investigations department.'

'Private...'

'Investigations,' Mabel finished for him. 'I will work with other Useful Women to undertake jobs for clients, such as finding lost things, looking into suspicious accidents and helping to sort out difficulties that may arise in all manner of situations. We'll discuss with the client the best way to address the problem.'

It was vague, but was it too vague? It was her intention to assuage any fears Mr Chigley – and by extension, her papa – may have about the venture, without being entirely obfuscating.

'You and your ladies will gather and talk about a client's problems?' Mr Chigley asked, grasping one piece of what Mabel had said and looking relieved. 'So, rather like a ladies club?'

A ladies murder club.

'Yes, Mr Chigley,' Mabel said, and smiled. 'Like a ladies club. Of sorts.'

A LETTER FROM MARTY

Dear reader,

I want to say a huge thank you for choosing to read *A Body on the Doorstep*, book one in my new London Ladies' Murder Club series. If you did enjoy it, and want to keep up to date with all my latest releases, just sign up at the following link. Your email address will never be shared and you can unsubscribe at any time.

www.bookouture.com/marty-wingate

I had a wonderful time writing about Mabel and the Useful Women agency, which really did exist in 1921 as did its proprietress, Miss Lillian Kerr. London was just the place for the modern, independent woman and it was great fun following Mabel's exploration of her freedom, from eating alone at a Lyons Corner House to going to a music hall.

I hope you loved *A Body on the Doorstep* and if you did, I would be very grateful if you could write a review. I'd love to hear what you think, and it makes such a difference helping new readers to discover one of my books for the first time.

I love hearing from my readers – you can get in touch through social media or my website.

Thanks,

Marty Wingate

www.martywingate.com

 facebook.com/martywingateauthor
x.com/martywingate

ACKNOWLEDGEMENTS

Writing the first book in a new series is full of both excitement and panic, and it takes not only the author, but also a host of others to get this book into the hands of you, the reader. For help, support and guidance creating the series the London Ladies' Murder Club and book one, *A Body on the Doorstep*, my heartfelt thanks go to my agent, Christina Hogrebe of the Jane Rotrosen Agency.

I'm thrilled to be publishing with Bookouture – the attention given to me and to my story has been magnificent – so here are more thanks to my editors, Rhianna Louise and Laura Deacon, and also to Jess Whitlum-Cooper and Imogen Allport.

My weekly writing group keeps me grounded and always asks the right questions – where would I be without them? Thanks to Kara Pomeroy, Louise Creighton, Sarah Niebuhr Rubin and Meghana Padakandla.

Special appreciation and love to my husband, Leighton Wingate, who is also my in-house copyeditor and proofreader ('Do you want to put a comma here?').

Thanks to these family members, fellow authors and dear friends who never mind listening to the latest results of my research, even if it is about the history of the envelope: Carolyn Lockhart, Ed Polk, Katherine Manning Wingate, Susy Wingate, Lilly Wingate, Hattie Bourne, Alice K. Boatwright, Hannah Dennison, Dana Spencer, Jane Tobin, Mary Helbach, Mary Kate Parker and Victoria Summerley. Cheers!

PUBLISHING TEAM

Turning a manuscript into a book requires the efforts of many people. The publishing team at Bookouture would like to acknowledge everyone who contributed to this publication.

Audio
Alba Proko
Sinead O'Connor
Melissa Tran

Commercial
Lauren Morrissette
Jil Thielen
Imogen Allport

Cover design
Emily Courdelle

Data and analysis
Mark Alder
Mohamed Bussuri

Editorial
Rhianna Louise
Nadia Michael